RIDING THE STORM

*How could she make Robert's children
accept her?*

When Kate Harper meets Robert Dengaul
she is amazed by the immediate passion
which flares between them. But Robert's
grown-up children present a few obstacles
to their happiness. And one of them is
prepared to go to great lengths to ensure
that Kate is off the scene for good...

RIDING THE STORM

Pamela Oldfield

Severn House Large Print
London & New York

This first large print edition published in Great Britain 2001 by
SEVERN HOUSE LARGE PRINT BOOKS LTD of
9-15, High Street, Sutton, Surrey, SM1 1DF.
First world regular print edition published 2000 by
Severn House Publishers, London and New York.
This first large print edition published in the USA 2001 by
SEVERN HOUSE PUBLISERS INC., of
595 Madison Avenue, New York, NY 10022

British Library Cataloguing in Publication Data

Oldfield, Pamela, 1934-
    Riding the storm. - Large print ed.
    1. Remarriage - England
    2. Large type books
    I. Title
    823.9'14 [F]

ISBN 0-7278-7045-9

Printed and bound in Great Britain by
MPG Books Ltd, Bodmin, Cornwall.

For Martin and Maureen
with love

One

As the departure time drew nearer, Robert's arm tightened around Kate's shoulders. All about them the platform was emptying as passengers hurried on to the train with a clatter of slamming doors and the murmur of a hundred farewells. Charing Cross station, Monday morning at the start of a June day. Dusty sunlight filtered down on to the platform and birds fluttered overhead among the roof girders. Kate watched the regal approach of a middle-aged matron who carried a small dog under her arm.

"In the luggage van? Certainly not!" she was saying. "Chitzy travels with me!"

The young porter, scuttling beside her, looked harassed as he tried to steer a trolley bearing a small trunk, a wicker basket and a leather hatbox.

"'Scuse me, sir ..." he stammered. "Whoops! Sorry, madam!"

Kate and Robert sidestepped hastily. A sweeper approached from the other direction, pushing a large broom. A small boy fought a losing battle with his mother as

7

his fingers were prised from the chocolate machine and he was tugged towards the waiting train.

"I want a choccy bar! I want a—"

"You shall have a penny for chocolate when we get to Auntie Dorothy's. Mummy wants to get on the train. Come *along*, Ernest!"

Kate smiled. "I suppose that will be me one day."

Robert laughed. "So you're not going to change your mind."

"Of course not."

In a first-class compartment Robert's jacket and a folded newspaper reserved his seat. The guard, pocket watch in hand, gave them a warning look as he strode past. The green flag was tucked under his arm as he tried to urge the last few passengers up the steps and into the waiting carriages.

With a sigh Kate turned to face her companion. She was reasonably good-looking – average height with brown eyes – but she had learned to make the most of her good features and wore her short brown hair waved close to her head in the style of the mid-thirties.

"I'll have to let you go, Robert," she told him.

Robert's smile was the saddest thing she had ever seen and her own heart ached as she studied the well-loved face, trying to memorise the details: the shrewd but faded blue eyes, the still thick but greying hair and the short curly beard. At fifty-nine Robert Dengaul was one of the most attractive men she had ever met.

She said, "I'm going to miss you, Robert – but then I always do."

"Not as much as I shall miss you."

A porter appeared and hovered nearby, a small book in his hand. He looked appealingly at Robert and said, "It *is* you, isn't it, sir?"

Robert smiled. "Yes, it's me." To Kate he said, "Excuse me, darling," and turned back to the porter.

"Is that what I think it is?" Robert asked, with a nod towards the book.

The porter grinned self-consciously. "If I *could* have your autograph, sir ..." He handed it over and Kate watched while Robert found an empty page and signed his name. The porter said, "It's for my wife, sir. Collecting autographs has always been a passion with her. Bit of luck me spotting you." He threw a shy smile in Kate's direction. "She's poorly at the moment so I said I'd look out for famous people. You see quite a lot on a station like this."

Robert returned the book. "I hope she'll soon be well."

The porter's expression changed. "I'm afraid she won't, sir. They discovered it too

9

late. TB, that is. Still, we keep cheerful." He patted the autograph book. "Robert Dengaul! She'll be thrilled with this!"

As he hurried away Robert stared after him with a strange look in his eyes.

Kate touched his arm. "What is it?"

He swallowed. "Nothing ... It's –" he took hold of her hand – "it's nice to be able to make people happy. Such a small thing ... Quite humbling, really."

"I suppose you get used to it – the autograph hunters."

He was still staring after the porter. "TB ... That poor woman. I suppose one day they'll conquer it."

The engine gave a long blast.

"These damned partings!" Robert's smile was rueful. "If you don't marry me soon I shall die of frustration."

"As soon as I've met the family," she reminded him.

The guard shouted a garbled version of "All aboard!" and more doors slammed shut.

"Robert, you must go, darling." She kissed him, hugging his thin frame to her for as long as she dared, then pushing him towards the train.

"I could catch the next train."

"I have to go to work! Please don't tempt me, Robert. It's Monday morning and I have to go to the office. You must go home.

Start on that synopsis. It will keep you busy and make the time fly."

They kissed again and Kate watched him climb into the train. He slammed the door and immediately turned, lowered the window, and leaned out.

"Friday evening, Kate, without fail. They'll be expecting you ... wondering about you. So don't miss the train. If I know Caroline, she'll be cooking something special for the occasion."

Kate smiled. "I won't miss it. Everything will fine. I'm sure I'll like them."

"I'm probably worrying too much. Caro had such a difficult childhood ..." He ran anxious fingers through his hair. "I just need you all to get along."

Kate squeezed his hands. "Friday. Twenty-one minutes past six. I'll be there. Cross my heart."

From the corner of her eye she saw the green flutter of the guard's flag. The whistle sounded and with a rush of steam the engine jerked forward sending a shudder through the line of carriages.

Robert reached out to her and Kate held his hand, walking alongside as the train gathered speed. When it was no longer possible, she stood breathlessly waving as the train dwindled and its gathering speed reduced Robert's head to a small dot. She stood alone, overwhelmed by the familiar

11

ache of loss and an illogical sense of abandonment. After a moment she turned and walked back along the platform, out of the station forecourt and into the city.

As she walked she thought about the man who had come so suddenly into her life and thrown all her carefully made plans into confusion. Six months ago, as a senior secretary with Gordon Brett Publishers, she had been offered the job of junior editor and had accepted with undignified haste. The first book launch she had attended in her new role had brought her into contact with Robert Dengaul and his obvious admiration for her had done wonders for her confidence. Thirty-six years old and widowed, she hadn't expected to meet anyone else with whom she wanted to share the rest of her life.

Passing the news stand, she bought a paper to read at lunchtime and, still puzzling over Robert's obvious anxiety, made her way along the crowded pavement with the rest of London's workers.

Robert had fallen in love with her and she with him, but very recently she had sensed a change in him and the intensity of his love was beginning to concern her.

"We don't have to rush into matrimony," she had told him. "I need time to get to know your children."

"They're adults, Kate, and we don't have

to wait! I *want* to rush into matrimony!"

He had tried to make a joke of it but, frowning now, she thought about his words and a small sense of unease settled at the back of her mind.

Determined to marry her as soon as possible, he had finally persuaded her to visit his home in Sussex and meet his family, two sons and a daughter. Nervously, Kate had managed to delay this fateful meeting but now Friday loomed ominously near.

A quarter of an hour later, Kate found herself in her office with a cup of tea in her hands, explaining her reluctance to a sceptical colleague.

"It's not that I don't want to meet them, Mu." She frowned. "It's just ..."

Muriel grinned. "It's just: do *they* want to meet *you*?"

"Exactly!" said Kate.

Her phone rang and she picked it up. "Gordon Brett." She listened for a moment and then said, "You really need to speak to the sales department but you've come through to editorial. If you hang on I'll try and get you transferred." A moment later she replaced the receiver and turned back to Muriel. "Why should they want their father to marry a woman who is only a few years older than they are? Why should they want him to remarry? Especially as their mother has only been dead two years. If I were in their shoes I'd be wary, too."

"You'll have to spell it out for him." Muriel sipped her tea and pulled a face. "No sugar! Are you trying to poison me?"

"Sorry." Kate pushed forward a bowl of sugar lumps and Muriel helped herself to three. "I have told him, Mu, but he doesn't believe me. He can't imagine that anybody would find me less than wonderful!"

"I wish somebody saw *me* like that." Muriel Burke, a senior editor in her early forties, was decidedly round with a figure that defied her expensive corsetry. "Fancy snaring Robert Dengaul!" She gave an exaggerated sigh. "He obviously likes the quiet ones. I'm probably too noisy for him."

"Mu, you're married! Or had you forgotten?"

"Married? Oh! You mean Eddie." Muriel rolled expressive eyes.

Kate stared at her over the rim of her cup. "Two years and three weeks since his wife died. It's what's known as 'unseemly haste' but I can't make Robert see it. Still –" she shrugged – "he's promised to tell them about me between now and Friday. And it's only for two days. I've insisted I must come back to my flat late Sunday afternoon. I've said it's so that I can wash my hair and do some ironing but actually I shall need to recover from the ordeal!"

Muriel said, "You'll survive."

"I hope so."

The telephone interrupted them again and Muriel rose reluctantly to her feet and left, taking her tea with her. Kate watched her go and wondered how she would have managed without her friend's support through the dark days following her husband's death. It was Muriel who had found her the job as secretary and helped her find a flat in south London near to the station.

Kate said, "Gordon Brett."

"It's me."

"Robert!" She smiled. "Long time no see."

"Now you're mocking me."

"Would I do a thing like that?" She glanced at the wall clock. "We've only been apart for fifty minutes! Are you home already?"

"No. I just had to phone you so I got off the train a bit further down the line."

"But why, darling?"

"I suddenly felt as though I couldn't breathe. Needed some fresh air."

Kate frowned. "Couldn't breathe? Are you all right, Robert?"

"Of course I am! It's the trains. They're never cleaned properly."

"I thought you looked tired."

"I'm fine. I'll have a cup of tea in the snack bar and catch the next train home. Kate,

15

I've been thinking about Caroline. She can be very difficult."

"So can I. So can you, Robert. Please darling. I'm nervous enough without you making it worse." Guiltily she noticed the pile of manuscripts on her desk waiting for her attention and heard the sounds of the cover being removed from a typewriter in the outer room. It still amazed her that she had become an editor and now had her own secretary. "I must do some work, Robert," she told him. "I'll ring you when I get home."

"I'll be waiting with bated breath!"

Kate returned the receiver to its rest with a niggling feeling of unease. Very difficult? Caroline might not like the new woman in her father's life but what could she do? In a few months Kate and Robert would be man and wife. She remembered the way she had waited for William to propose to her and how incredibly casual he had been about the relationship, ignoring all her hints until she was forced to seize her chance in a leap year and propose to *him*.

A young lad knocked and came in with the morning post.

"Morning, Mrs Harper."

"Morning, Tom."

Kate reached for a paperknife and picked up the first letter. Her own problems would have to wait.

Tuesday was an exceptionally fine day and Caroline lay on her back on an old rug, her face turned to the sun. Beside her, to her left, familiar brick chimneys reared up into the blue sky. To her right, the leads extended for two yards to the rusted rail which ran around the entire roof area. A book of poetry had been tossed aside. A half-empty bottle of barley water and two chunky glasses stood beside the book.

"Kate!" she muttered.

Her thick fair hair and blue eyes were inherited from her father although her mouth and nose were finer. At twenty-six she was pretty in a careless way. Today she wore blue shorts and a white sleeveless top. Born when her brother was nine she grew up adoring him although he did not return the compliment. Bernard had found a small sister both an embarrassment and an encumbrance. It was not until she was an adult that their relationship blossomed but this was soon shattered by the appearance of Alison, his girlfriend and future wife.

Caroline's consolation, however, was her younger brother Sebastian, born when she was four years old. This brother she could mother and the strong bond of affection between the two children had never wavered. Now Caroline was content to stay at home and care for Sebastian and her famous father and revel in the reflected glory.

In the distance the church clock struck three and she sat up reluctantly. For a moment she inspected her bare arms and legs but the June sun had made no difference to the colour of her limbs. Hugging her knees she stared down across the large garden, watching for Alison to arrive.

"You're not my favourite person, Alison," she muttered, "but you're all I've got."

How many times, she reflected, had her mother insisted that she "make the effort".

"Every girl needs friends, Caro."

"I don't. I want a pony."

"Ask one of your classmates to tea – or we could go out and take a picnic."

Poor Mother. Caro smiled at the memories. She had never wanted girl-friends. Seb had been all the human companionship she needed. A horse would have made life perfect.

"But now there's this wretched Harper woman." She squinted up into the sun. "Kate ..." So was it Kathleen or Katherine? Probably the latter. Kathleen would probably be shortened to Kathy or even Katy.

She waved at Alison who had now appeared outside the gates and was pushing them open. Caroline watched impatiently as her sister-in-law wheeled her bicycle through and closed them behind her. Dull as ditchwater, she thought with despair. A perfect match for Bernard.

She leaned over the rail. "Come on up."

A white dove settled briefly on the rail, decided against staying and flew away. A small white feather floated down to rest beside Caroline's bare feet. Moments later Alison stepped through the door and on to the roof. She looked pale, thought Caroline, and even less confident than usual. Probably had an argument with Bernard. Alison hated scenes.

"Caro! What on earth are you doing up here?" Alison stared out across the view and then joined Caroline on the rug. "I'd get vertigo if I dared look straight down."

"I'm used to it. We all came up here as children. It was our hideaway." Caroline grinned. "We used to dare each other to walk along the outside edge, beyond the rail."

"Good heavens! How could you!"

"How could we? I'll show you."

Suddenly she wanted to shock Alison, who cared too much about her appearance – always expensively dressed with her hair professionally set. Her father was the wealthy proprietor of a small chain of ironmongers but fortunately he was not as wealthy as Robert Dengaul and had virtually no claim to fame. The fact that

Bernard had been made a director of the company did nothing to appease Caroline. Alison had "broken up the family" and must never be allowed to forget it.

Scrambling to her feet, ignoring Alison's entreaties, she stepped over the rail and steadied herself with widespread arms.

Alison cried, "Don't! I can't bear it!" but she watched nevertheless.

Casually Caroline made her way along the edge, placing one foot in front of the other with practised ease. She reached the corner of the roof and glanced back, laughing at the look of fear on Alison's face. She stepped back over the rail and said, "That's how you do it."

Alison was breathing rapidly. "Oh God, Caroline!"

"D'you want to try it?"

"You must be *mad*!" Alison whispered. "Does your father know?"

"Of course he doesn't. Nobody knows. Just the three of us – and now you."

There were times when she felt almost sorry for Alison. Being an only child meant being pampered by your doting parents. No wonder she had grown up with so many inhibitions.

"It was our secret, that's all." Caroline filled two glasses with lemon barley water.

"Did Bernard do it?"

"Of course he did. He wasn't always the

way he is now." She meant the remark as a challenge but Alison let it pass.

Caroline said, "Anyway, you know now. So, any exciting news?"

Alison hesitated, then shook her head.

"Shame. I'm still hoping that I'll be an aunt one day."

Alison stared out across the lawn. "Stranger things have happened."

"Meaning?"

"Nothing."

Caroline glanced at her, alerted by her tone. It was no secret that Alison's failure to have a child was casting a shadow over the marriage and talking about it wasn't easy for her. Caroline was torn between showing a sympathetic interest and discreetly ignoring the problem.

"Well, *I've* got some news."

"Good or bad?" Alison kicked off her sandals. Her cream dress was immaculate and her face showed signs of subtle make up – a dab of lipstick and a hint of rouge.

Caroline's laugh was forced. "To tell you the truth I don't know. It's Father. He ..." she stared at her drink, "he wants to remarry."

Alison's shocked expression suddenly endeared her to Caroline.

"*Remarry?* But that's ... surely he ... Good heavens, Caro! Your mother's only been ..."

"I know. That's what I thought. About two

21

years. I couldn't believe it when he told me." She drained her glass then stared into it. "Kate Harper. That's her name."

Alison said sharply, "Why did he tell you? Why not Bernard?"

"I was handy, I suppose. Seb doesn't know either. He's staying with friends. He's been on one of his cross-country hikes. Don't ask me where."

She watched Alison covertly, longing for a sign that they were thinking along the same lines; that Alison too was disgusted by her father's betrayal. She went on, "Honestly Alison! How *could* he? It's so unlike him. You know how devastated he was when Mother died. There's never been anyone else—"

"That we know of." Alison picked up the dove's feather and twirled it between thumb and forefinger.

Caroline turned towards her. "You don't mean that, do you?" Her heart thudded. "Do you know something I don't?"

"Of course not, silly. I simply meant that – well, do we ever really know people close to us?"

"Don't we?" She stared at Alison, startled.

"Do you really know Seb? Suppose he was having an affair. Would he tell you?"

"Seb?" Caroline felt slightly hysterical. *"Seb?* Have an affair? Of course he wouldn't. Wouldn't have an affair, I mean. Seb's not like that. He's too lazy for a start!"

"But if he did."

"Of course he would. He tells me everything." Caroline was aware of a tightness in her chest. "Are you saying Father might have known this Kate *before* Mother died? That he was having an affair with her?"

"No I'm not."

Caroline poured herself another drink without offering one to her sister-in-law. She was aware of a growing anger. She had invited Alison round to offer comfort. Instead she was making her feel worse. "Apparently she's quite young."

"Good Lord! I can't believe it!"

They regarded each other with disbelief.

Alison said, "What on earth can she see in a man old enough to be her father?"

"His money? His fame?" Caroline spat the words out.

Alison considered, her head on one side. "He is quite attractive, I suppose, for a man of his age. He's worn well." Alison helped herself to what was left of the barley water. "Where is he now?"

"At the dentist's in London. A check-up. I was quite pleased to see the back of him," Caroline confessed. 'He's been wandering round the house like the cat that got the cream. 'Just wait,' he kept saying. 'You'll all love her.'"

They both watched a dove settle on the rail.

Caroline smiled. "It's come back, looking for the feather." She leaned back against the chimney and straightened her legs, admiring them half-heartedly. Would she know if Seb was having an affair? She felt a rush of jealousy at the thought of her brother with another woman. Blast Alison. Her sister-in-law looked as though butter wouldn't melt in her mouth but she could say some very unsettling things.

Alison clapped her hands and the bird flew away. She said slowly, "Has this Kate *said* she will marry him or is your father just hoping? There's a world of difference."

"He said they'll be 'getting married before too long'. He seems to be in an awful hurry. We've all got to meet her. You and Bernard are invited – to *dinner* – on Friday. Seven thirty for eight!"

She closed her eyes. That meant she would have to help Mrs Matthews tidy the house up – always a mammoth task. The daily woman came in for two hours most mornings depending on the state of her "rheumatics". In her mind's eye, Caroline saw the scattered magazines and newspapers, the dead flowers, the hearth full of toffee papers and the squashed cushions. Not to mention the spare room which would have to be dusted and polished. The bed would need to be made up.

As though reading her mind Alison said,

"I'll give you a hand if you like with the cooking."

"Would you?" Caroline brightened. "I thought I'd poach a salmon. That's nice and easy. Keep it simple. Salad. Might find a few new potatoes. Or not so new."

"I suppose it's only natural." Alison regarded her earnestly. "Your father might live another ten years or so and I daresay he gets lonely."

"Lonely? He's got me, hasn't he?" Caroline glared at her sister-in-law. "I look after him twenty-four hours a day."

"Unless you're out on Nutmeg."

Caroline hesitated. She knew exactly what her sister-in-law was suggesting – that she spent too much time riding and not enough managing the house. That was probably true, but it was not Alison's place to say so. A sharp retort occurred to her but she kept it to herself. She needed to keep Alison on her side. Ignoring the interruption she elaborated. "I help him choose his clothes. Cook his meals. Go with him to functions. Twice when Mother was ill I took her place. There's the summer party at Faber and Faber. I pay a girl to exercise Nutmeg morning and evening just so that I can accompany Father."

"Won't he take *her* this year?"

Caroline's heart skipped a beat. "Kate? But – but I *always* –" Now that she thought

25

about it, her father hadn't mentioned it. "He hasn't said anything but . . ." She shrugged, pretending indifference. No point in letting Alison see that the barb hurt. In an attempt to change the subject, she sought for something with which to discomfit Alison. "Would *you* know if *Bernard* was having an affair?"

"*Bernard*? An affair?" Alison's face broke into a grin. "I don't think the vicar would approve of that, do you? One of his church-wardens committing adultery?"

Caroline joined in the laughter. Her big brother. He had done so little after a promising start. She had to admit that, much as she loved him, he was dull company. He had done all the right things in an effort to please his father: church choir – he had a very good voice; good marks at school; a useful all rounder at cricket. He had even married well. Sebastian had done nothing but rebel. Even at school – and he'd never had any idea what he wanted to do with his life.

She said, "Chalk and cheese, my brothers. Seb was always a bit of a rebel. Did you know he was almost expelled from his last school?"

Alison nodded. "D'you know why?"

"No. Father wouldn't tell us and—"

"He was flirting with the head's daughter who was only fourteen."

26

Shocked, Caroline stared at her. "Who told you that?"

Alison opened her mouth, closed it, then said, "It must have been Bernard."

Caroline was speechless. Bernard *knew*! He'd always pretended ignorance. Another betrayal. Worse than a betrayal even – it was a *conspiracy*! Mother, Father and Bernard had all agreed to keep her in ignorance of Sebastian's crime. And Sebastian had been flirting with a young girl. Probably imagined he was in love with her. Her anger flared again. So much for the bond between herself and Sebastian. For a moment she felt sick with jealousy.

"Caro?"

Caroline became aware that Alison was talking to her and made an effort to speak normally. "Sorry. What did you say?"

"I said I could make a pudding if you like. One less thing for you to worry about. I could try out a new recipe I heard on the wireless. A sort of apple flan with the slices arranged in circles." She patted Caroline's arm. "Cheer up. Your father might be right. We might all love Kate Harper." She grinned. "She might even let you be a bridesmaid!"

Half an hour later Alison climbed on to her bicycle and set off for home. If only Caroline wasn't so prickly, she thought. She had gone to see her determined at last to confide in her but as usual Caroline's attitude had deterred her. Caro was unpredictable; so desperately possessive of both Seb and her father. Neurotic. That was the word Bernard had used. "Caro was such a neurotic child." Well, thought Alison, hardly surprising that she had grown into a neurotic woman. It was an uncomfortable thought.

Sighing she fought down a growing panic. Slowing down at a Belisha crossing, she faced the uncomfortable truth. There was no one with whom she could share her secret.

Robert sat at the desk in his study and stared at the blank sheets of paper which he had just rolled into his typewriter. Three sheets layered with carbon paper. "I like the sound of the new novel," Frank Brett had said, "a political scandal. Very topical. Look forward to seeing the synopsis." They made it sound easy. Take your time, they told him, while slotting it in for June 1936. A new novel every other year. He had made a rod for his own back by his prodigious output over the past years. He typed the words CHAPTER ONE and sat back. More than anything he wanted a whisky but it was only ten o'clock in the morning and what would Kate think if she were with him?

Vi would have understood because they

had been together a long time and she knew there were days when the words wouldn't come for him and had to be prised from his brain with a little help. There were days when *she* had needed a small glass of sherry to restore her good humour. Poor Vi.

He stared across the room to the only table that wasn't groaning beneath a pile of manuscripts and books – the one on which Vi had arranged family photographs. "In case you forget who we are!" she had teased him. He smiled at the memory. Whenever he became deeply involved in his story he would lose himself in his other world and forget the needs of his wife and children. It had been one of Vi's pet grumbles, but it was fair comment. He glanced at their wedding photograph – top hat and tails for him, creamy lace for her. He had wanted another wedding like that with Kate, wanting to see their marriage reported in every newspaper in the land and photographs in all the right magazines. But Kate, bless her, had refused, thrown into a panic at the idea of all the publicity. Poor darling! Marrying a well-known author was probably her idea of hell. A quiet wedding, she begged him, with just family and close friends. So be it. Kate could have whatever she wanted. If he could he would grant her every wish.

He stared at the page. For God's sake! He was supposed to be writing a synopsis. He sighed. Think, Robert. Concentrate. What had he decided to call his hero?

"Trenchard," he muttered. Yes. That was it. And he was setting it a couple of years ahead. In a rush of enthusiasm he began to type.

In May 1936 John Trenchard, a member of the Foreign Office, is approached ...

"By whom? By a Member of Parliament ... Maybe a Junior Minister ... First name? Something a little extravagant. Neil? Noel? Nigel? Yes." Nigel would sound right. And maybe a hyphenated surname Grant-Davies MP.

...by Nigel Grant-Davies MP who wanted to talk about ...

"About what? Oh bugger it!"

He pushed back his chair and crossed to the window. What was Kate doing? he wondered. He could imagine her at work, her shapely legs tucked under her as she leaned her elbows on the desk and tried to concentrate on the latest manuscript. Only two more days to get through and then she would be here and his desperation would fade.

There was a knock on the door and Caro came in with a cup of tea.

"Thanks, dear." He smiled at her. She had taken the news of his approaching marriage with an apparent equanimity but that made him nervous. Of his three children, he

30

thought Caro would be the most likely to resent a stepmother.

She held the cup aloft, waiting for him to clear a space among the jumble of papers that covered his desk, then set down the cup and saucer. "How's it going?"

"So so."

She read aloud what he had written, a habit of hers which she knew he deplored.

Robert let it pass. He asked, "So what did Alison have to say when you told her? I presume you did."

"About what?"

Wretched girl! "Kate, of course."

"Not much. She was surprised."

No enthusiasm there, then. "And Seb?"

"He doesn't know yet. He hasn't been home."

Robert found his irritation growing. "Hasn't been home? Where is he?"

"Staying with those friends in Roberts-bridge. They were doing one of those walks or hikes or whatever they are."

"He didn't tell me."

"You weren't here to tell. You were with Kate all weekend. Remember?"

He ignored the tone, but his spirits fell. How on earth would his daughter and Kate get along? Two women in one kitchen was a well-known recipe for disaster.

"What about Bernard?" he asked. "Is he pleased – about Kate?"

31

Surely one of his children would be happy that he had found a new love. He had never been really unfaithful to Vi – a few indiscretions perhaps, but Vi had been wise enough to look the other way. So his children had nothing with which to reproach him. Bernard would understand that a man needs more than fame and fortune. Bernard was married and Alison was a good wife to him. Bernard would approve of Kate.

Caro shrugged. "He just laughed and said, 'The sly old dog!'" Before he could react she went on hastily. "We've given the spare room a bit of a polish and made up the bed. I've swept out the conservatory. Half the flowers were dead."

He recognised the last remark for what it was. Vi had been so fond of her flowers and after her death he had devoted a lot of time to them. Since he'd met Kate the flowers had been forgotten.

Caroline went on. "I'm doing salmon for Friday and Alison is bringing a tart for pudding. Will you see to the wines?"

"I always do." He was also mortified by Bernard's remark. *The sly old dog*. Hardly complimentary and totally lacking in respect. *If* he had actually said it. He wouldn't put it past his daughter to exaggerate. Much as he loved her, he knew she had a talent for stirring up trouble. He sighed deeply. Perhaps he was over-reacting. It was only natural that they should feel like this. Once they met Kate it would be a different story. He decided that as soon as Caro had gone he would ring her. The sound of her voice would make him feel better.

Caro said, "By the way, I thought I should warn you. Seb wants to go to Art School. He's decided he wants to be an artist."

"An *artist*? Good God!"

She perched on the arm of one of the easy chairs. "He can draw, Dad. Don't you remember when he was at school? He always got good marks. Honestly, you should let him go. He'll be good at it."

"Over my dead body!" He put a hand to his head. *Could* Seb draw? It was news to him if he could. The boy couldn't do anything except lounge around and get himself into trouble.

"He's going to ask you to pay his way and then he'll repay the money when he's earning."

"An *artist*!"

Robert reached for his tea. He had always tried not to spoil his children although he admitted they had been too indulgent with Caroline. His own father had said, "Money shouldn't come too easily." While Vi was alive she had guided him, preventing his worst extravagances. Since her death he had been too casual with money as though it could fill the gap left by their mother's death. But Art School? He could imagine the wild types Seb would mix with there. They would surely bring out the worst side of his son's far from perfect nature. If only Vi were alive – she had always known how to deal with the children. He had left so much to her.

Without thinking, he said, "I'll talk to Kate about it and—"

Caroline sprang to her feet. "Talk to Kate! To *Kate*? Good God, Dad! What's it got to do with her? She's never even met Seb. How does she know whether he can draw or not?"

The eyes staring into his were full of accusation.

Cursing himself for his stupidity, Robert tried to repair the damage. He held up his hands in mock surrender.

"I'm sorry. That was stupid of me. Habit, I suppose. I always referred difficult decisions to—"

"To Mother. We all noticed. Well, she's dead, and Kate won't ever take her place! Not in our hearts, anyway. Just because she's pretty and smart . . ." Her voice trembled but she blinked furiously. "If Mother could hear the way you're carrying on, so soon after . . ." She faced him white-faced with anger. "If you want to know the truth *I* think it's disgusting!"

With a toss of her hair his daughter stormed out of the room and slammed the door behind her.

"Go to hell!" he muttered but he was shaken. He had brought that on by his own stupidity.

He drank the rest of his tea without tasting it and forced himself back to his novel. Trenchard. What a stupid, stuffy name. Surely he could come up with something better than that ... Frencham, perhaps? John Frencham. It was marginally better.

John Frencham. Jack Frencham? Jake Frencham?

Robert knew from experience that he wouldn't be able to visualise this character fully until he had found him a suitable name. Defeated, he stood up, pulled the cover over the typewriter and tucked his chair under the table. From the window he caught sight of Caroline heading for the stable. Her back was stiff and she moved with an urgency that he recognised as suppressed anger.

"That's it, Caro. Go ride your horse!" he whispered.

He had bought Nutmeg for her a month after her mother's death and had never regretted it. Whenever she was troubled she would ride – or maybe escape was a better word. Unfailingly she returned in a happier frame of mind but maybe not today.

Disgusting?

Was that fair? he wondered. Was he behaving badly? He swallowed, unable to cast off an unwelcome melancholy. He was in love with a wonderful woman and he ought to be happy. Kate had promised to share his remaining years, generously agreeing to give up her own work so that they could be together and Robert appreciated the sacrifice. Secretly he prayed they might have a child but he had kept this hope to himself. He was fifty-nine, after all, and was terrified he might fail her. And how would his resentful offspring take to the idea of a stepchild?

"God knows!"

Impulsively he turned from the window, reached for the telephone and asked for Kate.

"Mrs Harper is in a meeting I'm afraid. Can she call you back?" The voice was bright and impersonal.

Robert said, "Is that you, Brenda? Robert Dengaul here."

"Oh, sorry, Mr Dengaul. I didn't recognise your voice." He heard the awe in her tone. "She'll be in a meeting until three. I'll leave a note on her desk if you like."

"Don't bother. I'll try later."

He replaced the receiver and threw himself into one of the armchairs. He covered his face with his hands and whispered, "Help me, Vi! For God's sake, help me!"

Kate sat at the long table, five places from chairman Gordon Brett. Leaning forward she listened intently, the pencil stilled in her fingers. On her left was one of the sales reps, on her right a man from the publicity department. He was doodling on his pad – a series of cubes with heavily shaded ends.

The chairman was talking about Robert's latest published novel with more than usual interest. As an unknown writer, Robert Dengaul had been "discovered" by Gordon Brett many years earlier. The firm had carefully nurtured his career and Robert had remained loyal to them. Gordon Brett was enquiring about the initial subscription.

"I understand it's around three thousand and growing." He nodded his approval. *The Man From Milan*. I like the title." He glanced towards the man on Kate's left. "How did you rate the response?"

The man abandoned his doodling and sat up a little straighter. "Very positive, sir. Most of the buyers went for it. Very enthusiastic."

Gordon Brett smiled at Kate. "You must let Robert know. He was rather unhappy when we changed the title but I think he'll forgive us when he sees the sales figures."

Kate nodded. "I'm sure he will."

Robert had been furious, but he was too professional to do more than express regret.

As one of their top-selling authors of crime fiction, Robert had more influence than most but he was still unable to control aspects of the book's production. The choice of print, the quality of the paper, the selling price – all were beyond his jurisdiction and best left to the experts.

"Has he started on another novel yet, Kate?"

"I believe so." She tried to sound convincing although to the best of her knowledge he hadn't even *thought* about it.

A woman next to Muriel leaned forward. "We've had an invitation for him to speak at a luncheon in Derbyshire. The hall holds two hundred and they promise every seat will be taken."

"Do they give a date?"

"The middle of August."

"August? Oh!" Kate felt herself blush. "That might be – I'm afraid we ..." She faltered to a stop.

Muriel rescued her. "An August wedding," she told the chairman. "Might clash. Might not."

From around the table there were smiles and murmurs of interest which increased Kate's confusion. She had begged Robert to keep their impending marriage a secret until after the event but, elated by her acceptance, he had told virtually everyone. Now they knew the date.

She muttered, "I'm awfully sorry."

The chairman positively beamed. "Don't apologise. One of our up and coming editors marries our most illustrious author. It's wonderful. Keeps it in the family!"

Muriel caught Kate's eye and winked.

Kate said, "We'll let you know as soon as we have set a date – apropos the Derbyshire invitation."

They moved on to the rest of the agenda – a non-fiction imprint that was in its infancy and a new author whose first book was under consideration. The former was of no interest and Muriel was handling the second. Kate's thoughts began to drift. She would have to write to Will's mother and tell her about Robert – a task she was dreading. She and her mother-in-law had been very close and she was afraid that Margaret Harper might see the forthcoming marriage as a betrayal of her son's memory. The last thing Kate wanted was to hurt Will's mother in any way, but surely she would understand. Kate had been alone a long time.

The door opened softly and the tea lady pushed the trolley inside and withdrew discreetly.

"Time for some refreshment," the chairman announced and there was an immediate scraping of chair legs and a relaxed murmur of voices.

Kate poured two teas and carried them

over to where Muriel stood by the window.

"Thanks Kate." She sipped the hot tea carefully then lowered her voice. "You look a little down. Is anything wrong?"

"I am rather worried," Kate told her. "It's the Faber party. Robert's asked me to go with him."

"No problem is there? He can take a guest."

"But for the last few years he's taken his daughter Caroline."

"But then he didn't have you."

Kate frowned. "Caroline's going to feel slighted. She's that type of girl."

Mu shrugged. "She'll have to get used to the idea. She's an adult, for heaven's sake! It's her problem, Kate, not yours."

Before Kate could answer, Muriel was called away and Kate was left to her thoughts. After a few moments' reflection she decided to speak to Robert about it. Perhaps she and Caroline could *both* go. She also made up her mind about Margaret Harper. When she got home she would phone Robert, make a quick omelette and then write to her, inviting her to the wedding. Hopefully, she would make her understand that the happiness Kate had known with Will was treasured in her memory but that the time had come for her to move on.

Thursday evening Seb walked into the kitchen at Highstead. He was small and wiry with his mother's colouring – reddish brown hair and pale skin – and lazy good looks.

"Oh you've condescended to come home," Caroline said. "Very decent of you." She brushed a lock of hair from her face and glared at her brother.

He said, "What on earth's going on?" His gaze wandered round the large airy room to the scrubbed draining board, the pans arranged neatly on their shelf, the crumb-free floor and what looked suspiciously like newly washed curtains. He could smell a cake baking and on the table he saw flour, butter and lard and a basket of early purple plums. Curious, he asked, "Have I missed something?"

Caroline gave him one of those knowing looks which always made him nervous.

"You could say that," she told him. "I think the word is 'momentous'."

"Momentous?" He frowned. "Father's getting a gong for his services to literature."

"Don't be silly."

"A prize, then." She was shaking her head. "Why not? He's had them before."

He lowered himself on to a chair.

"Well, he isn't."

"Another American tour?" How typical, he thought. I need to talk to her and she's in one of her awkward moods which meant he

41

must tread warily. Caroline had a nasty temper.

She folded her arms. "His *girlfriend* is coming for the weekend."

"His *what*!" Had his big sister finally gone mad? She'd been weird for a long time now.

"His girlfriend." Caroline opened the oven door and pulled out a large fruit cake. She carried it to the table and tested it with a skewer. "Her name's Kate Harper and she's much younger than him. They're thinking of getting married so—"

"Getting *married*?" Suddenly she had his full attention. "Caro, are you serious? Because if you're kidding I don't find it funny."

She studied the skewer and then cursed slightly under her breath as she carried the cake back to the oven. He noticed that the floor tiles had been washed and there was a faint smell of polish. "Is that the reason for the big clean up?"

"Thanks for noticing. Mrs Matthews came in to give me a hand. Dad wants us to make a good impression." She shut the oven door and turned to face him, her hands on her hips. "So while you're off gallivanting *I'm* doing all the work."

"Serves you right. You should have kept Mrs Matthews on full time."

"She got on my nerves – always buzzing round Father. I never got him to myself."

"You don't mean she was *after* him! She's a bit too homely."

"And a lot too old, judging by this wretched Kate." She sank down on to a chair on the opposite side of the table. "Well, try to look pleased at the great news. Practise, if necessary, because Father's expecting us to welcome her with open arms. One big happy family."

In spite of his sense of shock he grinned at the look on her face. It reminded him of the way she had looked when, as a ten year old, she was given a torch for her birthday instead of a pony.

"Younger than him, you say?" he echoed. He was trying to believe what she had told him.

She nodded. "Anyway, where have you been?"

"None of your business."

"You *said* you were doing a walk."

"Then that's what I was doing." He prepared for a lengthy tussle – his sister hated not knowing what he was up to. All part of what he had long since termed the "mother-hen effect".

She said, "We're having dinner Friday evening – the whole family – I'm doing salmon and salad and—"

"You know I don't like fish. Are you serious – about Father?"

"I wasn't aiming to please you. I was

43

trying to find a simple foolproof menu." She rubbed her eyes, a habit she had when she was upset and for the first time Sebastian realised just how tense she was. "Of course I'm serious."

"Good grief, Caro. What's he playing at?" It was beginning to dawn on him that any problems he might have were being overtaken by something larger. He frowned, trying to imagine his father with another woman – a younger woman. The idea of a man nearing sixty flirting with anyone was rather repellent. He knew his father had always had a gleam in his eye for the fairer sex but planning to *marry* a much younger woman was incredible.

He said, "He'll never go through with it."

Caroline sighed deeply. "You haven't heard him going on about her. She's somewhere between an angel and a princess with a hint of film star. Kate. I already loathe the name."

"Does Bernard know?"

"I told him and he said, 'Sly old dog'. I told Father and he looked a bit taken aback. I really think he expected us to be pleased for him." Her mouth trembled. "What are we going to do, Seb? We can't just let it happen."

Sebastian felt the first frisson of real alarm. His sister was asking him for advice. He thought about it, trying to imagine his father with a lady friend. Presumably she couldn't be much to look at or she would have found someone her own age.

Caroline went on, "I mean, we live here. It's all right for Bernard because they've got their own home thanks to Alison's rich daddikins. What happens to you and me when this Kate moves in? Do we all live together? We'd cramp their style, wouldn't we? And she'd be our stepmother. Can you imagine it? She'd probably start trying to lay down the law."

There was a long baffled silence. Caroline seized a knife and started to attack the plums – pulling off the stalks and cutting out the stones.

"And don't think she won't make a difference because she *will*. I told Dad you wanted to go to Art School and—"

"Oh, you did. Thanks, Caro. You're a gem." He smiled at her with affection. "What did he say?"

"He said 'I'll talk to Kate about it.'"

For a moment Seb was speechless. His father had been so generous since their mother died. Caro had had her horse, Bernard had been given money towards his motor car, now his youngest son needed fees for the Art School his father was "going to talk to Kate".

"Hells bells!" he muttered. "He can't do this to me. It's not fair. Ask Kate? What does

45

she know about anything, for God's sake? I'm entitled to that money. You and Bernard have had some. It's my turn. He's always telling me to make my mind up and now I have he's—" he almost choked on the words, "he's *going to ask Kate*!"

He stared in dismay at his sister who had finished the plums and had started to make pastry.

She said, "If anything's wrong with this pie don't say a word."

"Caro! Who cares about the damn dinner? What matters—"

"I care." Her expression was anguished. "I'm doing my best here – working myself into the ground – but I can't guarantee everything's going to be perfect." She wiped her forehead with her sleeve, dropping flour on to her blouse as she did so. "Kate loves plum pie," he said. He said it twice, so I took the hint and offered to make one for Saturday lunch but you know what I'm like with pastry and if something's not right and anybody criticises I want you to say, 'No, it's fine.' I mean it, Seb." She drew a quick breath. "You've got to back me up. I'm not having him blame me if—"

"OK. I'll say it. OK?" He regarded her flushed face with growing concern. It was to be hoped she wasn't going to fall apart just when he needed her most. He preferred not to think about her breakdown all those years ago. The doctor insisted that she had made a full recovery but had warned her parents to watch for signs of a possible recurrence. The idea of another woman in their father's life was causing her to panic and that could be dangerous. He would have a word with his father about her when he got the chance. In the meantime he would try to allay her fears.

"Listen, Caro, let's just wait and see, shall we?" He smiled reassuringly. "This Kate person might be quite nice." He flashed his little-boy grin. "Who knows? We might even like her. She might be the sister you've never had." He didn't think this very likely. His sister didn't make friends easily and certainly not with anyone who might come between her and her father.

By way of an answer, Caroline rolled her eyes despairingly. "So you think we're going to love Kate Harper, do you?" She gave him a dark look. "Well, when Father dies and leaves her all his money you might not be so keen."

The thought had never even entered Sebastian's head. Now it did and he was shaken to the core. "He – he wouldn't!"

Her answer was a shrug.

Sebastian watched her knead the dough and begin to roll it out with thumps of the rolling pin.

"Hey!" he said. "What's that pastry ever

done to you? It's not Kate, you know."

She paused, then looked up at him. "I wish it were!" she said and burst into tears.

"Caro!" This was not the Caro he knew. He stared at the shaking shoulders with confusion. Could it be that his sister *was* as vulnerable as anyone else? "It's only a pie, Caro."

She sat down, rubbing at her eyes. "I just want everyone to be pleased." She sobbed. "And it's not only a pie. It's for Father. He wants it so I ..." She seized the handkerchief he offered and blew her nose. Suddenly she looked about seven and Seb was touched. He was also worried. Kate Harper's visit to Highstead was already stirring passions best left undisturbed.

Two

On Friday, as promised, Kate stepped off the train, straight into Robert's waiting arms. His hug was so fierce she could scarcely breathe.

"Robert!" she gasped as her weekend case fell from her hand to the ground.

"Kate!" He stepped back, looked into her eyes and then drew her close again. "I thought Friday would never come." He laughed breathlessly. "Say you've missed me."

"Robert! Of course I have." She couldn't tell him that the week had flown; that she had dreaded the passage of time which brought her closer to the meeting with his family. Instead she said, "I've been busy but I've missed you dreadfully." To change the subject she asked, "Have you made a start on the novel? I told them you had."

"Of course I have. A whole page of synopsis."

"I meant—"

"I know what you meant but I don't want to talk about the damned novel. You're here

49

and I want us to enjoy the weekend. All of us."

He picked up her suitcase and together they walked past the milk churns towards the gate.

"I haven't come by taxi. Bernard has his new motor and he offered to collect you. He can't wait to meet you."

"That's very sweet of him." Bernard, she reminded herself, was the eldest of the three. She mustn't muddle them.

"Isn't it? But I had to come with him. I didn't want you to be met by a stranger."

They joined the small queue at the gate and Kate handed over her return ticket which was duly punched and given back to her. Outside on the station forecourt she drew a deep breath and told herself to relax. Relax and enjoy yourself, Kate. Muriel had said, "They are just as nervous as you are and they don't bite." On the far side of the forecourt she caught sight of a young, fair-haired man leaning with feigned nonchalance against a brand new Morris.

"Is that Bernard?" she asked.

Robert smiled. "That's him."

Kate heard the pride in his voice. "He looks like you," she said, surprised and pleased by the likeness.

"Bernard's a brick," he told her. He withdrew his hand from hers and waved to catch his son's attention. "And Alison knows it. Steady as a rock, that's Bernard. Steadier than his old man, that's for sure."

Bernard came towards them. He walks like Robert, too, she thought and felt sure she was going to like this younger version.

A moment later Robert was making the introductions and she was shaking Bernard's hand with genuine pleasure. She said, "A ride in a new motor. I'm thrilled."

She walked slowly round the vehicle while Bernard pointed out its best features. She was aware that Robert's eyes were following her and when she glanced up he winked.

Bernard grinned with satisfaction as they finished making admiring noises. "So you like it?" He glanced at it with delight. "A couple of months old, that's all." He ran a hand smoothly over the bonnet, then gave his father a quick smile and opened the door. "Be my guest, Kate!" he said with a sweep of his hand.

Kate climbed in and settled herself on the seat. "What luxury! The smell of good leather! Mmm!"

Outside she saw Robert hesitate. "You go in the front," she told him. "I'll sit in splendid isolation."

Robert raised his eyebrows. "Certainly not. I shall join you."

While Robert climbed in beside her, Bernard carried her case round to the other side and put it on the floor in the front.

As they drove back through the narrow lanes Kate was able to consider the first of the Dengaul children. Bernard the brick. Eyeing the back of his head she noticed that his hair curled a little on the nape of a neck which was slimmer than Robert's. What she could see of his jacket was well cut and of good material. His hands on the steering wheel were slim with fine pale hairs. She found herself imaging the hands caressing Alison and wondered about a younger Robert with Violet. Apparently Bernard and Alison had no children and she wondered why that was. Presumably they could afford a family.

The three of them made small talk, but in a short time they were pulling up at a large Georgian house. Built of warm golden stone, its deep windows reflected the sun. The high square facade was topped by a slate roof and elegant chimneys. A large Victorian conservatory had been added at some time and the whole building was flanked by lawns and shrubbery.

"It's beautiful, Robert!" she exclaimed. "I can see why you're so attached to it."

Robert climbed out to open the door. "Highstead! We bought it with the money from my first novel. We took one look at it and fell in love with it. All the children were born here."

Bernard was removing her case as Robert

reached in to help her out.

"A very nice ride. Thank you," Kate said to Bernard.

"My pleasure, Miss Harper."

"Oh Kate, please!"

"Kate it shall be." He smiled broadly at her and she thought she could detect genuine warmth. Perhaps Muriel was right and she had worried herself unnecessarily.

Robert put a possessive arm round her shoulders. "So what do you think, Bernard. Isn't she lovely?"

Kate protested. "Robert! Don't embarrass me!" To Bernard she said, "Please don't answer that." She looked up at the house and saw a white dove swooping upwards to the roof.

"Doves! Are they yours?"

Robert shook his head but before he could reply the front door opened and a woman hurried down the steps. This must be the daughter, thought Kate. She had finer features than Robert but the colouring was the same. She was prettier than Kate had expected but her dress did not flatter her and her hair was drawn severely back and tied with a ribbon.

Caroline immediately took hold of her father's arm and kissed him.

He protested. "I've only been gone twenty minutes!"

She turned to Kate and held out a hand

with barely concealed reluctance. "I'm Caroline but everyone calls me Caro."

As they shook hands a trifle awkwardly Kate saw the strain in the other woman's eyes. She's wary, she thought, but so am I. She said, "I can see you and Bernard are brother and sister."

Caroline smile was thin. "Seb's different. He takes after our mother. She was wonderfully pretty with auburn hair. She died two years ago but it seems like yesterday."

Robert said quickly, "Where is Seb?"

"In the stable with Nutmeg and Hanlon."

Kate said, "Nutmeg. I've heard all about her."

Caroline turned to her father. "He arrived just after you left for the station." She turned to Kate. "Hanlon's the vet. My mare started coughing yesterday but Hanlon's only just shown up, lazy blighter. I don't suppose you ride."

"No. I'm rather nervous with horses although I do appreciate them. I mean they are such wonderful animals." She hoped the comment would count in her favour but Caroline was already drawing Robert up the steps and into the house.

Bernard and Kate followed. Inside the spacious hallway Robert detached himself from Caroline and took Kate's hand and led her into a large lounge. There, another young woman sprang to her feet and held out her hand.

"I'm Bernard's wife, Alison. I'm so pleased to meet you."

Kate looked at her appraisingly. Attractive with very dark hair. Good clothes. Rather formal, she thought.

Robert helped Kate off with her jacket and they all sat down except Caroline.

"If you'll excuse me a moment," she said. "I'll get back to Mr Hanlon and Seb. The kettle has boiled, Alison, if you want to make—"

Robert said, "Oh to hell with the kettle. I think we'll all have a drink. What will you have, Kate? A gin and orange, isn't it?"

Kate would have preferred a cup of tea but she saw that Robert was nervous so she nodded. On the train coming down she had reminded herself that a weekend could not last more than forty-eight hours. She was going to get through them one at a time – and for some of them she'd be asleep.

Kate took the drink which shook slightly in Robert's hand and watched him pour for the others. Before he had finished, his younger son came into the room wiping his hands on a large handkerchief.

"I'm all horsey," he said apologetically. "Old Hanlon's a bit past it if you ask me. If there's nothing wrong, why is the horse coughing?" He swivelled on his feet. "You must be Kate. *The* Kate." His tone and look were challenging as he took her hand. "The Kate who has stolen Father's heart!" His smile was another challenge and Kate felt her own heart speed up a fraction.

"And you're *the* Sebastian. I hope we're going to be friends."

The comment took him by surprise. He said, "Why not?" and turned to his father. "Whisky. Neat, please."

"Neat?"

"Yes."

Caroline returned from the stable and was handed a gin and orange.

Everyone looked at Robert who raised his glass. "To Kate!" he said.

For a long moment they all looked at her. Oh Robert! she thought desperately. Don't do this. Don't let them see how vulnerable you are. "To the weekend!" she amended.

Sebastian said nothing but downed half his whisky.

Alison said, "To a pleasant weekend."

Bernard lifted his glass. "I'll second that. And health and happiness to Father and Kate."

Caroline stiffened. Saying nothing, she put her drink down untouched. To her father she said, "Hanlon could find nothing wrong with Nutmeg, let's hope he's got it right."

Kate saw Robert register Caroline's challenge. He coloured angrily, opened his mouth to say something then thought better of it. Instead, he took Kate's free hand and gave it a reassuring squeeze.

"When you've finished your drink I'll show you to your room."

Kate nodded, but her heart ached for him. It wasn't going quite how he'd imagined and he was struggling to maintain his composure. She wanted to throw her arms around him and say, "Don't worry." Perhaps when they were alone. She glanced at the clock and saw with a sense of shock that she had only been in the house ten minutes. It seemed like an eternity.

That evening the family sat round the long dining table, which looked wonderful. Kate had already complimented Caroline on it in the hope that the compliment would help soothe any ruffled feelings. She had tried to put herself in Caroline's shoes and thought she understood Robert's daughter. The important thing was to forge friendly links but she was finding it harder than expected, not that that deterred her from further efforts. For everyone's sake, it was important that they should get along with a minimum of animosity, but Kate's priority was Robert's happiness. He wanted one big happy family and Kate would work toward that goal.

It was clear that Robert's success meant

that only the best was good enough. Delicate glassware sparkled, the elegant silver cutlery had been polished to perfection, there were expensive candlesticks and the tablecloth and napkins were of ivory damask. The extravagant floral centrepiece had been professionally arranged. Robert had confided earlier that they had argued about the seating arrangement. Robert had wanted his guest at the far end of the table opposite him but Caroline had protested that Kate wasn't yet mistress of the house so it was inappropriate. Robert pretended to find this highly amusing, but Kate agreed with Caroline and said so. Privately she found it worrying that the family was arguing over her already. It surely augured badly for the future.

Now she laid her knife and fork neatly together and gave a deep sigh.

"That was delicious, Caroline. Wonderful salmon. I wish I could cook like this."

Sebastian laughed. "I wish Caro would *always* cook like this! You should see what she serves up sometimes." He looked at his sister.

"Very droll, Seb. I keep hoping you'll grow up."

Bernard smiled at Kate. "Hope springs eternal! Are you plagued by any family, Kate?"

"None, sadly. I'm an only child of elderly

parents now both dead. I do have an aunt but she and my mother quarrelled and I lost touch with her years ago. But I do have Margaret, my mother-in-law. She's always been very good to me."

All the faces turned sharply towards her.

Before she could go on, Robert said, "Did I mention that Kate had been married before?"

Caroline said, "You know you didn't," in a tone that suggested there might be other untold secrets.

"Will Harper was my first sweetheart," Kate elaborated. "We were married while we were still students and he was killed five years later. He was a musician. Played tenor sax in a dance band." She smiled. "He was very unconventional. We did the oddest things. Once he decided we'd take up mountaineering but it didn't last more than a few weeks. We couldn't afford the equipment."

Alison said, "He sounds great fun."

"He was. One year it was judo. We both had six lessons, but he twisted his knee and we gave that up! Life was never dull with Will around."

Alison said, "How terribly sad, him dying so young."

"It was a nightmare. He'd been offered a much better job in London when the accident happened."

Sebastian refilled the glasses. "How did it happen?"

"He was riding his motorbike. He was so proud of that machine! A brand new Norton. There was a collision with a brewer's dray. A policeman came to my door to say he'd been killed instantly and didn't suffer."

Seb gave a snort of disbelief. "They always say that. It's to make you feel better."

Caroline gave him a withering look. "Honestly, Seb, you are *so* diplomatic! Go on, Kate."

"The policeman was so young. It was the first time he'd had to break bad news." She glanced at Robert who put out a hand across the table to take hers.

Alison shook her head. "Poor Will – and poor you!"

Seb looked at his sister-in-law and Kate was puzzled by an expression which flashed briefly in his eyes but then was gone. "Imagine how terrible you'd feel, Alison, if you lost Bernard. Could you ever love again?"

Kate saw that the conversation had suddenly taken an awkward turn and was trying to think of something to say when Robert spoke.

"No one wants to lose someone they love."

Caroline looked at her father. "But people *do* survive the loss. They live to – to fight another day. To find another love." She turned to Kate. "Don't they?"

Before Kate could reply Alison leaned forward. "Not everyone does, though. My mother's cousin killed herself when her favourite brother died at Mons. She couldn't imagine that life would ever be worth living without him. She left a terribly sad note. My grandmother's still got it." They were all looking at her. "Not everyone has the courage to go on."

Seb put his elbows on the table and stared into Alison's eyes. "The question is, would *you* go on? Would *you* ever want a new love?"

Bernard's expression hardened. "We're not talking about Alison."

Quickly Kate intervened. "I'm sorry. I didn't mean to depress everyone."

Robert said, "Of course not, darling."

But Caroline had recognised the cue and stood up. "Well, if we've all finished ...?"

Kate said, "I'll give you a hand. Bring some dishes out." She stood up but Alison put a hand on her arm.

"You're the guest tonight, Kate. Make the most of it."

Robert nodded. "I shouldn't argue with that, Kate."

She sat down again. No doubt Caro and Alison would want to compare notes about her when they were safely in the kitchen. She wondered what sort of marks she was getting but perhaps it was better not to know. She had no wish to be demoralised so early in the visit. At least Caroline had defended her when Sebastian made his tactless remark. There might be some hope after all, she thought.

She glanced at Bernard and then at Seb. Chalk and cheese, as Robert had said. Bernard had a certain smugness about him which she found a little disagreeable but at least he was being pleasant towards her. Seb was watchful and his intense expression made her a little uneasy.

Robert said, "Fate's a funny thing. We discovered recently that Kate and I had already met. Six years ago when *Angels of Darkness* came out. Kate was a humble secretary at that time and had been roped in to hand round the publisher's rotten little canapes. I turned a little sharply and knocked the plate with my elbow. Poor Kate was scarlet with embarrassment as the staff rushed to pick up the pieces!"

Seb said, "Was Mother with you? She always came to the 'do's."

"Yes she was." He smiled. "Five minutes later Vi found Kate crying in the Ladies Room and gave her a handkerchief. It was one of mine that I'd lent to Vi. I remember Vi said afterwards that she was so sorry for the girl. A blot on her copybook."

"I thought I'd ruined my career, but I kept

the handkerchief. Very impressed to have one with RMD in the corner."

"Not so impressed now, I daresay."

Kate smiled. "I wouldn't say that, Robert."

Caro had come in again and was listening to the conversation as she gathered knives and forks on to a small tray.

She said, "Then you and Father have known each other for some time – even before Mother died."

Robert gave her a sharp look. "I meant nothing of the kind, Caro. I'm simply saying that fate brought us all together on that one occasion. Then years passed until Kate and I met again."

"Which was when?" his daughter persisted.

Kate wished that Robert hadn't drunk three whiskies before dinner. His face was slightly flushed and his eyes were very bright.

"Which was about six months ago. What is this, Caro? An interrogation?"

There was a bright spot in each of her cheeks. "Of course it's not." She turned to Kate. "That's the trouble with writers. They always exaggerate. They over-dramatise everything. They—" She stopped abruptly, snatched up the cruet and left the room.

Kate closed her eyes briefly and uttered a silent prayer. Don't lose it, Robert, she begged. Don't say something indiscreet.

Robert needed to keep his wits about him.

For a long time nobody spoke and then Alison came in with a jug of cream and a cheeseboard and Caro followed with a large *tarte Tatin*.

She put it down and said, "Before you all congratulate me, it's Alison's contribution."

Everyone made the right noises, Robert refilled glasses and the meal continued.

Bernard looked at his brother. "How did the walk go – or was it a ramble?"

"The walk?"

"The rambling club. Alison said you'd joined something—"

Alison said quickly, "The South Eastern Harriers. Cross-country running. Honestly Bernard, your mind's like a sieve these days."

Seb said, "Oh that. Fine. Yes. We run at a steady pace. Great fun."

"So where did you go? From where to where?" Bernard's eyebrows were raised, his tone slightly mocking. He held up a forefinger on each hand. "From A to B."

Alison said, "Does it really matter where he went?"

Bernard looked at her. "I suppose not. Is it a secret, then?"

They were all looking at Seb who was looking at Alison. Kate stole a glance at Robert who had emptied his glass again.

Aware of yet another building tension she

said hurriedly, "My uncle used to belong to the Watford Harriers. He swore by it. Wonderful exercise and he enjoyed the social side of it. He must have been good because I remember he won a cup and I was allowed to hold it on one occasion. My aunt was very proud of it. She polished it religiously."

How on earth, Kate wondered, was she going to survive the rest of the weekend? Already her head was beginning to ache with the strain of trying to appear relaxed and happy. Maybe she would invent a cold and go home a day early. The familiar comforts of her small flat had never seemed so desirable as they did now. But leaving early would devastate Robert. It would be an admission of failure. Could she do that to him? He had waited so long for this family get-together and had expected great things. For his sake she would persevere. She poured cream over the tart, found it delicious and said so.

Alison said, "I could let you have the recipe. It's not too difficult. Tedious more than anything. Fiddling with all the little apple slices."

Caro said, "The salmon's easy, too. If you don't have a fish kettle the fishmonger will probably lend you one."

Seb turned suddenly to his father. "So what d'you think about Art School? Caro told you, I believe." Before his father could answer Seb turned to Kate. "I've decided to go to Art School if Father will finance the course for me. A loan, of course. I've always been interested but now suddenly—"

Robert said, "This is hardly the time, Seb. We'll have to talk about it."

"But I thought Kate would be interested. Getting to know the family and all that." He gave her a challenging smile. "An artist in the family, starving in a lonely garret! How does that appeal, Kate?"

She forced a light laugh. "It's different. I'll grant you that."

Caro said, "Actually he *can* draw. He's really quite good."

Bernard said, "It's news to me."

Alison gave him a withering look. "How would you know? Since when have you shown the slightest interest in Seb?"

He stared at her. "I could say the same about you. You never mention him from one week to the next. How would you know if he can draw?"

Kate watched the colour drain from Alison's face and knew she could bear it no longer. If she didn't get away from them she would say something she would regret.

She turned to Robert. "You promised me a walk in the garden before the light goes. Could we slip away for ten minutes now?" She smiled brightly at the rest of the fanily.

"Would you mind?"

There was no answer. Kate stood up and after a moment's hesitation Robert did the same. They walked to the french windows, opened them, and stepped out into the garden. As they began to cross the grass, conversation behind them started up again.

Robert slid an arm round her waist. "Kate, I'm sorry," he said huskily.

Kate said, "No need to apologise."

"Of course there is! They were bloody awful!"

She longed to agree but that would hurt him, she was sure. "Give them time," she said softly. "It's early days."

"They'll drive you away!"

"Robert! Of course they won't. We won't let them come between us."

He drew her closer and she was shocked to see panic in his eyes. "Oh God!" he whispered. "I wish I could believe you."

That night Bernard and Alison lay in bed, each keeping rigidly to their own side of it. Bernard wore navy-blue pyjamas, Alison a sprigged cotton night dress. Between them they had accomplished the nightly chores – Alison had filled the kettle and put out the mugs, milk and sugar ready for the morning tea and Bernard had locked up the various doors and put the empty milk bottle on the front step. This was the time of day when they felt able to talk, when they need not see each other's expression.

Alison said, "Well, I thought she was quite nice. She seemed genuinely fond of him."

"Yes. I thought so too."

"Bit of a shock that she'd been married before. Your father didn't say she was a widow."

"No. He kept that quiet. I wonder why."

"Probably didn't think it was important. Well, it isn't, is it?"

There was a long silence. Alison waited. She had made the first approach. It was his turn now.

He said, "The vicar has asked me to rejoin the choir. Bob Sanders is leaving and they need a baritone. Just as a temporary thing. I don't have to say yes."

"But you want to." The words spilled out.

"I knew you'd take it like that!"

"Like what?" She wanted to scream. It seemed they could no longer talk on any subject without friction.

"That tone of voice."

Did she want him to rejoin the choir? Would it really be a temporary thing? Another late night, but did she really care? If she couldn't love him any more he had only himself to blame. His attitude to what he saw as "her failure" had been the most hurtful thing she had ever endured. She had been so willing, in those early days, to resolve the problem. Visits to the clinics, the doctor, the hospital. All those awful tests and charts and the humiliating rituals. Her stomach knotted at the thought of her ordeal over all those months. And the final verdict? "Nothing wrong with you, Mrs Dengaul. Nothing at all."

She swallowed her rising anger, determined to prevent another row. Forcing a light tone of voice she said, "It must be interesting being an editor. Seeing all the manuscripts come and go. Some make it, others don't."

"She's only a junior editor. I don't suppose she gets to make any real decisions."

"Not yet, maybe. I thought Caro was a bit off with her. Rather rude, in fact." Too late she realised that this particular comment might give her husband further excuse. A disagreement, however unimportant, would be all he needed to put an end to any chance of lovemaking. Alison understood his reluctance without condoning it. If they never had sex, no one could ever suggest that her failure to conceive might lie with him. The consultant had wanted to talk to Bernard about it but Bernard had chosen not to attend.

"Trust you to pick on Caro. Can't you see how difficult it must be for her? She's got to live with Kate if Father does marry her." He threw back the covers. "It's hot in here. Are the windows open?"

"Aren't they always? It's those pyjamas. You should buy some thinner ones or sleep without the top half."

"Oh yes! You'd like that! Anyway, look at you."

"It's cotton. Cotton's cool." She turned her head slightly towards him. "It's not me that's hot. It's you."

"Good God, Alison! Do you have to argue about everything?"

Alison simmered in silence for a moment and then burst out. "Look! Just join the blasted choir. I don't care what you do." With a sense of shock she realised that it was true. She no longer cared for him. Did he care at all for her? In a way she hoped not. It would be so much easier if he no longer loved her.

He became aware that she was looking at him. "For God's sake, Alison. Why do you have to stare at me?"

She turned away with an exaggerated movement but she was still trying to avoid a major confrontation. With a change of tone she said, "You can see that they love each other. I think you should all leave them alone. Let them be happy. It's not much to ask. Your father won't live forever and I don't think your mother would have begrudged him a few years of happiness with someone else. Who knows if your mother had been left a widow *she* might have met someone else."

"Never. She had more sense."

"Who's talking about sense? Your trouble is there's no romance in your soul." That was true, she reflected with a twist of her mouth. No nonsense Bernard. Lived his life according to the book. So solid and dependable. That was what she had once loved about him.

"But then he's not your father, is he?"

"He's my father-in-law." She drew a long breath, trying to stay calm. If her husband turned away from her in a fit of temper she would never be able to get to sleep. No matter how logically she told herself that Bernard's mood need not affect her, it would do so. She would lie awake until the small hours and everything would seem ten times worse than it really was. *If* that were possible.

"I thought Seb was a bit obvious. Asking about his Art School fees right in front of Kate so that Father couldn't say 'no' without appearing tightfisted. Typical Seb, that. And he couldn't take his eyes off Kate." He turned towards Alison and propped his head on his hand.

"Did he? I didn't notice." Her heart began to race. Was it true? "I shouldn't have thought she was Seb's type. A bit too high-brow."

71

"Seb's not fussy where women are concerned."

"What's that supposed to mean?" He couldn't know anything, surely.

"What I say. He fancied a barmaid once – great blowsy creature at the Duck. He was only eighteen and she was nearly forty. That was before that trouble with Marion Whatsername – the bridesmaid at the Marklakes' wedding."

"You know that was nothing." She tried to keep her tone neutral. "Just the usual high jinks. Too much to drink and—"

"What d'you know about it? You weren't even there."

She felt his eyes staring at her through the gloom and a fine perspiration broke out on her forehead. "I heard about it from Caro. We do *talk*, you know. We are *friends*." She swallowed hard. She was being careless now. Time to stop before she went too far.

He grunted. "Caro doesn't know everything, and for your information the girl was only sixteen and she accused Seb of groping her under the table and trying to get his fingers—"

"Stop it! You know I hate that kind of talk." She was breathing fast. Not that she believed it for a moment. Seb had sworn the girl was lying to get attention and Alison preferred to believe Seb's version. "You're just jealous of him," she said, her voice rising slightly. Suddenly her control was slipping but she couldn't stop. "You've always been jealous because he was your mother's blue-eyed boy."

Abruptly he sat up. He reached for the bedside lamp and turned it on. As Alison saw the expression on his face she realised they had passed the point of no return.

"You ... you rotten cow!" He shouted. "You've been talking about me to *him*! Don't try to deny it!"

"I didn't know it was forbidden." Her voice shook. Somehow she had to extricate herself. "We talk about everybody. Every family does." It was a feeble attempt.

There was fury in Bernard's narrowed eyes as he leaned over her and for the first time in their life together Alison was almost afraid of him.

"What did the little wretch say about me, eh? What?"

"Nothing – only that you were jealous. He didn't go into details. It was a throwaway line. You know Seb."

"It seems you know him better! My God, Alison. If I find out – I shall have it out with him, and if I find – if you've said anything about our problem to him I'll—"

"Of course I haven't!" It was a lie. Guilt flooded through her.

He grabbed her shoulder and shook her violently. "If you've said – God Almighty!"

She tried to twist from his grasp but his fingers tightened, digging painfully into her chest. "Let me go, Bernard. You're hurting me."

"If I find out you've told him I'll *really* hurt you, and then I'll walk out on you. I *will*! I'll leave you!" He released her shoulder but he was still kneeling over her and his fist clenched as he struggled to restrain himself.

"If you're going to hit me, do it! Make it a good one so they can all see the bruises at church on Sunday morning. That should make interesting reading on the front page of next week's *Herald*!"

As the words tumbled out, Alison heard them with horror. What on earth was happening? What was she saying? Her husband had never laid a finger on her and never would.

With an oath she had never heard him use before he drew back his fist and hurled himself from the bed. Without a word he stumbled from the room and slammed the door behind him.

Slowly Alison sat up. She was shivering and icy cold. Gathering the bedclothes around her, she stared into the gloom, listening to the sounds Bernard made as he crashed around the house. The front door opened and shut, discreetly so as not to alert the neighbours and then she heard the engine of the car start up. He must be

74

wearing a coat over his pyjamas, she thought. Serve him right if he was stopped by a policeman.

Shocked by the speed of events, she shivered violently. She slid from the bed on legs that felt only partly connected to her body and reached for her dressing gown.

A cup of Ovaltine, she told herself. That would help.

While she waited for the milk to boil she watched from the window, anxious to know that he intended to return. In spite of her angry words, she was conscious of deep regret for the hurt she had caused. Worse, she wondered what Seb would say when he knew what had happened.

"Oh God, Seb!"

She had married the wrong brother.

The following morning Bernard, ignoring Alison's efforts at conversation, ate his breakfast without a word. Poached egg on toast and two cups of tea. When he had finished he went out, thankful for the committee meeting which gave him an excuse to get out of the house. An hour and a half later, unable to concentrate, he was longing for the meeting to end.

At twenty-five past twelve Reverend Scottley smiled at each member of his committee. "So now it's any other business. Ladies? Gentlemen?"

Bernard prayed that no one would raise another subject for discussion. Normally he enjoyed the company of his colleagues on the committee and found them intelligent and compatible. Today, they seemed small-minded to the point of foolishness. The church hall, usually bearable, felt airless and confined. He knew that the row with Alison was colouring his perceptions but he none-theless wanted the meeting to be over. He was also aware of a deep and uncharacteris-tic need for a pint of beer.

The vicar said, "Miss Hall?"

Miss Hall was putting her glasses back in their case. "No, vicar. I've nothing further."

"Mr Dengaul? Any other business?"

"Sorry?" Bernard looked at him guiltily. The vicar was just one of many who admired the Dengauls' happy marriage. "A good, sweet woman", was how he had once described Alison. How little he knew, Bernard reflected bitterly.

"Any other business? You did mention the church newsletter when we spoke on—"

"Oh no! Nothing urgent, Reverend."

Paul Catton said, "What *about* the newsletter?"

Bernard crossed his fingers. Catton was one of its editors and was already tugging his silly little beard and looking affronted.

Bernard said, "It was nothing that won't wait."

Miss Hall smiled. "I'm sure we can spare a few moments."

Bernard wanted to shake her. *"It will wait!"*

Reproachful faces turned towards him but while he was stammering his apology, John Somers spoke up.

"That's it, then, folks. We can all go home, can we, vicar?" His cheerful manner defused the tension, and the vicar nodded.

"Of course. I declare the meeting closed. Thanks to you all as usual and God bless!" He beamed on them.

Bernard turned to his rescuer. "Thanks awfully. I'm sorry about that." He lowered his voice. "The truth is I . . . I've got rather a lot on my plate at the moment."

"I thought you looked a bit down."

Surprised by his obvious concern, Bernard looked at him more closely, trying to recall what he knew about the man.

Somers, probably in his late fifties, was a widower. He had moved to the village just months before his wife died of tuberculosis. A large, comfortable-looking man with blue eyes, he lived alone in a large cottage on the Hastings road. After his wife died various single ladies in the village had paid him attentions but he remained politely aloof. Today he wore a shapeless linen jacket and a tweed hat.

Bernard rolled his eyes. "A *bit*!" He

pushed back his chair. "That's the understatement of the year!"

He regretted the admission as soon as the words were out, but Somers was nodding. "Fancy a quick drink? Stiffen the sinews, as they say."

Bernard longed to accept but he hesitated. As church warden he tried to maintain a certain standard of behaviour.

Somers lowered his voice. "At my place, I mean," he suggested. "Don't always feel like hobnobbing in the Duck."

Still Bernard hesitated. Alison would have the lunch on the table promptly at one. He came to a sudden decision. He *would* accept Somers' kind invitation, anything to delay the return home.

"Your place sounds fine," he said. "I've never been one for pubs, to be honest. I prefer a quiet drink at home."

"Me, too, but occasionally I need a bit of company, living alone." He shrugged, screwing the top on his fountain pen and clipping it into his jacket pocket.

Bernard was at once ashamed that he had never considered the man's plight. Loneliness must be terrible. He wished that he and Alison had asked him round for a spot of supper from time to time but it was too late now. She wasn't going to agree to anything now. He sighed as they made their farewells and went out into the sunshine.

Somers said, "There are times when Catton gets my goat!"

Heartened by this show of fellow feeling, Bernard nodded. "You'd think it was *The Times* instead of the parish newsletter!"

They glanced both ways and crossed the road.

"My wife was like that. Very quick to take offence. It made her life difficult."

Bernard lengthened his stride to keep up with his companion. "We saw you both in church, once or twice."

"She wasn't at all religious but she loved to sing. She had a fine soprano voice."

"You must miss her dreadfully." He wondered whether he would miss Alison if she suddenly died of something.

There was a long silence and then Somers gave him a quick sideways glance.

"Would it sound very callous if I said I didn't?"

They were leaving the village behind, walking along a grass verge with hedges on either side. Bernard could see the cottage at the bend in the road.

"No – that is, I suppose I'd be surprised, but callous? Not really."

"It surprised me, to tell you the truth. I expected to, naturally, but the truth is we'd sort of come to the end of the road several years before she went. We moved house to give ourselves a second chance. Thought it might make a difference. Fresh start sort of thing but it didn't help. Women can be difficult to live with, Mr Dengaul, and that's a fact of life!" He gave Bernard a rueful smile.

"Call me Bernard. Please."

"Right. Thanks. I'm John." He slowed down as they reached the cottage. "Ah here we are. *Chez nous*, as they say." He lifted the gate which was half off its hinges and Bernard followed him up a brick path that was sorely in need of weeding. To his left he saw a small dovecote with white doves perched around it.

John fumbled in his pocket for the key. "Ignore the state of the place. It's never dirty but it is untidy. Typical bachelor pad in fact." He laughed as the door swung open and he stepped into a darkened hallway. "I'll lead the way, shall I?"

They ended up in a small lounge. From one corner an elderly brown spaniel rose slowly to its feet, then hurried forward, wagging a stumpy tail.

"Meet Jasper. My wife wanted to call him Brownie but I won the toss." While Bernard patted the dog, John waved a hand to indicate the room. "Just big enough to swing a kitten! The estate agent described the room as 'bijou'. It's bijou all right but it gets very cosy in the winter so we didn't mind. There's a dining room that never gets used and we thought we might make them into one large room but didn't get round to it."

He waved towards an enormous sofa which was covered in some kind of patterned blanket and Bernard sank into its rumpled depth with a sigh of pleasure. Moments later, with John in an adjacent armchair, they were each holding a generous whisky. A dish of peanuts was placed strategically between them on the leather pouffe which served as an occasional table.

"Here's health!" said John.

"Cheers!" Bernard took a mouthful and swallowed it quickly. It hit his stomach with a reassuring jolt and he closed his eyes. "I needed that. Thanks, John."

"My pleasure. A bit of congenial company's always a treat." He stared at Bernard over the rim of his tumbler. "Having problems?"

Bernard nodded.

"I'm a good listener, if it helps."

Bernard hesitated.

John went on, "Women can be the very devil! Don't I know it. I loved her for years but in the end ..." He shrugged. "Well, it was doing neither of us any good. Can't live with them. Can't live without them. Only in my case I found I could." He crossed his legs and settled deeper into his chair. "The thing is we'd never have divorced. Too much of a stigma. The damned TB gave us both our freedom. I wasn't making her happy. She certainly wasn't good for me. I began to think I'd die first – of a heart attack!"

Bernard said, "I'm sorry." It sounded so inadequate. Doing neither of us any good. Was that a summary of his own marriage? he wondered. And how would he feel if they separated? He felt a rush of anxiety.

"We realised as the years passed that we'd got nothing in common, but we had our two sons and they held us together for a while. When they'd left home we were lost. Like two strangers."

Bernard nodded and for a moment they both stared into their drinks.

John said, "Sorry! I do go on, but it helps to talk about these things. Don't you think?"

Bernard was fighting an overwhelming urge to exchange confidences but something at the back of his mind was warning him against it. Instead he finished his whisky.

"Another? I never think one's any good." John drained his own glass.

"Oh well ... maybe just one more." He glanced at the clock.

"It's ten minutes fast. Wife expecting you back?"

"Lunch is always at one. On the dot."

"You've plenty of time. It's less than ten minutes from here." He refilled the glasses and settled himself once more.

The dog wandered over to Bernard and threw himself across his feet with a loud sigh.

"Alison hates dogs," he said. "She goes on and on about dog hairs!"

"A bit houseproud?"

"More than a bit!"

"Some women are." John smiled at Jasper. "We don't mind a bit of mess, do we?" The dog laid his head on his paws and closed his eyes. John looked at Bernard. "So what's the trouble – or shouldn't I ask? Tell me to mind my own business if you like."

Bernard drew a deep breath. He looked into the kindly blue eyes which met his with such warmth. He felt relaxed with John in a way he never had been with his own father. How old was John? he wondered. Late fifties, maybe? Much the same as his father. This thought led him to Kate. Another problem.

"I don't know where to start," he said. He needed to talk about Alison but that meant explaining about the lack of children and he didn't feel able to discuss that with anyone, not even a doctor. Instead he said, "My father's got himself entangled with a much younger woman."

"Your father? Good Lord! Met him a few times at the cricket club. Quite a useful fast bowler."

"He's quite besotted with her and – well, frankly, we're all rather worried for him."

"He's always seemed very level-headed."

"Level-headed. Exactly!" Bernard leaned back and crossed his legs, encouraged by his companion's interest. "Level-headed about most things but obviously not when it comes to women. This one's not unattractive, quite sweet, in fact. What you might call an intellectual." He took another mouthful of whisky. "She's thirty-six and her name's Kate Harper ..."

Three

On Sunday Kate woke soon after six and lay in bed, wondering about the rest of the household. Saturday had been no easier than Friday and Kate was counting the hours until she could go back to London. She rose before seven, washed and dressed and made her way quietly downstairs and out of the house. She had slept fretfully, weighed down by her anxieties and hoped to find the deserted garden soothing to her frayed mind. Wandering through the early morning sunshine, amid well-kept lawns and colourful shrubs, she tried but failed to shake off a growing feeling of apprehension. She and Robert might be happy here, but one day he would die and she would be left alone. It would all be hers, but she found the idea unutterably depressing.

Walking aimlessly, struggling with half-hidden emotions, Kate turned a corner in the path and discovered the stable. It was a small converted barn in which Nutmeg reigned in solitary splendour. The mare was a large roan with a darker mane and tail.

Kate was dismayed to find Caroline busy

about the yard but the latter appeared unfazed by the appearance of her father's fiancée. After polite greetings the two women regarded each other warily. Kate spoke first.

"I'm not too brave around horses," she said.

"Nutmeg wouldn't hurt a fly! She's a great softy," Caroline insisted, seeing the doubt in Kate's eyes. "Honestly, she won't bite you. Look here—" She produced a carrot from the pocket of her jodphurs. "Give her this. Hold your palm out flat and let the carrot rest on it."

Kate forced herself to obey and was pleasantly surprised when the horse's soft lips nuzzled her hand. "You're right." While the carrot was crunched between strong teeth, Kate risked a pat on the sleek neck. "She's rather lovely!" she admitted. "You must think a lot of her."

"I do. She saved my sanity when my mother died. It was so awful and I couldn't stop crying. I felt so bad about everything. I used to make my mother so angry as a child because I couldn't bear to see Father cuddle her. I used to struggle in between them. Once she called me a 'jealous little madam'." She gave an embarrassed laugh.

And you still are! thought Kate and wondered if Caroline was giving her a none-too-subtle warning.

Caroline went on, "I suppose I *was* jealous. Whenever we went out as a family I always insisted on holding Father's free hand – not that Bernard minded but Seb used to scream the place down! And I had to sit next to him in church. I was very close to Father. His little pet, you might say." For a moment she looked wistful. "Poor Mother. Looking back I think *she* must have been jealous – because Father paid me so much attention." When Kate made no comment she shrugged. "After Mother died I was in a dreadful state. Father dragged me off to the doctor although I told him it was normal. Everyone cries when they lose someone they love."

She opened the stable door and reached high up on the wall for Nutmeg's halter, which she slipped over the mare's head with practised ease. Proudly she led the animal out on to the paved area. "Isn't she beautiful?"

"Beautiful," Kate agreed as she hastily withdrew a few steps. Outside the stable the horse appeared much larger.

"The doctor gave me sleeping pills," Caroline continued, "and a tonic but they did no good. He said it was what they used to call melancholia in Victorian times but to me it was simply grieving."

Or guilt, thought Kate. She said, "Parents understand us better than we think they do.

I'm sure your mother knew that you loved her a great deal. My mother and I were never close. She always wanted a son and she miscarried two boys before I arrived."

"Here, hold her a moment."

Caroline thrust the rope into Kate's hand and dived back into the gloom of the stable. Nutmeg at once began to fret, moving uneasily over the ground with a clatter of hooves which Kate found unnerving.

Caroline returned with a large comb and brush. Seeing Kate's nervousness she said, "Oh give her to me," and quickly tied the mare to a convenient post. Beginning to groom her with slow strokes of the brush, she glanced up from one of Nutmeg's forelegs. "The doctor finally told Dad to send me abroad for a holiday to snap me out of it but I wouldn't go. So he suggested buying me a pet. A dog would be nice, he said. Company for me. I told Father – if you want to buy me an animal I'd like a horse." She laughed. "I'd always wanted one. I was always mucking out other people's horses just to be near them. Of course, it wasn't quite what Father had had in mind but to his credit he didn't flinch." She ducked under Nutmeg's neck and bobbed up the other side. "Hence Nutmeg ... Still, now I have Father all to myself – except for you, of course." She concentrated hard on her work, avoiding Kate's eyes.

"I'm not planning to come between you," Kate assured her. "I should hate Robert to feel he was being tugged in two directions at once."

"That's all right, then."

"We just need goodwill on all sides."

"We'll have to hope for the best."

Kate was considering this negative remark when she saw that Robert had approached unnoticed.

He smiled at his daughter. "I've never regretted buying Nutmeg. Life's never dull with a horse in the family. Feed bills, tack bills, vet's bills!" Grinning, he took hold of Kate's hand.

Caroline turned away sharply and Kate felt that any small rapport she might have built up with Robert's daughter had vanished.

To Kate he said, "I've been up since before six, ma'am, and I've finished the synopsis. Am I allowed to stop working now?"

Caroline looked up. "Honestly! You make Kate sound like a slave driver. She's only your editor, remember. Not your boss."

"Soon to be my wife."

Kate said quickly, "You've finished it? Robert, that's marvellous!"

"You haven't read it yet!"

"I know it will be."

"Pity you aren't a literary critic!"

Caroline turned to him. "When have the

critics *not* been kind to you? 'The best so far ... Another stunning plot from the pen of ...'"

They all laughed.

Kate said, "Would you like me to take it back with me or would you rather post it?"

"You take it, darling. I trust you not to leave the damn thing on the train."

Caroline said, "But you always have a carbon copy! Stop trying to frighten her."

She slipped an arm round Robert's waist. "I organise him – for his own good. I'm his secretary cum personal assistant. I stick on stamps, answer the phone, run errands. I even order the stationery." She looked up into his face. "I don't know what you'd do without me."

For a moment the words hung in the air, unchallenged.

Robert said, "You love it – and I pay you well."

"It's peanuts and you know it!" She tossed her head provocatively then looked at Kate. "It's just pocket money, but I'm saving up. I want to join the local hunt but it's very expensive. Father, old miser that he is, refuses to pay for me."

He disentangled himself. "I refuse because hunting's dangerous. All those hedges and gates. You'll fall off and kill yourself."

Caroline gave Kate a sly look. "He's terrified of losing his darling daughter!"

Behind her, Nutmeg shied suddenly as a dove flew low in a flutter of white wings. Caroline swung round. "Oh, poor Nutmeg! Have I been neglecting you?" She resumed her efforts with brush and comb.

Robert put an arm round Kate's waist. "I've come to take you away from all things horsey. I've something I want you to see." He began to lead her away, calling over his shoulder. "Don't be late for lunch, Caro. Bernard's going to pick the three of us up in the motor but Seb will have to bike round. You know what Alison's like if we're five minutes late."

"I'm surprised they haven't cancelled." Caroline straightened up, a hand to her back. "Didn't you notice what a funny mood they were in on Friday?"

Robert turned back. "I didn't notice anything. Maybe Alison was a bit quiet ... but then she was laughing with Seb about something."

Kate had noticed that, too. She had seen the glint in Alison's eyes and the flushed cheeks. Seb, also, had been over-reacting to everything Alison said. Here we go again, she thought.

Caroline said, "We'll see, won't we?"

Robert glanced unhappily at Kate. "I thought they were all right."

Caroline said, "You're the original ostrich!"

Kate, sensing friction, decided in favour of discretion. She squeezed Robert's hand. "So what is this mysterious something you want to show me?"

"Oh yes!" He brightened and they began to walk back through the garden towards the front of the house.

"Where are we going?"

He stopped and turned to survey the garden. "Now that we're alone ..." He took a small velvet box from his pocket.

Kate felt her heart beat faster with a rush of love and anxiety. "Oh no, Robert!" she stammered. "Not here!"

"Yes, here." He pressed the box into her hand. "Open it, Kate."

"Oh darling! Is this the right time?" Slowly she pushed up the lid and saw the large solitaire diamond ring. "Robert!" Her first thought was that it was too early; that the family was not ready for such a positive signal. "It's exquisite! Oh! You're too good to me!"

His eyes were shining with excitement. "Nothing is too good for you, Kate. Try it on."

It fitted perfectly. They both stared down at the beautiful stone.

"I want you to wear it to lunch. I'm going to tell the family that we are marrying in August. No arguments, Kate. I've made up my mind."

She whispered, "Oh God, I love you," and clung to him in a sudden panic. "All I want is to make you happy!"

"You do, Kate. You know you do."

She stepped back, looking up into his face. "And to make your children happy. I don't want to cause any trouble in the family, Robert. I'm prepared to wait until they can accept me."

"Well, I'm not!" His mouth tightened.

"You mustn't think like that. We can all get along if only you don't rush things. Your wife's only been dead a few years. It's natural Caro and Seb should resent—"

"Forget Caro and Seb!" he insisted. "They're not children and they have lives of their own. I'm old enough to be selfish, Kate, and I want you all to myself. Just the two of us. If they don't like it they must lump it." He put his arms round her again. "From now on it's just you and me. Nothing else matters."

Kate hesitated. Robert was so impatient and she felt the need to urge caution but was this the right time? she wondered. Any argument would spoil the romantic moment. Held tightly in his arms she waited in vain for inspiration until a voice disturbed them.

"Oh dear! Am I interrupting something?"

Startled, they sprang apart and turned to see Sebastian only yards away. Kate regarded him with dismay. There was a mocking smile on his face but his eyes were hard. Instinctively she clutched Robert's arm. How much of their conversation had Sebastian heard?

Sunday lunch with Bernard and Alison promised no relaxation from the tension. Kate sensed the atmosphere from the moment they arrived. Bernard was hearty to the point of desperation while Alison was subdued. Kate, noticing her heavily powdered face, assumed that she had been crying at some stage. Caroline was wary, Sebastian determinedly cheerful. The meal, less than inspired, suggested that Alison's attention had been directed elsewhere. The topside of beef had been overcooked and the Yorkshire pudding hadn't risen. Conversation was strained and Kate's heart ached for their hostess, imagining the hours of preparation taking place in an atmosphere of bad feeling.

At last Alison looked round at the plates and said, "Well, if you've all finished I'll clear."

Kate said, "I'll give you a hand, if I may." Anything to get out of the room, she thought. Anything to avoid the cheated look on Robert's face. His proud announcement of their engagement was still to come but Kate sensed his growing irritation with the situation. She was hoping he would wait for another opportunity but suspected that he would force the issue today.

Without waiting for permission, she stood up and reached for Sebastian's plate.

"That was delicious, Allie."

Caroline said, "Don't be sarcastic, Seb. It doesn't suit you."

Bernard glared at his brother. "And you know Alison hates to be called Allie."

"Does she?" Sebastian turned to Alison but she was hurrying from the room with a tureen in either hand. "That's news to me. She never objects."

Caroline's expression was frosty. "You never do call her Allie. You're just trying to make trouble."

"Caro's right," Bernard said, "but then you always have, haven't you, Seb? You've always tried to make trouble, even as a kid."

Robert snapped, "Do we have to put up with this? For God's sake, grow up, can't you!"

Kate beat a hasty retreat to the kitchen. It was small but airy with a modern cabinet standing against one wall. She put the plates down on the draining board.

"Alison, I—" She stared at the slim figure silhouetted against the sunlight, her head was bent and her shoulders were shaking. Kate stepped forward and put an arm round her. "Alison, it doesn't matter. Please don't upset yourself. Beef can be dry sometimes – I've had the same trouble."

Alison shook her head then drew in a long sobbing breath. "It's not that. To hell with the beef! I don't *care* any more ... about *anything*!"

Kate swallowed. "Can I do anything to help you? I mean *anything*? Nothing's that bad, Alison. Truly it isn't."

Gently she tried to pull Alison round to face her but Alison resisted. She ran the tap and began to splash cold water over her face, gasping and uttering small cries of distress. Glancing round the kitchen Kate found a hand towel and handed it to her.

"Won't you let me help?" she asked softly. "You can talk to me."

Alison scrubbed fiecely at her eyes. "You *can't* help me. You don't *know*—" She stopped abruptly. "I can't tell anyone."

At that moment Caroline appeared at the kitchen door with the gravy boat in her hand. "Oh no! There's Father carrying on in the dining room and you grizzling in the kitchen! I've had happier Sundays."

Kate looked at her coldly. "Are you always so insensitive?"

Caroline blinked, taken aback by the rebuke, but recovered quickly. "What's it got to do with you? She's *my* sister-in-law."

"Then you should care about her."

They stared at each other.

Alison said, "It doesn't matter. Honestly." She gave Kate a watery smile and her eyes a final dab with the towel. "Let's forget it." She drew a long breath and glanced around the kitchen but at that moment Bernard came into the kitchen, his expression thunderous.

"Your bloody brother!" He threw Kate an apologetic look and said, "Pardon my French!"

Caroline said, "Oh he's *my* brother now, is he? He's your brother too."

He glared at his wife. "Oh, not again!" he muttered. "Not the 'poor little Alison' bit again. Pull yourself together, can't you?"

Kate's patience was fast disappearing and with it her good intentions to stay out of the family frictions. She said, "I really can't take any more of this. Excuse me!" and stalked out of the kitchen. Reluctant to return to the dining room she made her way to the bathroom and once inside, locked the door. Pink curtains tied back with silk ribbon and a frieze of pink seashells. Very "Alison", she thought with a wry smile. She used the lavatory and washed her hands. While she was drying them on the pink towel she stared at her reflection. Not surprisingly she looked unattractive. Her eyes were narrowed and her jaw set.

"Oh Robert!" she whispered. How could he bear this fractious family of his? she wondered. More to the point – how could *she*? And how could he have been so wrong about them? "They'll love you!" he had insisted. Well, they didn't – and the feeling was mutual. How could she tell him that, faced with the dreadful reality, she doubted that she could ever share a house with either Caro or Sebastian.

"Are they always like this?" she asked her reflection, "or do you bring out the worst in them?"

She closed her eyes. Her head was thumping unbearably and had been ever since she woke. She sat down on the edge of the bath. What a relief to be away from them, she thought guiltily. What had Robert done to deserve such difficult offspring?

"Poor darling!"

A little later she stood up. There was no way she could skulk in the bathroom waiting for the storm to blow over. She owed Robert her support. She took a couple of deep breaths to calm herself and tried to smile. It wasn't easy but she persevered, telling herself that it might never again be as bad as this. On that hopeful note she went back downstairs and into the dining room. In her absence a large trifle had appeared and there was a platter of cheeses. Everyone was waiting for her and she returned to her seat rather self-consciously.

Robert said, "I missed you!" and gave her

an anguished smile.

She laughed, waiting for a snide remark from Sebastian, but he said nothing.

"Kate? Some trifle?" Alison said.

"Please. It's one of my favourites."

Caro said, "Alison always puts in plenty of sherry. Likes to get us all tipsy."

Kate accepted her helping and Caroline passed her the cream.

Robert was helping himself to Stilton and Bernard passed him the cheese biscuits. When they were all served Robert caught Kate's eyes and winked.

She stammered, "Oh! No. No, I don't think—"

Her apprehension was so obvious that all heads turned towards Robert.

He looked slowly round the table. "It seems as though no one has noticed the ring Kate is wearing on her left hand. Rather unobservant, I must say."

Caroline said, "I noticed it."

"It's an engagement ring. Kate has promised to marry me and we're having a quiet wedding in August."

Kate stared down at her trifle and waited.

Alison said, "Congratulations!"

"Thank you." Kate smiled at her. A possible ally? she wondered with sudden hope.

Caroline said, "I hope you'll be very happy." Her voice was flat and unemotional.

She exchanged a glance with Sebastian and then said, "Great news."

Kate wondered whether Sebastian had passed on the conversation he had over-heard earlier.

Sebastian smiled at Kate. "You'll be a stepmother. How exciting. Not a wicked one, I hope." Before anyone could take offence he leaned forward and seized Kate's hands.

"Congrats and all that!"

Robert glanced at Bernard who took the hint.

"Wonderful news!" he said. "You're a very lucky man."

Sebastian said, "I'll second that!"

Robert put an arm round Kate's shoulders. "I *am* lucky. Kate's a wonderful girl!" His voice took on a more serious note. "I think I'm extremely lucky. I had more than thirty years with Vi and we were happy together. Now I've found Kate who is prepared to put up with me. I like to think Vi would approve."

No one spoke. Kate's heart almost stopped beating. Couldn't Robert see that this was dangerous ground?

Undeterred he went on, "I've got a bottle of champagne hidden in the larder, Alison. Would you rustle up some glasses?—" He leaped to his feet and hurried from the room.

Slowly all eyes turned on Kate. Her stomach was churning but she glanced at them in turn as calmly as she could. "I'll do my best to make Robert happy," she said. "I was prepared to wait but ..." She shrugged.

"He's always been very impetuous," Caroline said, "Mother was always nagging him about it."

Alison said, "I'll get the glasses."

"At least you've been married before. Forewarned is forearmed!" Bernard said, and he forced a tight smile.

"That sounded straight from the heart!" Kate gave him a direct look. "I was happily married, so I've been lucky too."

Sebastian rolled his eyes. "I'm told it's very over-rated. Marriage, that is."

Bernard said, "Really? Who told you that?"

"A little bird!"

Caroline looked at Sebastian. "You're not the marrying kind, Seb."

"Fortunate for some poor girl!" Bernard pushed his half-eaten trifle aside, helped himself to a couple of cheese biscuits, spread them with butter and ate them.

Alison brought a tray full of glasses from the sideboard.

Bernard looked at her. "We were just saying that Sebastian should never marry. Too selfish by far. Don't you agree?"

"Not really."

Caroline said, *"He* agrees."

Alison gave Sebastian a quick look but he avoided her eyes.

Kate said, "I must keep an eye on the time. I wouldn't want to miss the train."

"Don't worry. We won't let that happen." Caroline gave her an ambiguous smile.

Sebastian grinned. "We'll get you to the station on time. Come hell or high water, as they say!"

"I hoped to catch the four fifteen." Kate wanted to knock the mocking smile from his face. Her head was aching and she was desperate to escape. The thought of her own flat and solitude filled her with a treacherous longing.

Robert came back into the room and Kate breathed a sigh of relief. She knew she was being baited but she was unsure how to deal with it. If she fought back, Robert would be upset. Her only alternative was to pretend not to notice the hostility. At this particular time, she wasn't going to risk spoiling Robert's big moment. He opened the champagne and filled the glasses.

Alison took the tray round and Kate was glad to see that she showed signs of recovering. She decided that before she left for the station she would give Alison her telephone number.

Dutifully the family raised their glasses. Robert took Kate's hand and held it tightly.

102

"To my future wife!" he said.

There were indistinct murmurs of congratulation. Only Alison said clearly, "To you both. To your happiness!"

Sebastian said, "To the future."

Which could have meant anything. Kate thought of the aspirins in her sponge bag. She would take two more before she left for the station. If only she could get some relief from this headache. She couldn't imagine how she would cope with Monday in the office but an evening alone and a good night's sleep might restore her flagging spirits.

Robert leaned down and kissed her and she heard Sebastian whisper something. Bernard laughed and Kate sneaked a look at the clock. One hour and eleven minutes still to go.

It had been one of the longest days of her life.

Two days later Muriel was back at work after dealing with a family crisis. She came straight into Kate's office and perched herself on the edge of the desk.

"So how did it go?" she asked. "Was it very bad? The family, I mean." Kate rummaged in the drawer for a notebook before answering. She had promised herself that she would never tell a soul about the humiliations she had suffered but as Muriel

103

spoke, her good intentions flew out of the window.

"It was absolute hell, Muriel. Wild horses wouldn't drag me down there again." She scribbled something, tore off the page and slipped it into an envelope. She looked up, her face drawn with fatigue. "They hated me. I know it. Robert knows it. They know I know! They are just an awful family."

Muriel frowned. "It couldn't have been that bad!"

"It *was*, I tell you. If that's what they're like when there are visitors, God knows how they behave when they're alone! I was worn out, Mu. They almost reduced me to tears at times. I came back to London with a terrible headache."

"You look like death!"

"Thanks!"

Muriel fiddled with an elastic band. "You'll have to tell him."

"I think he knows." Kate reached out her left hand and waited.

Muriel's eyes almost popped out of her head. "Kate! The ring! Oh, it's beautiful!" She took Kate's hand and turned it this way and that.

"I'm totally committed now, Mu. He's even announced the date of the wedding. Of course I'm happy but—"

Quickly she described the events of the weekend while Muriel listened spellbound.

"You'll have to do something!" she said at last.

Kate slid paper and carbons into her typewriter. "I'm going to suggest that we live most of the time at my place. It's the only way we can be on our own. I can't live with Caro and Seb – I'd go mad – and I can hardly expect Robert to turn them out of their own home." She sighed deeply. "Not that I'd want him to. Is it selfish of me not to want to share him? I feel so guilty about it all."

Muriel shrugged. "Pack the son off to Art School. That would get rid of him."

Kate raised her eyebrows. "Brilliant idea, Mu. Do they have an Art School in the Outer Hebrides?"

The telephone shrilled but Muriel put a hand over it before Kate could reach it. "You're not in your office!" she told Kate. "And when you've waved Sebastian off you can find a lusty young husband for Carrie."

"It's Caro, short for Caroline. And she doesn't seem very interested in men. There was no sign of a boyfriend."

"Does she like to travel? Send her to France for a few weeks."

"Or *years*!" Kate grinned. "Perhaps I'm being paranoid. Mind you, there's something wrong between Alison and Bernard, that's for sure." She glanced at her watch. "Blast! I promised to ring the copy-editor just after nine. Much as I love you I'll have to throw you out."

With a sigh Muriel slid from the desk. "I've brought some sandwiches. There's enough for two, I thought we could share them in the park. Interested?"

"Thanks, Mu, I'd love to."

"About twelve fifteen, then." With a wave of her hand she was gone.

Kate nodded. She was already dialling the copy-editor's number.

Doctor Harris glanced through his notes with pursed lips. It was a very warm day and he had loosened his tie. He wiped his face with a handkerchief and then took off his spectacles and polished them on his special yellow cloth. Dora, the young receptionist, waited silently beside him but when he still showed no signs of readiness she moved to the window and stared down to the street below. Harley Street was never bustling but nor was it ever deserted. She saw one or two pedestrians, an elderly woman in a wheelchair being pushed by a young companion, a boy carrying a birdcage and a number of taxis delivering or collecting patients.

Doctor Harris said, "You say he's here already?" He put his spectacles on again.

"Yes, Doctor. Mr Dengaul has been waiting twenty minutes. He came early. He always does." She smiled. "He says he likes to read the magazines."

"Better show him in then."

He looked nervous, thought Dora – which meant that the news was not good.

She crossed to the door and opened it. "Mr Dengaul? The doctor will see you now." She gave him a cheerful smile, confident that she was looking trim and neat in her white and grey uniform. Not that she was a real nurse. The uniform was to reassure the patients. Robert Dengaul had once told her that she had a wonderful smile. Everyone said he was a bit of a charmer and she could vouch for that. She'd read an article about him once that said he'd been a bit wild when he was younger, drinking heavily and suchlike, but that was before he met Violet Sherwell. A wife and three children had calmed him down. Or so they said.

As he passed her he winked and whispered, "How's my favourite nurse?"

"Mr Den*gaul*!" She felt herself blushing. She had read most of his books and so had her mother. True, they were always about crimes, but they weren't gory like some novels although sometimes people got stabbed or strangled, but there wasn't too much nasty detail and sometimes the crime was embezzling or theft where there was no violence at all. They did occasionally have some foreign words or phrases, which Dora hated. It was rather like showing off to put in something in Latin which nobody could understand but then he was famous and the article said he'd been to Oxford University so that probably accounted for it. Not that she would ever tell him she minded. She respected him too much for that and what did she know, anyway?

Dora took his jacket and hung it carefully on a hanger behind the door then settled herself discreetly at her desk in the corner. Here, she dealt with the patients' files, answered the telephone and made entries in the diary. She had been working for Doctor Harris since she had left secretarial college nearly two years ago.

"So, Doctor, tell me the worst."

She turned her head slightly so that she could watch the two men.

Doctor Harris sighed. "I wish it were better news but I'm afraid my first diagnosis has been confirmed. The test's results are quite clear. It *is* nephritis, Mr Dengaul, but we—"

"And is it going to see me off? I need to know the facts."

She found it so distasteful when the patients insisted on knowing, especially when she had looked up the disease in the doctor's book when he was out at lunch. She did that sometimes. She knew that nephritis wasn't very nice, but Doctor Harris was clever with words. He could be so reassuring if they would allow him to tell it in his own way. He could make any disease sound bearable.

Now Doctor Harris raised his eyebrows. "Will it see you off? I suppose it will eventually but—"

"So the answer's yes."

"It is. As I explained last time you were here, there's no cure, Mr Dengaul, but we can certainly hold the disease at bay and alleviate the—"

"So how long have I got? It's important."

Mr Dengaul sounded irritable but that wasn't unusual in the circumstances. Hearing bad news was difficult for anyone. Dora wished it were better news because she admired Robert Dengaul and because he wasn't exactly old and was still good-looking.

The doctor consulted his notes. Playing for time, she thought, trying not to rush it. "You must let the patient accept one unpleasant fact at a time." That's what he had told her. That way it lessened the shock.

"Hard to say exactly," Doctor Harris said finally. "At least a year. Possibly two. I'm afraid the damage to the kidneys is already quite severe but we can see what a better diet can do for you. Best to stay off alcohol. Eat more protein and maybe take a slight reduction in fluids."

"Oh God!"

Dora was watching the patient struggle with the knowledge that he might have less than two years to live. His head was bowed and his hands were tightly clasped in his lap.

Then his head jerked up. "And if I don't bother with the damned diet?"

Doctor Harris raised his eyebrows. "Oh, but you *must*! You'll soon get used to it. It's simply a matter of establishing limits. Nurse Brown will type it out for you. Your wife will find it quite easy to follow."

Abruptly Robert Dengaul stood up, glaring down at the doctor. "I thought I'd explained that I don't want my future wife to know about – about this problem. I want time for us to be together free of any anxieties. I certainly don't want to frighten her with thoughts of imminent widowhood."

Doctor Harris frowned. "But Mr Dengaul, is that fair, do you think? Hasn't she a right to know? She must love you a great deal. She should be given the chance to care for you. How would you feel if the situation were reversed?"

He hesitated. "But it's not." He crossed to the window. "I want to know how it will be at the end. Exactly."

The doctor caught Dora's eye and gave an almost imperceptible shrug.

She stared at the famous author. He was like one of his own characters, she thought.

A bit like Andrew Carstairs in *The Courtney File*. Tough, hating to admit to any weakness and keeping his troubles to himself. Although, of course, Andrew Carstairs had dark hair and he was a lot younger. Still, Doctor Harris was right, Mr Dengaul's wife ought to be told. Knowing you were going to die would be a lonely business.

The doctor spoke gently "Today your blood pressure is almost normal but later it will rise dangerously. You may suffer dizzy spells."

"I already do!"

"Then your wife should be prepared. She will need to recognise the signs. There will be some vomiting and maybe convulsions."

"God Almighty!"

Dora sighed. If she were Robert Dengaul's wife she'd want to know what to expect. That way there would be no sudden shocks and no dreadful panics.

The doctor said, "Nobody can pretend that renal failure—"

"Stop it!" Robert sank down into his chair, his face pale. "I don't want to hear any more."

"But Mr Dengaul, a moment ago you were insisting on—"

"I've changed my mind." He swallowed hard. "I take your point. I'll tell my wife – when the time is right."

"It's right now!"

111

"It's right when *I* think it's right, dammit!" He caught sight of Dora, who was watching him anxiously. "For God's sake! I don't feel ill, just a little tired at times. I can slow down. Just write in the mornings. Do I *look* like a sick man to you, nurse? Eh?"

She didn't know what to say but Doctor Harris would expect her to support him. She said, "You are rather pale, Mr Dengaul."

Immediately she regretted her candour.

He cried, "Pale? Of course I'm bloody pale! I've just been told I'm going to *die*! You'd look bloody pale—"

Affronted, the doctor half rose from his chair. "*Please*, Mr Dengaul. Watch your language! There are ladies present."

Dora said, "It doesn't matter. Really."

"I'm sorry, nurse." Robert ran agitated fingers through his hair. "Please forgive me."

She was beginning to feel rather pale herself. "It's my fault," she stammered. "It was a silly thing to say." A new thought struck her. If his wife became pregnant he might not live to see the child.

There was an awkward silence. Then Robert Dengaul straightened in his chair.

"I can't accept this, doctor. I *won't* accept it. There must be *something* I can do. Somewhere I can go. A new treatment. I don't care what it costs."

112

Dora turned away, unable to watch.

"I'm afraid not, Mr Dengaul. In Harley Street we keep abreast of all research wherever it is. If there was a miracle cure I would know about it, believe me, and I would have told you. Please listen to me, Mr Dengaul. For your own good. You've just entered what we call the oedematous stage and, although you've lost a little weight, your blood pressure is still normal. You are, however, rather anaemic which is why you feel run down. I'll give you an injection of iron and we'll test your blood regularly. It's what we call monitoring the disease and—"

"Oh God!" Robert Dengaul put his head in his hands. "Injections. Diets. Blood tests – they're worse than the bloody disease!" He glanced at the nurse. "Sorry again! I'm a bit overwrought."

Dora nodded, blinking fiercely. Of course she understood and he was such a lovely man. It was all so *terribly* sad.

Four

When Robert arrived home he went straight into his study and locked the door. He leaned back against it and stared for a long time, seeing nothing and shivering with delayed shock. In the consulting room and during the train journey back, anger had kept the fear at bay; anger and a determination not to break down in front of anyone. The sight of his familiar room and well-worn chair undermined him completely and he moved towards his desk on leaden feet. Sinking into his chair he felt like a frightened child and his thoughts went round at a dizzying speed in a search for an escape. He longed to cry; longed for his mother to put comforting arms around him. If only someone could kiss it better.

"You're done for, old son!" he muttered.

He attempted a wry smile but knew that it failed. It seemed incredible. So much fame, so much wealth and what good would it do him? He couldn't prolong his life by so much as an hour let alone a day. If only he could make a deal with the devil and surrender his success for a few more years with Kate.

He heard footsteps. It was Caro. Damnation. He couldn't tell her. Couldn't face her tears.

"Father?"

Poor Caro. She had always adored him, never making any attempt to hide the fact that Vi would always come a poor second. When she was seven she had flown at her mother in a jealous rage, biting the arm Vi had draped so casually round his waist. A very nasty bite, in fact. The scar had still been faintly visible when Vi lay on her deathbed.

A rattle of the doorknob. He would have to speak, she knew he was in there.

"I'm busy. I'll be out later." He wanted to say "Leave me alone" but that was so uncharacteristic she would be immediately suspicious.

She called, "Are you all right? Why is the door locked?"

He supposed he should be pleased that she was concerned but her insistence irritated him. "I've said I'm busy!"

"I've made a pot of tea."

"I don't want tea." He pushed himself up from the chair and after a moment's hesitation, decided he would have to open it.

Caro came into the room carrying a small tray. "What's going on?" She stared at him, her eyes narrowed. "Have you been drinking?"

"Drinking? For heaven's sake! I've only just come back from—" He stopped just in time.

She moved some books and set the tray down on the windowsill. "From where?" Her expression changed suddenly. "You look terrible."

"There's nothing wrong with me."

He felt himself sway and then she was steadying him, guiding him back to his seat. Robert felt a fine sweat break out on his body. Was it simply the shock or was it starting already? Maybe this was the beginning of the end. He put a hand over his eyes and forced back tears.

She was kneeling beside him. "Something's happened," she said. "I can tell. You're white as a sheet. Where have you been? I got up soon after six and you were gone."

"I went to London. Pour me a whisky, will you?" The doctor's warning about alcohol rang in his ears but he told himself this would be the last drink. And surely he deserved one, he had been given a death sentence.

"London?"

She handed him the glass and he took a large gulp. Thank God!

So where should he say he'd been?

116

He emptied the glass. "Yes. I popped in to Gordon Bretts to verify something." Oh God, now she'd be asking awkward questions which he couldn't answer. She would assume he'd seen Kate. Better come up with something else. "And then I called in on Nathan."

"Feeling a bit better?" She stood up and patted his shoulder. "I thought you were going to faint." She sat down on the sofa. "What did Nathan want?"

Nathan & Ruff were the family accountants and Derek Nathan was almost a family friend.

So what *did* Nathan want? More damned lies. "Nothing in particular. It was my idea to meet up. Haven't seen the old rogue for nearly a year."

Caroline grinned. "Does he still smoke like a chimney?"

Robert forced a smile. "Still smoking that disgusting old pipe! And wearing those awful pullovers. Thank heavens Vi wasn't a knitter."

He finished his drink and looked with longing at the empty glass. Would another whisky shorten his time with Kate? If so, he owed it to her to resist.

"Been out with Nutmeg today?"

"Not yet. I've been talking to Seb, who is in a very difficult mood. Dad, he's really set on the Art School idea."

"The Art School." Robert rubbed his eyes. "He'll get over it. Last year it was restoring antiques. I despair, sometimes – but don't tell him I said so."

But she would, of course, and he cursed his careless tongue.

"But this time he's *really* keen." She leaned forward with an earnest expression on her face and he thought that she could be attractive if she wanted to make the effort. How pleasant it would be if she had found herself a husband. Isn't that what daughters were supposed to do? She could be running her own house and producing a family instead of staying at home to spoil his own chances.

"He's talking about fabric design or silk-screen printing. Or even photography. Taking people's portraits. Apparently there's a developing market for that sort of thing and he thinks he stands a real chance. All he needs is some encouragement and I'm sure—"

Robert interrupted her. "Caro, I'm not saying no but I can't deal with this right now. I'll talk to him about it some other time."

He struggled to speak normally, to hide his desperation. He needed time to come to terms with his future – or lack of it; time to overcome the fear; time to think of ways to hide his growing weakness from Kate.

The doctor's words had troubled him. Was he being unfair to her to hide the extent of his problem? And what was his real motive? To spare her anguish or to spare himself the shame of being a sick old man who wanted to marry a healthy young woman.

"He doesn't think you will, Dad." She was looking dogged. "Seb thinks you are so wrapped up with Kate that you won't bother with him."

Robert looked at her and was surprised to feel no anger. Wrapped up with Kate. So that was how his children saw his relationship. He sighed. They had no idea of the depth of feeling they had for each other, no wish to understand the part love played in the relationship. No doubt they found it all a nuisance. Or a joke. Father making a fool of himself.

"His words or yours?"

She frowned.

" 'Wrapped up with Kate'. Are they his words or—"

She had the grace to look guilty. "Mine, maybe. Does it matter? Why can't you just say yes and let him go?"

He tried to imagine the place without Sebastian and was agreeably surprised. "Wouldn't you miss him?" he asked.

She shrugged. "He's got to do something and he's never here anyway. Always off with his stupid harriers." She stood up. "Well, I must go. Nutmeg will think he's been abandoned. I'll love you and leave you." She bent down and kissed him on the forehead.

He caught her arm as sudden tears blurred his eyes. How would she manage when he died? Losing Vi had been bad enough for her. Losing him might well push her into another breakdown. There was so much he wanted to say before it was too late.

"What is it?"

Words failed him. Instead he held up his glass and muttered, "Pour me another before you go."

Kate sat at the table feeling far from happy. Pencil, paper and chocolates were to hand – the latter to help her through the ordeal. She had already made one false start and now stared helplessly round the small familiar room. Her mother's favourite picture hung on the wall. There were photographs of family and friends, a sewing machine she never used, a heavy cut-glass vase which had been a wedding present from Will's parents and the carriage clock that Will had bought on their first anniversary. Kate found it wonderfully comforting. By comparison, she thought, Highstead was an alien planet.

"A very alien planet!" she murmured and was immediately racked with guilt. With a deep sigh she started a second letter.

Dear Robert,

I am such a coward. I do hope you will understand why I cannot say this to you face to face. It's because I hate to hurt you in any way ...

He wouldn't understand, thought Kate, but she must try and explain her reluctance. She bit into a Turkish delight, savouring the scented sweetness as she struggled for the right words. She must write nothing ambiguous. Honesty was the key.

I know we hoped to live together at your home but I now see that it won't work. It is nobody's fault and I am certainly not criticising any of your children. Far from it. They do you great credit.

That wasn't quite true but she felt the lie necessary to save Robert pain.

I can see how difficult it would be for Caro and Seb to have me thrust upon them and, naturally, they would see me as as an intruder. It would be difficult for me, too, darling ...

It would be impossible. Kate reached for another chocolate and slowly chewed a nougat surprise without tasting it. The pencil hovered as she hesitated.

121

It would also be cruel to expect Seb and Caro to move out ...

She rubbed out the word cruel and wrote unkind instead.

...before they are ready to fly the nest. I'm sure they would resent the suggestion. I know I would in their shoes.

She was aiming for a calm, common-sense attitude with a minimum of emotion. Carefully she read through what she had written and groaned. "Write to him," Mu had insisted over the sandwiches. "He's a grown man. He'll understand." Kate drew a long breath. The trouble was that Robert loved Highstead. He had bought it with the money from his first best-seller and had shown it off to her with obvious pride. He and Vi had created a comfortable home and she, Kate, could live there with him – but not with Caro and Seb. But where could they go and who would exercise and care for Nutmeg if Caro moved out? If the animal had to be sold Kate Harper would get the blame. It was unthinkable that Caro should be expected to move out.

"Oh Lord!" It was so complicated. Yet falling in love with Robert had been the easiest thing in the world.

May I suggest that for a while, at least, you move in to my flat and live with me? I know it would be a squash but I could bear it if you could. I'd be out most of the day and you could write in the spare bedroom. Eventually – and it may be only a year or so – Seb and Caro will move out to live their own lives and then we would have Highstead to ourselves, which would be wonderful.

You know how much I love you, Robert, and how much I want us to be together but I can see frictions arising if the four of us are forced to live under one roof for any length of time. I don't think it's reasonable to assume Seb and Caro will automatically take to me and you might well find yourself pig in the middle! I am so afraid that family quarrels could affect our love for each other. Dearest Robert, do please try and understand. I don't want anything or anybody to come between us.

Kate ate the chocolate cream while she read the letter through and made a few last minute alterations, then she made a fair copy in ink. It wasn't perfect but it wasn't too bad and she didn't feel she could improve on it. She folded the letter then unfolded it and tried to read it through Robert's eyes. How on earth would he react? she wondered. Disheartened, she ate three more chocolates, found an envelope and addressed it. Feeling slightly sick from too many chocolates she stuck a stamp on to the envelope and set off for the post box with a heavy heart.

Two days later, a Saturday, Sebastian and Caro sat at the kitchen table, regarding each other morosely. Between them was the lunch Caro had prepared – Brie, bread, tomatoes and a jug of lemonade.

"Did you make this?" Sebastian demanded, sipping the lemonade.

"What's wrong with it?" She tried some and wrinkled her nose. "It's the lemon zest. I may have used too much."

"It's bitter."

"I know it is! Just stick some more sugar in it and stop fussing."

They ate in silence until Sebastian bit into a whole tomato with a deliberate slurping sound.

"You really are a baby," Caro told him. She regarded him through narrowed eyes. Would she know if he were having an affair? Of course she would! She knew Seb better than anyone else did.

"You were saying?" he prompted. "About the letter?"

She sighed heavily. "If you let on that I said anything you'll be sorry. It was from Kate. I recognised the handwriting on the envelope."

"You went through Dad's pockets?"

"Of course I didn't! I found the envelope in the waste-paper basket. The point is that Dad had been crying. Whatever she said in the letter really upset him."

"He *cried*?"

She nodded. "I was almost ready to like her—"

"No, you weren't!"

"I'd love to read that letter. D'you think it would be reasonable, in the circumstances, to try and get hold of it?"

Sebastian balanced a piece of cheese on the tip of the knife. "Maybe she's changed her mind and isn't going to marry him after all. We could say three cheers all round and forget about Kate Harper." He popped the cheese into his mouth.

Caro added sugar to her lemonade and stirred it briskly. "If you could keep him talking somewhere I could take the letter, read it and put it back before he knew it had gone."

"There'd be hell to pay if he found out!"

She was silent, weighing up the risks.

"Why don't we just make sure she doesn't marry him – by making her life so miserable that she can't face life with the Dengauls?"

"I think we already *have*! And without even trying. She must have hated last weekend."

Seb looked thoughtful. "She's not bad-looking. I can see why he fancies her. If I met her elsewhere *I'd* fancy her."

125

Caroline felt a rush of resentment towards her future stepmother. It was bad enough that her father was making a fool of himself over Kate without Sebastian falling under her spell as well.

"You would – but then you never did have much taste where women are concerned. Or good luck, either!"

He laughed but she sensed that the barb had hurt him.

"I wouldn't say that, Caro. I don't do too badly," he said, raising his eyebrows.

Caroline gave him a quick look. "How can you say that? You haven't even got a girl-friend." When he didn't answer, she regarded him closely. Something in his expression alarmed her and she went on with less confidence than before. "Alison asked if I would be able to tell if you were having an affair. I said I would – but now I'm not so sure." She drew a quick, nervous breath. "Are you, Seb?"

He grinned. "I wouldn't tell you if I were because you'd never stop badgering me for details."

"I wouldn't badger you." Her eyes widened. "Does that mean ...? Oh my God! You *are*, aren't you! Tell me, Seb."

"You're badgering me already!" He mimicked her voice. " 'Tell me, Seb.' It's none of your business, Caro."

So he *was* having an affair. She pushed

her plate away, sick at heart. Kate's letter to her father was forgotten. Her beloved Seb had found someone else and the shock was tremendous. Her thoughts raced as she tried to put a name to the mystery woman.

"Do I know her? You can tell me that, surely."

He put a hand over hers but she pulled hers away.

He said, "Look, I didn't tell you at first because I didn't – I don't – expect it to last. It's just a bit of a fling. Nothing serious."

Seb was having an affair. The phrase hammered at her brain. *An affair*! Did that mean the woman was married?

"If Father finds out ..."

"He won't, will he?"

"She's not married, is she?" If the newspapers got hold of the story ...

"Yes, she is."

She stared at her brother, still hardly able to credit what she was being told. Her brother had been having an affair and she hadn't had an inkling! Tears filled her eyes and she covered her face with her hands. Through her fingers she whispered, "You told her but not me." She felt betrayed.

"I didn't need to tell her, Caro. She already knew."

Startled she lowered her hands. "She *saw* you?"

"No ... Well, I suppose she did in a way."
He looked ill at ease, she thought, as well he
might. She had never imagined he would be
involved with a married woman. "I'd like to
tell you but I don't know how you'll react –
or if I can trust you to keep it to yourself."

"Oh Seb! Of course you can trust me."
She held her breath. Whoever she is, say
something nice about her, she told herself.
Don't alienate him or he will never confide
in you again.

"It's Alison," he said.

"What is?"

"The married woman is Alison."

Her heart began to thump erratically.
Alison? I don't believe ..." She couldn't
understand what he was saying. Alison and
Seb? It was impossible. "No. It can't be." At
the back of her mind she heard Alison's
voice. "Would you know if Seb were having
an affair?" And she, Caro, had been so
certain that she *would* know. How Alison
must have laughed.

She looked at him dazedly. "But Bernard?
What about Bernard?" Before he could
reply another thought struck her. "So you
weren't with the harriers!" He'd lied to her.

"I'm afraid not." His expression was
defensive. "He shouldn't have left her on her
own so much. All those days away. She was
lonely."

"Bernard was *working*! You know he has to

128

go away." Her voice was shaking. Seb and Alison – on top of everything else. Poor Bernard. What had he done to deserve this? And how on earth had it happened? Bernard could be pompous at times – and boring, even – but didn't they love each other any more? Was it because of the non-existent baby? This thought gave rise to other thoughts of Seb and Alison in bed together. She swallowed hard.

"And if Bernard finds out?"

"He was never right for Alison."

"She must have thought he was. And Father! He'll go mad when he finds out!"

"If he does."

Seb was poking the point of his knife into a hole in the tablecloth. In a flash of anger she snatched it from him and hurled it across the room. It hit the window and a crack appeared.

"Damn and bugger!"

"Temper! Now see what you've done." He laughed.

Caroline jumped to her feet, picked up the milk jug and tried to hit him with it. He ducked easily and took it from her. They both looked at the spilt milk.

"Calm down, Caro! You're making a fool of yourself."

"And you're not? Fooling about with your brother's wife! You disgust me, Seb!"

"I don't disgust Allie." He gave her a sly

look. "She rather likes ... what we do."

"I shall tell Father and he'll put a stop to it." The shake in her voice spoiled the effect of her threat. She felt choked. Sebastian and Alison. Together they had betrayed her and she hated the pair of them for their conspiracy. She tried to breathe naturally but there was a pain in her chest and tears threatened. "I think you're both ... utterly despicable!"

If she stayed she would break down and cry and her brother would tell Alison and they would have a good laugh at her expense. Tears spilled down her cheeks as she stumbled blindly from the room. With murder in her heart she ran out across the yard in the direction of the stable.

On the same day, Kate lingered in the grocer's shop, aware that she was delaying the moment when she must return to the flat and get the inevitable phone call from Robert. He would have received her letter the previous day but she had stayed overnight with Muriel and Eddie after supper. Arriving home, she had hurried out again to the shops but she knew she had to make herself available to talk. Robert would be horribly upset by the knowledge that she didn't want to live at Highstead and he would do his best to change her mind. She hoped she had all the arguments ready but as she turned the corner into her own street she was shocked to see Robert standing outside her front door, waiting for her.

When he saw her, he pushed himself upright and hurried forward. "Where were you?"

"Robert!" Kate was shocked to see how drawn he looked. He hadn't shaved and his hair was tousled. "What on earth is the matter?"

He made no move to kiss her but she told herself that was probably because her arms were full of shopping.

Smiling she said, "Let's get inside first!" and, trying to hide her concern, fumbled in her pocket for the key.

He took one of the baskets from her and followed her inside. He was saying nothing, Kate noticed with alarm. Robert was so rarely lost for words. One of the newspapers had once described him as garrulous.

The moment she reached the kitchen she put down the rest of the shopping and turned to face him.

"Robert, are you all right?"

"No, I'm not all right!" There were dark shadows under his eyes.

"I'll put the kettle on," she began.

"I need a whisky," he told her. "Where were you last night? I waited for hours." He slumped into a chair.

Kate stared at him. "You waited last night?

131

What do you mean? Where were you?"

"On the doorstep. Where else?"

"I mean, where did you sleep?"

"I didn't. I walked around and I waited. I slept on the step – or tried to!"

"For heaven's sake, Robert!"

"When I woke I went in search of a lavatory, came back and waited some more. Where *were* you, Kate?"

"So you've had no breakfast?"

"Where *were* you, for heaven's sake? I came as soon as I could. Your letter about Highstead … We have to talk."

He ran agitated fingers through his hair and Kate's heart ached for him. She fetched a bottle of whisky from the sitting room and poured a generous helping, annoyed to see that her hand trembled.

"You were out all night, Kate. I have to know where you were."

"I went to Mu and Eddie's for supper." She handed him the drink. "I told you I was going."

He, too, had been invited but had declined with a bad grace. He had wanted Kate all to himself and had been put out when Kate insisted on accepting.

"Mu and Eddie! Of *course*!" His relief was apparent.

"I said if it got too late I'd stay the night." She sat down next to him. "Where did you think I was, Robert?" The exchange was shaking her confidence. Did this mean he didn't trust her? "Who did you think I was with?"

"Nowhere. No one. Forget it." He drank the whisky greedily and held out the glass for a refill.

Kate ignored it. "You thought I was spending the night with another man?" She stared at him. "You *did*, didn't you? Look at me, Robert. You *couldn't* have thought that, could you? Tell me."

His sigh was deep and ragged. "My imagination got the better of me. I'm sorry."

Kate swallowed, her anger tempered by his obvious distress. No wonder he looked so tired and ill. "My poor darling!" She moved closer and put her arms around him. "All those hours in the dark and cold. I can't bear it." She imagined him, alone and wretched, praying for the dawn but dreading the unpleasant revelations it might bring.

"I'm such a fool! My lovely Kate, you must forgive me."

"Of course I forgive you." Now she almost wished that she hadn't accepted Muriel's invitation although it was the timing of her letter that had created the problem. With hindsight she knew that she should have foreseen what might happen, but it was too late now.

She poured him another drink and decided she needed a small sherry.

"We are a pair!" she said softly, touching her glass to his.

"If only we were. Why do we have to wait so long?"

"Darling, it's only a few weeks."

"I want us to be together all the time. At Highstead."

It was out. Kate braced herself. "You don't understand, then, how I feel?"

"No, I don't. This place is too small and Highstead is my home. It has to be *our* home. Yours and mine. If you can't stand the children—"

"Robert!" Dismayed, she counted to ten. "I didn't say that. You're being unfair. Twisting my words."

"They'll have to get out."

"No, Robert!"

She had never seen him like this, so intractable. His face was set in stubborn lines. Well, she had expected resistance to the plan but not this intensity. He was going to fight her all the way. Leaning back she closed her eyes. Part of her understood, even admired, his determination but another part insisted that she should not be bullied into surrender.

Opening her eyes, she said, "If you're so set on Highstead then let's agree to wait a little longer. Christmas, maybe, or—"

"*No!* No more delays, *please* Kate. I want us to marry and live at Highstead. Seb and

Caro must find somewhere else. It's time they did. They're just lazy. Young people are these days. When I was Seb's age I'd been on my own for years."

Kate took a deep breath. "Robert, the whole point of my letter was that I *don't* want to turn your son and daughter out of their home. That would make me some kind of ogre. All I want is for you and me to be happy together. I don't—"

His eyes widened suddenly and he gripped her hand. "We could sell Highstead! We could buy somewhere new. You can choose the house, Kate."

She hesitated, totally undermined by his desperation. "But how will that solve the problem of Seb and Caro?"

"You're right! It won't. Then I'll keep Highstead and find them a flat. They can live together. We'll be on our own then."

Kate regarded him with despair. "Suppose they don't want to live together? I thought Seb wanted to go to Art School. Anyway it will take time and—"

"Listen Kate." He was brightening. "We'll marry and you'll move in with us at Highstead and meanwhile I'll talk them round to the idea of a flat. I can afford it. I'll let them go house hunting together. It'll be fun for them. There now!" He grinned at her. "All settled." His expression was triumphant and the fear had gone from his eyes.

He finished his drink. "Actually I do feel rather hungry. Wouldn't say no to egg and bacon."

Kate came to a decision. She would let the matter rest for the time being. She didn't want to quarrel and she could see how much Highstead meant to him.

"Let's think about it some more, Robert. But not now. Now we *are* together and I don't want to spoil things." Pushing her reservations to the back of her mind she smiled. "Eggs and bacon coming up! Mushrooms, maybe?"

He took her hands in his and kissed them. "Throw in a slice of fried bread and the answer's yes."

Alison was making their bed. She loved the bedroom with its Wedgewood-blue curtains and blue and white striped wallpaper. They had decorated it lovingly and with such care all those years ago. A doll dressed in a blue sprigged dress sat on one of the chairs. Suddenly, Alison paused, her head on one side, listening for Sebastian. Surely someone was down there. She went to the top of the stairs.

"Who is it?" Please, she thought, let it be Seb. I have to see him. I must talk to him.

"It's me. Caro. Sorry to disappoint you."

Alison stiffened. What did she mean by that? "I'll be down in a sec." Delaying the moment, she smoothed the patchwork counterpane and pushed her slippers further under the bed.

Downstairs she found Caroline staring out of the kitchen window. "It's started, Alison," she said. "I knew it would."

"What's started?"

Caroline turned. "Kate! She wants us out. Bitch! I *knew* she would!" She leaned back against the sink. "Father's offered to buy a flat for me and Seb to share. 'You must be mad!' I told him. 'I don't want to live with Seb. Nobody in their right mind would want to live with him.'"

Her expression was unfathomable. Alison began to pull down washing from the ove-head airer. She folded each garment and piled them neatly.

"I thought you and Seb got on well."

Caroline shrugged. "It seems Lady Kate doesn't think we can all live together. Well, I saw that coming a mile away. In other words, she wants everything for herself. Father pretends it's his idea but I don't believe him. It's her."

"What does Seb think?"

"He just goes on and on about Art School. It's become the Holy Grail to him!"

She sighed heavily. "Personally I wish he'd push off and go to Art School. There's one in London called the Slade but the new term starts in September and he thinks he's too late to apply. Pity." Absentmindedly she picked an apple from a dish on the table and bit into it. "If you must know I'm tired of him mooning about the house. He thinks I don't know what's eating him but I do." She gave Alison a sly look. "He's taken a fancy to Lady Kate!"

Alison felt as though she had been punched. *Seb and Kate?* With an effort she kept her voice steady. "I find that hard to believe." It couldn't be true.

"You don't have to listen to him. On and on about her and how Dad's too old for her. How easy she is to talk to and how intelligent. He's so pleased because she's coming down again next weekend."

Alison took the dry washing to a chair next to the ironing board and plugged in the iron. "I rather liked her actually. She seemed to want to please." It was true, she thought. Kate had seemed a friendly person and Alison had felt sorry for her, thrust into the bosom of the Dengaul family. But if Seb had taken a fancy to her ...

Caroline said, "There's no accounting for taste!"

Alison changed the subject. "If I were in your shoes and someone offered me a flat I'd jump at it."

"Where would I put Nutmeg? Not many flats with adjoining paddocks and stables!"

"Nutmeg. I forgot." She began to iron a

nightdress. Blue with pink ribbons. She heard herself ask, "Have you heard anything in the village – about Bernard?" and was startled. She had intended to bide her time on that particular problem. "Fools rush in ..." It was one of her mother's favourite quotes.

Caroline stopped eating. "Bernard? No. What about him?"

Now Alison regretted the question. She applied herself to her ironing. "Nothing really. He's been a bit strange lately. Mrs Green said she saw him coming out of John Somers' cottage."

"So what? He's entitled to have friends, isn't he?"

"I suppose so. But last weekend he was over an hour late for Saturday lunch and when he came in he was – he was tipsy." She stopped ironing and faced Caroline. "It seemed a bit odd."

Caroline frowned. "Bernard *tipsy*?"

"It's not like him. He'd been to one of his meetings. You know Bernard and his stomach. He's never late for lunch. I just wondered ..."

"I'd worry if he was with another woman but not another man. You've often complained that he's got no friends. This John Somers might be good for him. Why don't you invite him round to tea? Give him the once over."

Alison thought about it. On the face of it, it sounded reasonable. She said, "Maybe I will. He's re-joined the choir, too. Bernard, I mean. I hardly saw him before because of all the meetings but at least we had Friday evenings. Now that's gone."

Caroline tossed the apple core through the open door and on to the terrace and Alison bit back a sharp comment. Perhaps when Caroline had a flat of her own she would be a little more houseproud, she thought irritably. Not that she wanted her to move away. They had always been friends and she had been hoping to confide in her about Seb.

Alison spread a white shirt and began on the collar. Collar, yoke, sleeves, fronts and back. In that order. Her mother had taught her well.

There was a long silence which finally grew uncomfortable. At last it was broken by Caroline. "I know about you and Seb. He told me."

Alison felt her legs grow weak. The iron grew heavy in her hand and ironing a shirt seemed immensely difficult. She wanted to continue with her ironing but couldn't concentrate. She set the iron upright, bent to switch it off and sat down heavily. Outwardly calm, her insides churned. This was not at all how she had imagined it. She had intended to join Caroline on the leads above Highstead and break the news gently. Seb had broken his promise to let her do the telling and she was angry as well as frightened.

"He had no right to tell you." It was almost a whisper.

"Why not? I'm his sister. I know him better than you ever will." She was watching Alison closely. "Does Bernard suspect?"

"Of course not. At least, I don't think so." She forced herself to look at her sister-in-law. What is upsetting Caro most? she wondered. The fact that Seb had kept the affair a secret from her for so long, the fact that he loved Alison more than her, or the fact that they were deceiving Bernard?

Caroline's expression was unforgiving. "If you want to know what I think about it all—"

"I don't think I do, thank you!"

Caroline was in an awkward position because both her brothers were important to her and she wouldn't want to be alienated from either. She went on as though she hadn't heard Alison's last comment. "I think Seb's an absolute rotter and you're as bad for encouraging him, for allowing it to happen. You can't blame it all on Seb. If you must know I'm seriously thinking about telling Bernard."

Alison felt cold but she was determined not to let Caroline see how frightened she

141

was. "If you must know I don't much care if you do."

"I will then."

"You really think he'll thank you for humiliating him? Nobody loves the bearer of bad news, Caro."

Caroline wavered visibly. "Maybe ... but at least he could put a stop to it. God knows where it will end."

Little does she know, Alison thought wearily, that it was already too late to put a stop to it. Much too late. She said, "I hope you won't do anything so stupid. It's between me and Seb and Bernard. We'll work it out in our own time."

"They're my brothers. It's my family. You're the outsider."

"But Seb's my lover and Bernard's my husband!" She knew she was being small minded but she was beginning to realise that she had never really been close to Caroline.

For a moment they glared at one another. Alison longed for her to leave so that she could recover from the shock of Seb's betrayal. Having Caroline opposite her with that hateful expression on her face made thinking impossible. Helplessly she muttered, "You don't understand, Caro. How could you? You're not married and you've never been in love."

"How do you know?"

"Well, have you?"

"None of your business."

Her expression was defiant but Alison sensed that she had hit a nerve.

She said, "I think you ought to go now, Caro. This conversation's going nowhere. My advice to you is to say as little as possible in case you make things worse."

Caroline's eyebrows shot up. "Is it really? You think things could get any worse? You're married to one brother and – and committing adultery with the other and you think it could get *worse*?" She jumped up, almost knocking over her chair. "I might decide that my father has a right to know."

"Why not place an advertisement in the local paper?" Alison smiled coldly. "Tell everyone."

"Do *your* parents know?"

"Not yet. Why? Are you planning to tell them too?"

The air between them bristled with antagonism as they faced each other, both white faced and slightly breathless.

Alison longed to know exactly what Seb had told his sister about them, and why he had told her anything. Was he tired of the affair? Was telling Caro his way of forcing matters into the light so that Bernard could step in and put a stop to it? She felt a surge of rage at the thought that he might treat her so shabbily.

Caroline turned to leave then turned back. She looked a little less sure of herself.

"Are you going to leave Bernard?" she asked. "You know what it'll do to him. The scandal of a divorce, I mean. He's never done anything to deserve this and he's – he's so well respected."

Alison shrugged. Unspoken between them was the fact that Bernard's livelihood and his comfortable lifestyle depended on her family's firm. Her father's money had bought their house. Bernard had more to lose than a wife.

She said, "I'll talk to Seb. We'll decide what to do. We might do nothing. It depends on how much trouble you've stirred up. The more people who know, the less likely it is to die a death."

That would give her sister-in-law pause for thought and maybe it would keep her silent for a few days. Alison couldn't entirely blame her for her anger. It was Seb who was to blame – he should never have told her.

As she opened the back door, Caroline's mouth trembled. "Alison, *please* don't do anything rash. That's all I ask. I really hate all this ... this nastiness. I hate everything changing. Why can't things stay the same?"

"It's the way of the world. You've been very sheltered, Caro – until your mother died, that is. A rich, famous father. A united family. Everything going for you in fact."

Caroline stepped outside and stared around the garden with its neat lawn and colourful flower beds. She turned and her face was troubled. "I'm sorry I called you a tart."

Startled, Alison frowned. "A tart? I don't remember."

"I did – to Seb. I called you a hussy and a loose woman. I called you both a lot of things. I expect Seb will blab. But I was in a state of shock ... Alison, please try to get everything right again. I don't know how but just try. Will you?"

Alison sighed. "I can't promise anything," she said.

She walked through the house to watch from the lounge window as Caroline climbed on to her bike and cycled quickly away.

"I can't promise, Caro," she whispered, "because I'm expecting Seb's baby."

Five

In Gordon Brett's conference room, now thinly disguised as a party venue, the book launch was in full swing. About forty guests mingled in small groups as Marie Jayne's latest novel made its appearance on the literary scene. An arrangement of a dozen or so copies of the new book with an accompanying display board trumpeted "a story of anguished love set against a background of desperate odds". A little overblown, Kate conceded silently, but Marie Jayne was an extremely fashionable writer and her name on the cover was enough to ensure satisfyingly large sales both in Great Britain and overseas.

Kate glanced across at the author, who stood in the middle of the room with her agent Tom Cross. A birdlike figure, Marie Jayne was in her early seventies. The photograph on the display board was cunningly designed to flatter her but that, thought Kate, was how it should be.

Her own companion, Clive Peebles, was a reporter for *The Times*. He was talking about the literary scene in general but Kate, for once, listened with only half an ear. Robert had been invited to the launch and she was surprised that he hadn't arrived. As the minutes ticked by, she became uneasy. It was so unlike him to miss any kind of party.

"I hear congrats are in order," said Clive. "Quite an achievement – snaring Robert Dengaul!"

"Actually, he snared me!" she told him, a smile softening the reproof. It annoyed her that some people assumed she had set her cap at Robert. Several women had, of course, and according to gossip a few hadn't waited for Vi to die before offering to replace her. True, Kate had always found Robert amusing but when they first met she was still recovering from losing Will and was certainly not looking for a second husband. In the early days of their courtship she had warned Robert that she might never remarry. It was Robert who had been the hunter. She had been the reluctant prey until without warning and to her great surprise, she had fallen in love with him.

"Lucky old Robert!"

Kate didn't miss the "old" but it no longered bothered her.

"We're expecting him at any moment," she said.

At that moment Tom Cross detached himself and drifted towards them. A bulky man with an untidy moustache and hair to match, he laid an arm across Kate's shoulder.

"Don't believe a word this man tells you!" he told her. "Clive was born to cause chaos and dismay and he wields his pen accordingly!" To Clive he said, "Didn't see you at the Hodder bash last week. Quite a decent do, actually. I met a South African who's writing the definitive account of the Zulu uprising ..."

Thankful for the opportunity, Kate made her excuses and left them to enjoy each other's company. A waitress offered a tray of canapes. She chose a vol-au-vent filled with mushrooms and was still chewing when Marie Jayne came up to her.

"My dear Kate, I was so thrilled by your news. Bob is such a darling man. I call him Bob just to annoy him, you see." Her laugh was a soft trill. "We go back a long way. His father knew my aunt in the far distant past. He came to a couple of parties with Violet and I've watched his career with interest, and *envy*, if I'm honest."

Kate recognised the need for reassurance and said, "You have no need to envy anyone, Marie. You and Robert are among our most popular authors and long may it continue."

"Thank you, my dear." She contrived to look surprised by the compliment. "Anyway, you'll make a very handsome couple and hopefully he'll help you with your writing."

"My writing? Oh no! I'm not a writer. I was never serious about—"

Marie wagged a sticklike finger. "Then you *should* be. You sent one of your first attempts to Heinemann – remember?"

Kate stared at her. "But that was years ago! I realised I didn't have what it takes."

"Oh, but you do!" Marie insisted. "You sent it to Evelyn Noakes, I remember. Poor soul. She died of blood poisoning. Anyway, I know she was very impressed because she showed me the manuscript and it *was* promising, Kate. She was quite excited about it and she was going to talk to you. Of course it needed a lot of work but she was going to point you in the right direction."

Kate shook her head. "I remember her kind letter but it was just around the time when my husband died. I lost interest in the idea and Muriel was kind enough to find me a job here."

Marie reached out and took another glass of champagne from a passing waiter. "Have to wash the food down with something," she explained. "Why do you serve these dreadful snack things? Nobody serves a decent lunch any more. It was so much more civilised when I started." She sighed. "Well, think about it, my dear. You *can* write." She glanced round the room. "So

149

where is Bob? I thought he'd be here."

They both looked for him among the chattering crowd and Kate again felt the prickle of unease. She glanced at her watch. An hour late? Robert loved these literary gatherings, thriving as he did on literary gossip. "You have to keep abreast," he had once told her. "Nothing stays the same in this business. Publishing is becoming very commercialised. You need to keep your wits about you." That was true enough, Kate reflected. Only a month ago a best-selling author had been poached by a rival publisher, lured by a large sum of money. "Hardly cricket," according to Robert, "not the gentlemanly thing to do." She smiled at the memory of his indignant expression.

Tom Cross hurried through the crowd to retrieve Marie Jayne, promising to introduce her to a new book reviewer. Finding herself alone, Kate decided to telephone Highstead and slipped away to her office. The telephone rang for some time before being answered.

"Yes?" It was Caroline.

"It's Kate. I was wondering where Robert is."

"He's had a fall. The doctor's here now."

"Oh *no*!"

"He tripped and fell down the stairs. He was rather shaken up and the doctor insisted he shouldn't travel. I was supposed

150

to have phoned you but I forgot. Sorry."

Kate was not convinced. She suspected that Caroline had "forgotten" deliberately.

"And you're sure he's not hurt? May I speak to him?"

"No." There was a hint of triumph in her voice. "He's supposed to be sleeping. The doctor's given him something."

Kate pressed her lips together. Don't antagonise her, she told herself. "Then perhaps I could speak to the doctor."

There was a slight pause and Kate knew what was coming.

"He's just gone. Sorry."

"I see. I'll ring the doctor myself if you give me the number."

Another pause. "I can't remember it offhand and I was busy with Nutmeg when it happened. I'm sorry, Kate, but I've got to rush. I'll ring you back later."

Kate said, "Would you ask Robert to ring me as soon as he feels up to it?"

"It will probably be some time tomorrow."

"Tomorrow? Can I do anything to help if I come down?"

"Such as?"

"I don't know but ..."

"There's nothing that I can't cope with. I've been looking after my father for some time now."

Which translated, meant, "And we don't need *you*!"

Kate muttered a rude word then stared at the telephone as the line went dead.

"Caroline Dengaul!" she muttered. "You are an uppity little madam!"

Fuming, she replaced the receiver. It was the first time any of Robert's offspring had been quite so antagonistic towards her and she was shaken. She was also worried about Robert. How bad *was* the fall? Presumably Caroline had not lied about that. It would rebound on her when the truth came out and Robert would be furious with her.

Undecided, Kate tapped anxious fingertips on the desk top, wondering what to do. Best to leave it for an hour or so, she decided. When the launch was over she would ring again. Or maybe Robert would wake up and decide to ring her. If she didn't hear anything and was unhappy about the situation she would take the train down, stay overnight in a nearby hotel, and see Robert in the morning. There was no way Caroline could refuse to admit her to see Robert if she turned up on the doorstep.

Thoughtfully she made her way back to the conference room.

"Can I tempt you?" The waiter offered his tray.

Kate took a sausage roll. The pastry was hard and the filling tasteless. Marie was right: the buffet was not exactly inspired. She looked for Muriel but her friend was chatting to an editor from Macmillan.

"Ah there you are!" Michael Deen hurried towards her, hand outstretched. He was a senior buyer for a small chain of lending libraries in the Midlands and to be encouraged at all costs. Fixing a smile, Kate pushed all thoughts of Robert and his daughter to the back of her mind. She had a job to do, she told herself, and moved forward to greet their guest.

As soon as Sebastian arrived home, Caroline sat him down in the kitchen with a cup of tea and told him about their father's fall. She had decided they must stand together and she now had to persuade her brother to co-operate.

"The point is we don't want Lady Kate descending on us," she declared. "She's already been on the telephone fussing and I gave her short shrift. We don't need her."

Seb stirred sugar into his cup. "Father might *want* her to come down."

"Maybe *he* will but *we* don't."

"Talk for yourself. I've nothing against her. To be honest I quite like her. Aren't there any biscuits?"

Caroline's mouth tightened. "You're just a pushover for anyone in a skirt! I tell you we don't—"

"OK. So *you* don't want her here. Then you'll just have to look after him yourself. If he needs it." He frowned. "How did he manage to fall down the stairs anyway? You said he tripped over something but what?"

She sat back, her expression anxious. "Actually he said he felt dizzy and then found himself on the floor at the bottom of the stairs. I didn't want to tell Kate that. The doctor thinks it was a blackout."

They exchanged startled glances. Caroline fetched a tin of biscuits from the dresser and watched her brother sort through them.

"No digestives?" Munching a pink wafer he asked, "A blackout? Is that bad?"

"Well, it's not good. The thing is we don't have to say anything to Kate. If she thinks it's serious she'll come over all Florence Nightingale."

"Suppose he'd been crossing a road – he might have been run over!"

"So what I'm saying is if you answer the phone to her, make light of it."

"I can't see what she sees in Father. She needs someone nearer her own age." He grinned. "Like me."

"You've got Alison!" she snapped.

"But you want me to give her up, don't you?"

"Not in exchange for Kate!"

"Well, you've got a choice. You can have her as a stepmother or a sister-in-law!"

"That's assuming she'd even look at you!"

It was a thought, though. A sister-in-law

wouldn't inherit everything. And Bernard's marriage wouldn't suffer.

She watched Seb as he helped himself to more biscuits. Would Kate have fallen for him if she hadn't met his father first? Withdrawing the tin, she replaced the lid and put it back on the dresser. "What worries me is that Father might change his will. He might leave everything to you know who."

"We're his natural heirs. Why don't we simply ask him. We're entitled to know, surely."

Caroline hesitated. "*Ask* him? Wouldn't it seem rather mercenary?"

Sebastian sat back. "If he won't tell us we could ask Jones. It might not be too ethical but we could try."

Jones was the family solicitor.

Caroline frowned. "How would he know if Father's ill?"

"He won't know that but he'll know what's in Father's will." Sebastian clasped his hands in front of his chest. "Maybe we could trick it out of him – Jones, I mean. Ring up and phrase a question so that he thinks we already know."

"He wouldn't tell us and he might tell Father."

A voice from the doorway asked, "Might tell me what exactly?"

They looked round in alarm. Robert was

still in his pyjamas and dressing gown and their dark-blue colour deepened his pallor. He looked at Caroline. "Did you ring Kate?"

Shocked, Caroline managed to collect her wits. "I spoke to her. I told her not to worry. I said we can manage."

He moved carefully across the kitchen and Sebastian leapt up and pulled out a chair for him.

"How're you feeling now?"

"So-so. Who might tell me what?" He looked from Caroline to Sebastian.

Neither spoke.

Finally Caroline said, "The doctor. If we asked him if you're ill, he might tell you that we'd asked." Without waiting, she fetched another cup and poured him tea. "Did you ask him what was wrong?"

"There's nothing wrong. Dizziness on it's own isn't serious. Not at my age."

Caroline thought he was lying. His tone was too hearty; his expression too cheerful.

She said, "So you can still go ahead with the wedding?"

"Of *course* we can!"

He gave her an angry look and she knew she must step cautiously.

"That's good," she said and smiled.

Seb said suddenly, "That money Mother left for us. The five hundred pounds each. Why does it have those restrictions? The home-buying clause? Because if you're not prepared to help me I'd like my share now – to pay my way through Art School."

"Have you got a place then?"

Robert sounded pleased, Caroline noted with surprise.

"Not yet but I've got an interview next week. Several people have dropped out at the last minute."

"Your mother wanted you to have some money for a deposit on a house or a flat. She didn't want it frittered away on fast cars or flashy clothes."

Sebastian looked at him indignantly. "Paying for a form of training isn't like that. It's education, isn't it? I don't think she would have objected."

Their father shrugged wearily. "She wanted to be sure you had a roof over your head. If it's of any interest, I had no hand in Vi's will. She drew it up without my help."

As he sipped his tea, Caroline shot her brother a warning glance which he ignored.

"Because if I can't have it, could I have some of the money you said you'd be leaving for us? I really do have to find the money from somewhere."

Caroline recognised the ploy immediately and wanted to applaud. Seb was testing their father.

Seb went on. "What I mean is, if you marrying Kate changes anything – I mean,

157

if you've changed your will or anything –
well, you'd tell us, wouldn't you?"

Caroline watched him with admiration.
His expression was a clever mix of
innocence and apprehension.

When their father didn't answer he
stumbled on. "The fact is that if Kate
expected—" He stopped abruptly. "What I
mean is we'd understand if you had to cut us
out. A new wife ... she would expect it all, I
suppose." His voice trailed off and Caroline
held her breath.

Normally her father would have reacted
angrily to such questions but hopefully he
was feeling low and might sympathise with
his children's anxiety. On the other hand he
might know them better than they
imagined. In that case he might put Seb's
questions down to avarice or, worse, see
them as an indirect attack on Kate Harper.

She said, "Biscuit?"

Her father shook his head. Then he said, "I
have changed my will to include Kate. That
is the only fair thing to do. I shall sign it on
the eve of the wedding. I will leave you both
something substantial, of course, but –" he
forced a smile – "don't get your hopes up. I
intend to live for – for as long as possible."

Caroline was suddenly fearful. Something
in her father's voice – or was it his eyes –
troubled her. *Was* he ill? She jumped to her
feet and put her arms around him.

"Please don't talk about dying! You know how I hate it. I know you'll do what you can for us." She crouched beside her father, looking up into his face. Whatever her feelings about Kate she couldn't bear to think about losing him. "Kate won't ever stop you from loving me, will she?" The words were out before she could stop them.

"Stop me from loving you?" her father said gruffly. "You silly girl!" He put his arms round her. "You and Bernard and Seb are very precious to me and always will be. Kate knows that. She would never try to come between us."

Sebastian said, "She's very lucky, Dad. So are you! Kate's a stunning girl."

"I just want us all to be happy and get along."

He sounded so tired. Caroline stood up. There was no way she could let Kate spoil their special relationship. Leaning down, she kissed him.

"Stop worrying. We *will* be happy," she told him. "So, will you ring Kate later? She's obviously a bit of a worrier. We don't want her to panic and come rushing down here."

He stood up. "I'll ring her now from the bedroom and then I'll put myself back to bed. The fall shook me up but a few bruises won't kill me."

Sebastian asked if he needed any help up the stairs but the offer was refused.

When he had gone they looked at each other and Sebastian held up a thumb in a gesture of triumph. "We did well!" he said in a low voice.

Caroline nodded but her satisfaction was muted. The money was no longer a factor, she realised. What mattered most was that Kate should never come between her and her father. If he *were* to become ill she, Caroline, would be the one to care for him. There was no place for Kate in the equation.

Kate put down the phone and looked up.

"Is he OK?" Muriel asked.

Unable to wait any longer, Kate had slipped away from the launch to make another phone call. She nodded slowly. "He was on the point of phoning me. He says he's fine but he sounded ... different. A bit shaken, I suppose." She had detected a certain reluctance on his part to admit that anything was wrong. Probably his pride, she thought, with a rush of affection. Once, at her flat, he had caught his hand on the iron and it must have hurt because it came up in a huge blister, but Robert had pretended not to feel it. Men were funny, she reflected. Will had been just the opposite. The tiniest bruise held his interest for days and when he got a head cold he had been impossible.

Muriel picked up a newly sharpened

pencil and began turning it to and fro. "I'd slip down there if I were you. If you're worried, that is."

"Caroline doesn't want me there. She made that quite plain."

"Does *Robert* want you there? That's what matters, Kate. Don't let a bad-tempered daughter cramp your style." Muriel began to tap the pencil point on the desk top.

Kate tried to recall the nuances of the conversation. "I don't think so. I think he'd like to be in London with me, but the doctor's said he's not to travel today. He has to take it easy." She wondered if there was any way she could bring him up to London without over-tiring him but to Caroline that might seem rather high-handed. It might be better if she didn't meddle. They weren't yet married and he was still very much part of his family.

Muriel said, "Why the frown? Something on your mind?"

"I don't quite trust her."

As soon as she uttered the words, Kate knew that she *didn't* trust her future stepdaughter. She had no real reason to doubt her but something about Caroline set alarm bells ringing in her subconscious mind. Something in her eyes perhaps or a trace of deceit in her voice.

Muriel pressed on the pencil point and it snapped off.

"Give that to me!" Kate snatched it from Muriel's hands and dropped it into the top drawer.

Muriel surrendered the pencil without protest but she raised her eyebrows. Ashamed, Kate said, "Sorry, Mu! I'm not thinking straight."

"You *are* worried, aren't you?"

Kate tried a smile but it failed miserably. "I am but I don't know why. Am I becoming paranoid? You'll tell me if I am, won't you?"

"You could go down on the train and bring him back to London in a taxi. Bit expensive, of course ..."

Kate sighed. "I've thought of that and I'd love to, but Caroline would never forgive me. I don't want to make matters worse than they are already." She came to a decision. "No. I won't interfere. I'm sure he'll survive without me. Let's get back to the party. It'll take my mind off things."

That same evening, Bernard was in the church hall where choir practice was in full swing. Bernard sang with as much energy as he could muster, his strong baritone blending easily with the other two men. The choir consisted of eight people altogether – three baritones, one bass, one tenor, one contralto and two sopranos. This arrangement was not from choice but from necessity. Anyone who was willing to give up

162

Friday night for rehearsal and most of Sunday for services (plus the additional duties at weddings, funerals and the like) was welcome – as long as they could sing – but there were never enough volunteers.

Ian Stewart, better known as Stew, had run the choir for at least twenty years. Over the years his red beard had turned grey and his hair had thinned, but his enthusiasm had never faltered.

"For all the saints who from their labours rest ..."

Bernard glanced at the man in front of him. John was also a member of the choir and as the only bass singer was seriously cherished. "Stew's favourite," Bernard had teased him. "Teacher's pet." The good-natured banter which both men could give and receive reminded Bernard of his schooldays. There, as a boarder at prep school, he had had a friend named Phinbar. The boy, so close to him in age, had been more like a brother than Seb had ever been. When Phinbar left to rejoin his parents in India Bernard had watched his departure through eyes blurred with tears. It was the only time in his life he had ever had a friend and confidant – until now. Now there was John Somers. Part friend, part father figure. Why was it, Bernard wondered, that he had never felt close to his own father? Never able to confide in him, always struggling to earn his admiration. His relationship with John was wonderfully relaxed.

The practice continued until the result was to Stew's satisfaction and they embarked on another hymn written with differing parts.

"We'll take it right through without a stop. All three verses." Stew beamed at his choir. "I think everyone knows it except our new member. Here you are Mr Dengaul." He handed over a hand-scored sheet. "Just follow it for now. You can practise at home."

Bernard was content to listen, watching the man in front of him, noting the fact that the collar of his jacket didn't fit as snugly as it should. He wondered what it was like to live without a woman. He tried to imagine John washing out his smalls or making the bed. Hopefully, after choir practice, John would invite him back for a nightcap. Alison wouldn't like it but he no longer cared.

The piano stopped again. This time Stew's complaint was that the contralto was a fraction behind the beat.

"Sorry Stew."

"Last verse with feeling then. Build gradually then let go for the last line."

Bernard was toying with the idea of suggesting to Alison that they invite John Somers round for a bit of supper but he wasn't sure whether he wanted to share his friend. If John and Alison got on really well he would lose his newfound ally, but if they hated each other on sight Alison would object more loudly about the time they spent together.

"Walking the dog?" she had protested. "I didn't know you liked dogs that much. I can't see you cleaning up after a puppy—"

On and on. It was one of her faults – the way she would never let go. He had never cared that much about animals, but walking along the lanes and through the wood with John and the old spaniel had proved so pleasant that he was longing for the chance to do it again.

Suddenly Stew was staring at him and John was turning round, grinning.

"Sorry!" Bernard mumbled. "What did you say?"

He became aware that the choristers were preparing to go their separate ways, collecting up hymn books and heading for the door.

Stew laughed. "Mrs B will bring the vestments round on Thursday."

"Mrs B?"

A plump soprano turned, smiling. "That's me. Mrs Beddowes. I wash and iron them every other week. I hope Saint Peter has made a note of it!"

Stew said, "Think of all the sins you can offset!" He smiled at Bernard. "See you in the vestry Sunday then. Ten o'clock sharp."

"I'll be there."

It dawned on him that the service would make them late leaving for Alison's parents' house. Normally they skipped morning church in order to be on time. Alison would have to ring them and explain and ask them to make lunch half an hour later. Something else for her to grumble about. Serve her right, he thought spitefully. She had been less than loving for the last few months and increasingly moody. Twice he had caught her crying and once she had uttered the dread word "divorce". Only to frighten him, he was sure but it had provoked a sudden terror in him.

"Oh Alison!" With a start he realised that he had spoken aloud but glancing round it appeared that no one had noticed. Women. They had always been a mystery to him. Left to his own devices he would probably never have proposed to Alison. He had looked upon her as a friend but she had seen him as a husband. Accused of leading her on he had given in gracefully and agreed to marry her.

Thank the Lord for simple male friendship, he thought. If it hadn't been for the pleasure of his time with John he might well have slipped into depression. Instead, he was able to suffer Alison's behaviour, knowing that he could arrive at any time on

John's doorstep. Whatever Bernard's mood, his friend would be a willing and sympathetic listener because his own marriage had been less than perfect.

Spilling out of the hall the choristers found themselves in a night still heavy with the remains of the day's heat.

"We could have a storm," said Bernard.

John glanced up at the sky. "Let's hope so. It would clear the air." Glancing at his watch he lowered his voice. "I made some sloe gin last winter and it's just about drinkable. Have you got time to help me sample it?"

Bernard grinned broadly. "I thought you'd never ask!"

An hour later, Alison lay in bed struggling with mixed emotions. Fear and anger kept her in a state of permanent tension and she glanced frequently at the alarm clock. Nearly eleven. No choir practice ever lasted this long so presumably he was with John Somers ... unless there was a woman involved and he was being terribly clever. Letting her *think* it was Somers.

She sat up, slipped from the bed and made her way downstairs to the kitchen. While milk boiled she stirred sugar and cocoa in a cup. She would wait here for Bernard, letting him see that his late nights were causing her problems. Not that this was a problem compared with other areas of her life. The problem was Seb who hadn't been near her for days. She had to tell him about the child and although she was certain he would do the decent thing and marry her, she had to be *sure*. If he abandoned her then she would have to pretend the child was Bernard's and live with the lie and that thought appalled her. It involved so much deceit and worst of all the child would grow up calling his father Uncle Sebastian. What a ghastly mess it would be. Worse still was the thought that at some time Seb would marry someone else and have other children whom he *would* acknowledge. Would her own son or daughter be a "love child"? she wondered, with a fresh stab of fear. And if the truth ever came out ... A chill clutched her as she imagined the recriminations. Her child might well turn against her.

"Oh God!" she whispered, close to tears. Suppose that by her selfishness she caused her unborn child untold anguish at some time in the future. How would she ever explain it? After so many years her feelings for Sebastian would appear tawdry and entirely without merit.

With a shaking hand, she poured the frothing milk into the cup and carried it into the sitting room. What exactly *was* a love child? she wondered. Was it an illegitimate child, born to a mother who was unmarried or one born to a mother married to a man who wasn't the father? Her stomach churned. How on earth had she allowed this to happen? Or rather, how had Seb allowed it to happen? He had sworn that he knew what he was doing – that he would never make her pregnant. So much for his promises ... Yet she knew she must shoulder some of the blame because she had known Seb since before her marriage and she knew how unreliable he could be.

"*Please*, Seb," she whispered, "don't let me down!"

She sipped her cocoa which was too hot and burnt her tongue. Her despair grew as she thought about other ramifications of the small but significant life growing within her. If Bernard divorced her, everyone would know why. Her parents would have to know and they would be so ashamed and upset. Her father would look at her with that hurt expression as though she had done it deliberately to cause them pain. Her mother would never stop crying.

She had just finished her cocoa when she heard a key being turned in the front door. Footsteps in the hall. Alison felt her fear turning to anger. It was Bernard's fault in a way. If he had given her a child none of this would have happened. At least she was pregnant and he could no longer pretend that *she* had failed *him*. Resentment for past humiliations boiled within her.

The moment Bernard stepped into the room she knew he was drunk. With a thin cry she hurled herself at him, raining blows against his chest and arms, slapping his face, hurling abuse. Bernard, caught off guard by the onslaught, held his arms in front of his face to ward off the worst of the blows and struggled to make sense of the situation.

"Stop it, for God's sake, Alison. What's got into you?"

Your brother, thought Alison hysterically. Your damned brother.

"You don't love me," she shouted. "You don't want to be with me. Any excuse to stay away from me. Don't think I don't know what's happening!"

Exhausted, she dropped her arms and burst into tears. Bernard took his chance. He grabbed at her hands and held them tight.

"Alison, stop this! Tell me what the hell's happened."

Alison jerked her hands free and stumbled backwards. Her legs came into contact with the coffee table, she lost her balance and toppled backwards. She fell heavily and lay there, winded, gasping and coughing. Bernard stumbled to kneel beside her.

"I didn't touch you!" he said.

"Nobody said you did."

"Are you all right?"

Alison looked at him with dislike. His cheeks were flushed and there were two scratches on his face.

"Are you hurt?"

She closed her eyes. Am I hurt? she thought with a rapid descent into a deadly weariness. More to the point – is the baby hurt? Could a fall like this kill Sebastian's child? And if it had, would she be relieved or sorry? At that moment she honestly didn't know.

She allowed Bernard to help her into a sitting position.

The shock had sobered him. "Take a deep breath," he told her. "Breathe slowly. You're going to be OK."

She said, "I'll never be OK again." Her voice trembled. She put a hand to the back of her head. A bump was forming already. Had she struck her head as she fell?

He said, "Let's get you into a chair."

As he made to take her hands she snatched them away. "Don't help me," she told him. "Don't even touch me. You won't want to when you know."

"When I know *what*?" He sat down on the nearest chair, one hand to his heart. "You scared me."

Alison was aware of an overwhelming pity for him. Whatever he had done or had not done to make her happy, he didn't deserve what was coming. Suddenly she had to tell

171

someone. Seb was absent so it would have to be Bernard.

"I'm having a baby," she said, her voice unnaturally loud. "I'm three months pregnant and—" She hesitated.

"A baby? But Alison ..." His eyes widened. "Oh my God!"

"Seb's the father. I'm sorry."

She could see that the implications of her words had not yet registered.

He rubbed his face. "What do you mean ... about Seb?"

Abruptly the words sank in and she saw dreadful realisation strike deep into his heart. His mouth opened and closed. His expression changed several times. Disbelief, disgust, anger.

He whispered, "You and *Seb*?"

She nodded.

"No, Alison, you *wouldn't*!"

Alison began to shiver. "I'm sorry but I did."

She tried very carefully to stand. Was she still pregnant? she wondered fearfully. It dawned on her that the baby might be the only child she would ever have. If she had killed it she would never forgive herself.

"Oh God, Bernard!" She clutched her abdomen. "That fall!" Was it her imagination or was she feeling a dull ache? She tried to remember what she knew about miscarriages, which was remarkably little. She felt a fine perspiration break out on her forehead and she sat down again.

Bernard was eyeing her with something akin to horror. He had backed away and was standing beside the unlit fire, clutching the mantelpiece with one hand. For a long moment they regarded each other with dismay.

He said, "Shall I call the doctor?"

"No!" She winced as the first pain shot through her.

"Who then? Caro? Dad?"

"Are you crazy? What do they know?" Tears slid down her face.

"You can't just sit there and let it happen. For heaven's sake, I have to call *someone!*" Colour was returning to his face in odd patches.

Alison doubled up with the next pain. When it faded she raised her head. "Call Kate," she told him.

Six

Next morning Kate left it until just after eight before ringing Highstead. Caroline answered.

"Caro, it's Kate. Is Sebastian there?"

"He's in London for his interview at the Slade."

"Good. Then I'd like to speak to Robert, please."

"I'm afraid he's still asleep. Shall I—"

Kate rolled her eyes. "Caro, I can hear him whistling."

"Oh!"

Kate could imagine her cursing under her breath.

"He must have just got up then. He was asleep."

"It's rather important, Caroline."

"I'll ask him to ring you later."

Kate longed to snap at her but instead she took a deep breath. She was already more involved with the Dengauls than she wanted to be. Quarrelling with Caroline would only make things worse. She said, "I'm afraid I have to insist. Your father will want to talk to me."

174

"He's got your number. He—"

"*Caroline*! Will you please ask your father to come to the phone. Tell him I'm not in London, I'm with Alison."

The silence, she reflected, was deafening.

In a different tone Caroline said, "With Alison? Is there something wrong?"

"Obviously there is. That's why I want to speak—"

She heard Robert's voice. Then Caroline's, "She says she's with Alison."

Robert said, "Kate? What's this about Alison?"

He sounded much stronger than when they had spoken the night before. Hiding her relief, Kate explained briefly, making it as undramatic as possible. She didn't say that it was Sebastian's child nor that Bernard had stormed out into the night within minutes of her taxi drawing up at their door. She wanted to lessen the shock for Robert but she imagined Caroline standing nearby listening. "I've just rung the doctor and he's promised to call in but I think she's been lucky."

"Lucky!" he exploded.

"I mean I don't think she'll lose the child." Before he could say anything she rushed on. "She's quite comfortable and sleeping. There's really nothing you can do for her but I thought you'd want to know."

"I'll be round in about twenty minutes."

"Only if you feel up to it, darling. I'm quite capable of cooking a bit of breakfast."

She heard Caroline's voice and then Robert's and hoped he was refusing to bring her with him.

"Come alone, Robert. The fewer the better at a time like this." Perhaps that would help spike Caroline's guns. "I'll see you soon then. Have you eaten yet?"

"Not yet."

"I'll raid Alison's larder."

She put down the phone, her fingers crossed. Robert would be furious when he knew all the facts but her own presence might soften his wrath. She went upstairs to the bedroom. Alison was awake, sitting up, her hair tousled, her eyes still reddened from last night's tears.

"I'm going to cook us all some breakfast," Kate said cheerfully. "We'll all think better on full stomachs." She smiled. "You look so much better. More colour in your face but until the doctor's seen you I want you to stay in bed."

Alison started guiltily. "But I've already been to the toilet!"

"That's OK. I meant no standing around in the bathroom or taking a bath. I'll bring you some washing things and a bowl of warm water. It's amazing what a soapy flannel will do for morale. I'm surprised doctors don't prescribe it." She bent down and hugged the slim figure. "Look Alison, right now it may seem like the end of the world but you'll be surprised how these things work themselves out."

Twenty minutes later when Robert arrived bacon was keeping warm on a plate in the oven, tomatoes were under the grill and Kate was waiting to put the eggs into the frying pan.

Robert held her close in his usual bear hug. "My poor Kate!" he said. "You'll be wishing you'd never met this bloody family!"

"Never!" Kate assured him with a reassuring kiss. "Now come into the kitchen and eat, darling. Alison's got a breakfast tray upstairs so we have a bit of time to talk."

While they ate, Kate said, "Alison has asked me to tell you what's happened and Robert – I'd like you to hear me out in silence if you can. It's not going to be easy for either of us." She then explained the whole situation as simply as she could while Robert listened with an expression of incredulity. She finally came to the end of her account. "As soon as I arrived, which was sometime around midnight, Bernard said, 'Well, I'm not staying where I'm obviously not needed' and rushed out of the house."

"God Almighty! What a shambles!"

"I'm afraid it is!" She put a hand over his

and said, "Finish your breakfast, Robert. You'll need all your strength!"

He didn't even smile. "And where the hell has Bernard gone? He could hardly knock on the door of a hotel in the middle of the night." He sighed heavily. "Probably gone to her parents' place to spill the beans."

"Alison thinks he may have gone to a friend – a chap called John Somers. Does the name ring any bells?"

"I've heard of him. Wife died." His grim expression softened. "Poor Bernard! He must be going through hell." It hardened again. "And as for Seb! He needs a bloody good hiding! What can have possessed him? His brother's wife, for God's sake! He's a good-looking boy. He could have any woman."

He buttered more toast and Kate was pleased to see that his appetite was unimpaired.

"I think you should feel flattered, Robert, that Alison wanted to see you. I offered to visit her parents but she can't bear them to know just yet."

He groaned. "She probably thinks I'll talk Bernard round." He glanced up. "She does want him back, doesn't she?"

Kate hesitated. "I rather gather she'd prefer Seb."

"But how does she *know* it's his child?"

"It seems they haven't had – haven't been

intimate for months. They had a quarrel and it was never resolved. Weeks became months. I'm sorry, Robert."

"*You're* sorry? Kate, it's me that should be sorry. Dragging you down from London like this for something that's not your problem."

"But it almost is, Robert. I'll be Mrs Dengaul in a few weeks' time. I think it's rather nice that she trusted me enough to send for me. Look on the bright side, darling."

She spoke confidently, keeping her doubts to herself. It seemed very probable that Caroline would see her presence as unwarranted interference believing that *she* should have been sent for instead.

As if reading her mind Robert said, "Caro could have come round on her bike. You must let me pay for the taxi. No, Kate! I insist. It's the very least I can do." With a heavy sigh he carried his empty plate to the draining board, sat down again and reached for more toast and marmalade. "God, I could strangle Seb!"

"But a grandchild would be nice."

"You think so?"

Kate put a hand over his. "In a few years, Robert, you'll look back on this day and wonder why we were all so upset. You'll be pushing your grandchild on the swing or—"

"*Don't!*" He avoided her eyes. "Nothing is ever that easy. You should know that by now." He ate in a thoughtful silence and Kate decided to let him be the first to break it. Perhaps he was right. Perhaps both Bernard and Seb would reject Alison and she would go back to her parents, taking the child with her.

He said, "Where's that ruddy doctor?"

Kate swallowed. Make allowances, she told herself. He's angry and humiliated.

"He'll be along soon I'm sure. Do you want a word with Alison?"

"Do I have to?"

"I think she'd be grateful for a few reassuring words."

"Reassuring words?" He shook his head, "Thank God poor Vi isn't alive to see the mess the family is in. God, I'll have something to say to Seb. I'll give him Art School! He won't get another penny out of me unless he does the decent thing by that girl!"

Kate said nothing.

"I've got to talk to Bernard," he said abruptly. "I'll ring her parents."

"But if he's not there ... Robert, wait, please."

Ignoring her, he went out into the hall to the telephone. Kate heard him speak to the operator and then he was obviously through to Alison's parents.

"... He's not there? Damn him! ... Look here, before you go blaming Seb just

180

remember it takes two to … What's it about?" He sounded incredulous. "Oh! Of course, you don't know."

Alone in the kitchen Kate shook her head. *"Not* like that, Robert," she whispered. "You will alienate everybody."

He said, "Trouble? Yes, you could put it like that …"

Kate crossed her fingers. "Don't tell them about the child!" she whispered.

A note of caution crept into Robert's voice. "There's been a – a bit of an upset. She'll tell you about it herself … They've had a quarrel and he's walked out … No, that's all I know. Sorry."

Kate heard the receiver being banged down and then Robert came back into the kitchen.

He said, "I couldn't tell them." He sat down, his expression subdued. "Bernard's not there." He looked at Kate. "Where could he have gone? He wouldn't … wouldn't do anything rash, would he?"

"Robert, I told you earlier. Alison says he has a friend – a man friend – who lives in the village. He might have gone there."

He still wasn't listening, she thought, as he ran a shaking hand over his face.

"We had such hopes," he said. "You live for your children, in a way, and then … this happens."

"Darling, they're still your children.

They're just making mistakes. We all make them. We'll get through this, I promise."

There was a ring at the front door and Kate hesitated.

Robert said, "It'll be the doctor. You'd better go. I'm in no mood to be civil."

A strange man stood on the doorstep.

"Come in, Doctor." Kate held the door open.

He shook his head. "I'm not the doctor. I'm John Somers, a friend of Bernard's." An elderly spaniel trotted up the path and stood beside him. He patted the dog. "This is Jasper. He loves everybody."

She bent to pat him. "Hullo Jasper." She glanced up. "Does he shake a paw?"

"He used to but he's getting lazy in his old age."

She smiled. "I'm Kate Harper. Won't you both come in?"

"No thank you. I thought Alison should know Bernard's staying with me for a few days. Didn't want anyone worrying about him and wondering where he is. You've all got enough to think about. He doesn't want to see anyone at the moment. He's had a rather nasty shock."

"It's all very sad. I'm so sorry."

"Not your fault, is it?" He raised his hat. "I'll be off then."

She hesitated but he had turned away. The dog hurried after him.

When Kate went back into the kitchen there was no sign of Robert so she guessed he had gone upstairs to talk to Alison. A moment later he came down the stairs with the full breakfast tray in his hand and set it down on the table.

"I can't talk to the poor girl. What on earth can I *say*?"

"What did you say?"

"I said 'How're you feeling?' and she said 'Sick. I can't eat that,' and I said, 'Right' and walked out!" He leaned dejectedly against the cupboard. "I wanted to say, 'Bernard not good enough for you, then?'"

"I'm glad you didn't, Robert." Kate crossed to him and slid her arms round his neck, pressing herself close. "Don't take it too hard, darling. It will only defeat you if you let it."

"Oh God! Homespun philosophy! That's all I need." He kissed the top of her head and a heartfelt sigh shook his entire frame. "Why don't we just run away and leave them to it?" he whispered.

"Because they may need us. We can run away later."

The bell went again and this time it was the doctor. Kate took him upstairs and left them together. He came down fifteen minutes later.

"Baby's still fine," he told them, "so no harm done. Plenty of rest. A day in bed with

183

a little pampering will do wonders." To Kate he said, "If there's any sign of blood loss lay her flat and call me. I'll send the nurse round in the morning. I'll let myself out."

"No harm done?" said Robert, when he had gone. "You could have fooled me."

Kate laughed. "Never mind. I'm here and I'll stay with her for the weekend if you like."

"You'll do no such thing! You'll stay with me at Highstead!"

Her heart sank. "Someone should be here with her."

"Caro can stay with her. I need you more than Alison does."

She stared at him, hearing the desperation in his voice. "I'll just fit in," she offered. "If Alison wants Caro here ..." The truth was that staying at Highstead held no appeal for her. She could imagine the scene there would be when Sebastian finally came back from London.

Robert said, "That's settled then. I'll run you back and then Caro can cycle over with a bit of lunch for the two of them."

Seeing that argument would be useless Kate agreed and broke the news to Alison who took it remarkably well in the circumstances. Five minutes later they were at Highstead. The house looked beautiful in the morning sunlight – beautiful and deceptively tranquil. Kate studied it as they went up the drive and wondered if it would ever feel like home.

From the leads above them, Caroline and Sebastian watched without being seen as Robert and Kate arrived back. Seb wore a pair of khaki shorts, a shirt and sandals. Caroline was dressed in slacks and a blouse.

"Here comes trouble!" said Caroline as Kate stepped out of the car.

Seb leaned back against the chimney stack. "I stumbled on them once and I heard Father say, 'It's just me and you from now on.' or 'It's just the two of us now.' Words to that effect."

"Meaning we don't matter? What a bitch."

He shrugged. "It was Father who said it, not Kate."

"We've got to *do* something about her We were perfectly happy before she came on the scene. I was thinking in bed last night. We could try and put him off her – or put her off him. Drop a few hints here and there."

"Tell a few lies, you mean."

Her eyes widened. "Look who's talking about telling lies! You've been telling them for months. Off with the harriers, indeed. All you were harrying was Alison."

He stretched his legs. "I can't marry her, Caro. I've got no money and no job and I think I'm going to get that place at the

185

Slade. I'm not giving that up just because she's going to have a baby."

"Well, you should."

"Bernard will take her back. You'll see. He won't want people laughing at him. He'll hush it all up and pretend he finally made it! A father at last! Alison will be eternally grateful to him and promise undying devotion. He should be thanking me."

"And you'll swan off to Art School and leave me stuck here playing gooseberry to Father and Lady Kate! Thanks very much. You're a real sweetie, Seb."

"He's offered us a flat. We could get one in London – the most expensive we can find. I'll go to college each day and you can cruise Knightsbridge in search of a rich husband."

"I don't want to live with you and I don't want a rich husband. I want to live here with Father and Nutmeg and *without* Kate. Blast the woman! I wish she'd never been born."

"Then steal the family silver, leap on to Nutmeg and gallop away into a golden sunset."

"Honestly Seb, you're not even vaguely amusing."

They fell silent, watching a white dove walk the rail along the edge of the roof, occasionally fluttering its wings to correct its balance. When it flew away Seb turned towards his sister.

"You could marry a farmer with plenty of

stables and have half a dozen Nutmegs."

"No thanks. I'm going off men. He might turn out like you or Bernard!" She sighed. "If only Kate would fall down the stairs. Then we could all pretend to be sorry, comfort Father and live happily ever after."

"Grease the stairs."

"They're carpeted."

"Dad fell down them."

"So he did. I could get Kate drunk and push her down! We'd say it was an accident."

"It would be rather a waste."

"What would?"

"Killing her. A waste of a gorgeous woman!"

"Kate is *not* gorgeous." Caroline rolled her eyes. "You are so cheap, Seb. You'd sniff round anyone. You've already got Alison into trouble. Isn't that enough? Anyway, if I want to get rid of Kate I wouldn't need your help."

Seb stared out across the garden. "I've got a better idea." He turned to face her and his eyes gleamed. "Let me see if I can seduce her. Then Father can find us in a compromising situation. You could make sure that he does. You could lead him to us. He'll throw a fit—"

"And throw Kate out!" Caroline was aware of a great lightening of spirit. "That's perfect, Seb. *Perfect*! But do you think you can?"

He laughed. "My charm has never failed me before."

"You are *so* conceited! It's sickening." The more she thought about it, the more the idea appealed. It was a wonderful idea. "And of course you'd be willing to co-operate in this little scheme."

He closed his eyes and beamed. "Let's say I wouldn't object – and she won't either!" He leaned across and gave Caroline a quick brotherly kiss. "What a team!" he whispered.

Caroline felt her pulse quicken. It was so simple. They could do it. She began to laugh.

Later, while Robert and Sebastian had their heart to heart in the study, Kate made herself scarce. Caroline, with a great show of reluctance, had gone round to Alison's to take her a bowl of salad and half a cold chicken pie. Kate had promised to rustle up an omelette for whoever remained at Highstead. Meanwhile she made her way slowly around the garden which would one day be hers. She really couldn't find fault with any of it. Robert's novels had provided an elegant home for his family.

To one side of the house there was a formal rose garden which had been Violet's pride and joy and this led on to a rectangular pool in which fish swam among waterlily stems. She watched them for a moment then wandered under an old sycamore and round the side of the house to the kitchen garden. All this was too much for one pair of hands, she reflected, there must be a gardener. Rows of lettuces and beetroot had been planted with military precision, also onion and leeks. Tomatoes were ripening against a trellis and there was a well-filled cucumber frame. She pulled a handful of carrots, skirted what looked like a potting shed and made her way towards the stables. Nutmeg accepted her offering with delighted snuffles and loud crunching noises and she found herself wondering whether she would take riding lessons. Maybe she could persuade Robert to do the same. Perhaps they could buy a miniature pony and stable it for Alison's child. A vague picture presented itself. She sighed. Was it possible that with enough goodwill it could all turn out well?

"Poor Robert," she whispered. No doubt he was finding this hard. Just when he was trying to persuade her that she could live happily with the Dengaul family they were doing their best to prove otherwise. She longed to be able to offer help and advice but she was totally out of her depth. It might be best if she returned to London but Robert might see that as negative and be plunged further into gloom.

She wondered what Alison and Caroline

were talking about. Was the crisis drawing the two women together or forcing them apart? Stroking the horse's smooth neck, Kate allowed herself, for the first time, to wonder if she and Robert would have a child. Or two or three. If they did, she imagined that Seb, Caro and Bernard would resent them. They would almost certainly see the newcomers as rivals.

"What a charming picture! A beautiful horse and a charming woman."

She swung round to see Seb a few yards away, hands held up as though framing a picture.

"Thank you." She was immediately on her guard.

He laughed lightly. "For your information, I've survived. Dad's said his piece and he didn't use the horsewhip. It was what we schoolboys used to call a 'wigging'. No physical violence just withering scorn. It's like water off a duck's back to me."

Kate was astonished. Seb appeared completely at ease, almost cheerful. Either he was genuinely unconcerned or he was a superb actor.

"Don't you care about Alison?" she demanded.

"Of course I care." He sauntered towards her, slipping his hands into the pockets of his shorts. "I gave her what she's always wanted."

"Alison wanted an *affair*?" She stared at him, baffled.

"A *child*." His gaze didn't falter. "Not that it's anything for you to worry your pretty head about. The Dengaul family can shoot itself in the foot without help from anyone else." He propped himself up against the stable door. "Actually, I'm sorry we dragged you through all this. Alison had no right to involve you."

Kate moved her hand to the horse's head, avoiding his gaze. "But shouldn't you be talking to Alison? She thinks you love her. She trusts you." She was trying not to sound too censorial.

"Of course I'll talk to her. I'm giving her time to recover from the shock." He put up a hand and stroked the horse's muzzle, managing as he did so to touch Kate's hand.

She withdrew her hand. "Are you planning to marry her?"

"Shouldn't think so."

"I can't believe you are really as selfish as you pretend." Immediately she cursed her stupidity. Comments like that simply fanned the flames and would not help matters. She should say as little as possible. "Forgive me!" she told him. "Forget I said that."

He gave her an intense look and said, "I'd forgive *you* anything, Kate. Anything. Hadn't you realised that? Am I being too subtle?"

191

A coldness seized her. Sebastian was dangerous. He was clever and manipulative. She said, "I'll forgive *you* for those stupid remarks!" and involuntarily stepped back, putting a greater distance between them.

Noticing the small retreat, he laughed. "Oh Kate! Have I scared you? I'm sorry. I thought you'd have seen that I'm consumed with jealousy. Have been since the first moment I saw you with Father."

"Stop this!" She tried to sound more confident than she felt.

"She's much too good for the old bugger, I thought. I knew—"

The shock deepened. "I said stop!" she snapped. "I won't listen to talk like that."

He raised his eyebrows in mock astonishment. "Can't you recognise a compliment when you hear one? Why is it such a shock, Kate? You must be used to men falling for your not inconsiderable charms." He shook his head lightly. "If I promise to admire you from a distance will that suit you? Will that make you—"

"That's enough, Seb!" She was losing her composure and that made her angry. "I know exactly what you're doing, and I know why. This is your way of taking revenge on Robert for whatever he has said to you about Alison. Well, I can see through you and I'm not impressed."

His boyish laugh rang out. "We could run

away together! I wonder just how many scandals this family could survive."

Looking into the handsome face, Kate thought: How can he look so good and behave so badly? Was it merely bravado on his part or something inherent in his nature?

She swallowed. "You really are a selfish brat, Seb! It's about time you grew up."

"That's exactly what *he* said. I asked why. I don't see that adults are any happier than I am. He isn't. He's got wealth and fame and *you*. Is he happy? He doesn't look very happy. He's been moping about the place for weeks now."

"Because you are spoiling everything for him!"

Sebastian shrugged. "But he's spoiling things for me, isn't he? He doesn't want me to go to Art School because he's terrified I might make a success of it. Might even become famous. Might bag a little of the attention he enjoys. He has to be the big cheese, Kate. The famous father with all the money. He's afraid—"

Kate slapped his face hard. He deserved it, but she regretted it instantly. She was making an enemy of him. She drew in a sharp breath as he touched his cheek and she saw the triumph in his eyes. He had been deliberately provoking her and she had fallen for it. Still reeling from her mistake she was unprepared as, without warning, he stepped forward and pressed her roughly against the stable wall. His kiss was long and harsh and his fingers were tight around her upper arms as she tried desperately to free herself. She could smell his sweat mingled with expensive aftershave.

When he released her she was breathless with anger.

He winked. "My God, Kate, you're really something!" He turned and began to walk away. He turned back and called, "Lucky old Father!"

With a sickening feeling of defeat, Kate resisted the urge to run after him and beat him with her fists. He would be too strong and she would lose the undignified struggle.

Instead she shouted after him, "Damn you, Sebastian!" and closed her eyes as tears threatened. Helplessly she leaned back against the stable wall. Nutmeg whinnied and she opened her eyes. With a trembling hand she patted the glossy neck. She longed to take the next train back to London and the security of her own life. But she was going to marry Robert and *this* was to be her life. How could she run away when Robert was going to need all her help to cope with his mounting problems. He was probably looking for her right now.

"Pull yourself together, Kate!" She breathed deeply, tidying her hair with her fingers and smoothing her dress. How much of this, she wondered, could she confide to Muriel? She had guessed that the family might resent her but this avalanche of betrayal and deceit had found her unprepared. Were they always like this or had she somehow acted as a catalyst? The thought troubled her deeply as she made her way back to the house, but not as deeply as the decision whether or not to tell Robert about Sebastian's behaviour. If she didn't tell him and Sebastian did it would look very odd. On the other hand she would have preferred to forget the incident which had shaken her more than she cared to admit. She didn't want to cause more trouble between father and son, but on balance, she thought unhappily, honesty was probably the best option.

Robert had hidden himself away in the study. He had resisted the temptation to lock himself in while he wondered what to do next. When Kate entered the study he said, "I'm going to have to bring Alison to Highstead. She can do her resting here. I'll pop over shortly. We have to sit her down with Seb and thrash this thing out. He's promised to go to round to see her but I know he won't. He'll put it off until someone else deals with it." He sighed. "Vi called him woolly headed once but that's a kind way of putting it. He hates facing up to his mistakes. When he got into scrapes as a boy his way of dealing with the reprimand was to stay in bed. I had to literally drag him out sometimes. Bit of a coward really. Vi used to take his side against me and then *we'd* argue." He sighed heavily. "The joys of family life!"

He glanced at her to see how she was taking this revelation but her expression was unreadable. He noticed that she was rather pale but his mind was on more immediate problems.

"Actually, Robert, I need to talk to you."

He looked at her in alarm. She probably wanted to go back to London! Poor Kate. She was taking it all very hard, but then she was an only child and had no experience of the down side of family life. He said quickly, "So I'm off. We'll talk later, darling."

She hesitated.

He said, "You will be here when I get back?"

"Of course I will, but before you go—"

"I'll make it up to you, Kate."

She gave him a strange look, then nodded. "Shall I rustle up something for us all to eat tonight or will Caroline be offended?"

"She'll be delighted, I should think. Give her more time to spend with Nutmeg."

He gave her a brief kiss and hurried out before she could reconsider. When this business with Seb was straightened out he would take Kate away. Paris or Vienna. Just for a week. The thought of some time together many miles from Highstead was something to cling to.

As soon as he reached Alison's doorstep he smelled it. The faintest wiff of something like gas. *Like gas?* For a moment he remained stock-still, frowning. Then a terrible thought struck him.

"My God! She wouldn't!"

He hammered with his fist on the front door without result then rushed round the side of the house to the back door. Here the smell was stronger and he was seized by a cold dread.

"Alison!" He tried to open the door but it was locked. "Alison! Open this door!" Peering through the glass his view was spoiled by the net curtain gathered across it. Glancing round he spotted a smiling garden gnome and, snatching it up, smashed the window with one blow. Lifting the curtain he saw the crumpled figure on the kitchen floor.

"Christ Almighty!" He reached through the window and unlocked the door and stepped inside.

"Alison! Oh my dear child!" A deep groan escaped him as he knelt beside his daughter-in-law. Alison's head lay on a cushion which had been propped beside the open oven door. She was very still. While he stared at her in shock the gas invaded his own lungs and he began to choke.

Gasping and spluttering he gathered her body into his arms, staggered upright with difficulty and struggled outside. He laid her in the middle of the lawn while he sucked in clean air. He was overcome by a wave of dizziness but that might have been caused more by his exertions than by the gas. As soon as he could he leaned over the prone figure and listened for signs of breathing. He heard nothing but thought he saw a slight movement in her chest. Was she still alive? He stared round him helplessly.

"Is there something wrong?

A woman was shaking a duster from an upper window in the house next door.

Unwilling to explain he said, "She's fainted. At least I think so."

"I'll come round if you like. I used to be a nurse."

"Oh thank you! Please. The side gate's open."

While he waited he shook Alison gently. "Wake up, my dear!" he said to her. "It will all be sorted out. I promise you. Alison ... *Alison*! For God's sake, wake *up*!"

It seemed an eternity before an elderly woman appeared, the duster still in her hand.

"I'm Mrs Ferris. Fainted, has she? Such a

nice couple." She knelt beside Robert who moved back slightly, grateful to surrender to more experienced hands.

"She smells of gas!" She glanced up.

Robert nodded. "I'm afraid so. I'm sorry ..."

"Oh dear! The poor soul." She shook her patient. "Mrs Dengaul! Open your eyes!" She patted the pale face then leaned over her to listen to her heart. "She's still breathing." She began rubbing Alison's right arm and Robert, copying her, worked on the left one.

He said, "She won't die, will she?"

"I don't think so. I think she'll pull through."

"She – she's expecting a baby." He regretted the words as soon as they were out but it was too late. He wondered how much she knew or had guessed. Presumably she would have noted Sebastian's too frequent visits.

"Oh dear!" She avoided his eyes. "That rather alters things. I mean, it does rather complicate matters."

Before he could reply, Alison's eyelids flickered and then she opened her eyes.

"She's coming round. A bit of luck you turning up when you did." She gave him a pitying look. "I said to myself earlier that I could smell gas. Maybe the two flues join up somewhere in the chimney. I thought at first it was a leak in my house. I opened the windows and it cleared and I thought maybe I'd imagined it. I said to myself, I'll tell George the moment he gets home, he'll know what to do because one doesn't like to call the man out for nothing."

Alison looked round dazedly.

They both looked at her. Mrs Ferris said, "You're going to be fine. Your father-in-law arrived just in time."

Robert hesitated. "She and my son ..." He stopped.

She lowered her voice. "These walls are rather thinner than one would like, Mr Dengaul. I did realise things were not quite how they should be but *this*!" She shook her head. "When one's young these things are always such disasters, aren't they? My favourite uncle threw himself under a train. I was only nine and I've never forgotten what it did to the family. He was terrified of going into hospital and he had a tubercular hip, poor man." She patted Alison's hand then glanced suddenly at Robert. "You *did* turn off the gas, I hope."

"Christ no!" He leaped to his feet, stumbled and righted himself. He ran indoors, switched off all the gas taps and threw open the windows. When he returned to the garden Alison was sitting up, talking to Mrs Ferris who looked up, smiling.

"So you're *the* Mr Dengaul. My husband

loves your books. Funny, all this time and I didn't once make the connection. I suppose—"

Alison said, "I'm going to be sick!"

Before either of them could help her to her feet she threw up on the grass. Robert passed her a handkerchief. To Mrs Ferris he said, "I came to take her back with me to Highstead. We'll fetch the doctor to check her out."

He was longing to be home. He felt that he could deal with almost anything if he was on his own territory. While Mrs Ferris helped Alison in to the back of the car he threw a pail of water over the vomit on the lawn and locked the house. He thanked Mrs Ferris profusely and climbed into the driving seat.

Mrs Ferris leaned down. In a low voice she said, "As far as I'm concerned none of this happened. The gas, I mean. You realise a suicide attempt is an offence."

"Good God!" He stared at her helplessly. "I'd forgotten."

"Just a faint," she repeated, putting a finger to her lips.

"Thank you," he said. "You've been an absolute angel. I'll send someone to make good the broken window." He forced a smile. "Do you think your husband would like a signed copy of my latest novel?"

Her face lit up. "A signed copy? Oh Mr Dengaul, he'd be *thrilled!*"

Robert drove slowly, glancing repeatedly at Alison in the rear-view mirror. She was slumped against the seat, crying silently into the handkerchief he had lent her.

Suddenly she said, "Bernard came round to collect some clothes and Caroline wouldn't stay. He wouldn't listen. Wouldn't let me say *anything*. He was so terribly polite."

Robert said, "You've hurt him. What do you expect?" It sounded harsher than he had intended.

"I wanted to say how sorry I was ... to ask him if he could forgive me. Each time he passed me he said, 'Excuse me', as if to a stranger." She began to cry again, loud racking sobs. Vi had hardly ever resorted to tears. She was either icily silent or throwing something. He thanked God she hadn't lived to see the trouble they were in.

He said, "He'll never forgive Sebastian. Never. You realise that?"

He wanted to be softer, more understanding, but the words wouldn't come. His family was being torn apart and this woman was to blame. Or partly to blame. Damn her. Damn Seb. And why hadn't Bernard seen what was happening? Was he blind?

"Please stop crying. You'll make yourself ill."

He promised himself that the moment they reached Highstead he would pass her over to Kate. More than anything he wanted to take his two sons and bang their stupid heads together.

Watching Robert drive off to collect Alison, Kate felt herself at a loss. Sebastian was upstairs somewhere and Caroline had returned and had gone out riding. She wandered into the kitchen and started to look in the various cupboards in search of something she might prepare for the evening meal. There was a well-stocked larder full of jams, marmalade and chut-neys, all of which bore a small decorative label with a description of the contents and the date it was made. All written in a neat script, presumably Violet's. Staring at them made Kate feel as though she had encountered a ghost. She sighed. If Robert's wife were looking down on them she must be full of despair.

In the meat safe she found the remains of a joint of beef and some cold sausages. In another cupboard she found a collection of vegetables to which dry earth still clung and which had recently come from the Highstead garden. What could she cook, she wondered, which was idiot proof? Shep-herd's pie was entirely unoriginal and she had no wish to serve an unappetising meal. She was already unpopular and had no desire to see her rating fall even further.

"For heaven's sake, Kate!" she muttered with a faint smile. Her own self-esteem was totally unimportant in this household, racked as it was with internal strife.

Feeling vulnerable, she stopped worrying about the evening meal and made her way upstairs and into Robert's study. She sat down in his chair behind his desk and was comforted. For a few moments she closed her eyes, telling herself to relax. At last she opened her eyes and took a leisurely look round Robert's "den". So this is where the famous novels were created, she thought. The study was a reasonable size and the walls were shelved and groaning with books of all sizes. Only one wall remained clear and this one contained several paintings. Had Violet been an artist? Were they hers? She crossed the room and searched for a signature. Harold Dengaul. Was that Robert's father? If so maybe Sebastian had inherited artistic talent and if he hadn't become involved with Alison, Kate might have persuaded Robert that Art School was a promising option.

Moving round the room, she picked up several photographs of the family and studied them regretfully. She had wanted so much to become part of the family but instead she felt herself an intruder. Had she not cared for Robert so deeply she could have walked away from all this but she was passionately in love with him and nothing could alter that. She sat down again and looked curiously at Robert's typewriter. The sheet of paper rolled into it was depressingly blank and Kate understood how distracting the family crises must be proving. Vague memories returned, unbidden, of her own attempt at fiction. At the time she had been inspired with a need to get the words on paper; to present the story in a way that would intrigue the readers. Snatching every spare moment she had worked on the manuscript on a second-hand machine and she could still recall the flaws in its performance – a slightly raised "m" and an "e" which punched a hole in the paper.

But the story hadn't been that bad, had it? According to Marie Jayne the work had shown promise. Smiling, she imagined Robert hiding himself away in here when the pressures of life became too great to bear and she reminded herself to urge him back to work as soon as the immediate problems had been resolved. Violet, presumably, had known when to urge her husband on and when to leave well alone. Kate had no such knowledge.

The door opened and she was surprised to see Sebastian in a paisley dressing gown, barefooted and carrying a towel. Grinning at the look on her face, he gave his hair a brisk rub.

"Forgive the undress," he said. "I wanted to catch you before you disappeared."

Unsmiling she said, "I'm not going to disappear, Seb. I don't want to disappoint you but I'm here to stay." She wondered what he was wearing, if anything, beneath the dressing gown. Was he being deliberately provocative?

"I meant today." He came further into the room and Kate caught a whiff of perfumed bath salts.

"I was curious to see where Robert works. To—"

"I came to apologise," he told her. "I behaved abominably this morning. I've come to ask you to forgive me." He sat down in one of two leather armchairs and crossed his legs. "I know you ought to tell Father about what happened, but I hope you won't."

"How do you know I haven't told him already?" If he wanted to throw her off balance he was succeeding, she thought furiously, but she could hardly order him out of his father's study.

"Because you're a very nice person and you wouldn't want to hurt him. You're probably still trying to decide what to do about it."

Baffled, Kate searched for a suitable reply. His expression was earnest and he sounded contrite but could she trust him? Her instincts warned her against it but if he *was* genuine this might be an opportunity to make a fresh start. She said, "I haven't said anything yet. If you are truly sorry—"

He put a hand on his heart. "As God is my witness, Kate! I *am* sorry. I can be awfully stupid at times. Caro will bear me out. But I know how much you and Father mean to each other and I don't want to cause any problems. I'd hate to come between you."

"Don't flatter yourself, Seb. You could never do that!"

He raised his eyebrows. "Bernard probably thought the same way, but I've upset the applecart there with a vengeance. I can't seem to put a foot right at the moment."

"Don't expect sympathy, Seb. Not from me." She wondered how long Robert and Alison would be.

"I don't want *sympathy*, Kate, I want a little respect although I doubt anyone is going to give me that."

His glib smile had gone, she noticed. "You have to earn respect," she said.

He appeared unfazed by the rebuke, however. As he had told her, harsh words were like water off a duck's back. He gave his hair a final rub with the towel, which he then draped around his neck. "The fact is that I do admire you and I do wish I had met you first but—"

She had jumped to her feet but he held up a placatory hand.

"Kate, listen to me, please. I promise I will never mention my feelings again and that I won't do or say anything to upset you. I just wanted to say it. I wanted you to know that what happened earlier was not simply lust. It was something deeper and altogether—"

"Seb *please*!"

"It's my loss, Kate. You've got a much better bargain with the father than the son." He stood up. "There. I've said my piece. Please say you understand and that you truly forgive me."

She felt trapped. "I do."

"So I can join the queue, can I?" He grinned wickedly. "If Dengaul Senior changes his mind – or if *you* do – Dengaul Junior is in with a chance?"

She felt a frisson of alarm. "Seb! I didn't *say* that. You know I didn't All I said—"

"But you don't despise me. You haven't crossed me off the Christmas card list."

Her instincts had been right. She dare not trust him. "Let's just say Alison has a prior claim to you."

"Alison? Poor girl. She doesn't really want me. She knows me too well. Anyway, she deserves better."

"And I don't?"

His smile faded. "I didn't mean that! Dammit, Kate, I'm usually so good with women but being with you – you confuse me." He leaned forward and she could see the pale hairs on his chest. "Seriously, we *are* friends now, aren't we?"

Reluctantly she nodded.

"Good friends?"

"Hopefully." She could see how hard it had been for Alison to resist him.

"More than good friends?"

"Certainly not!"

"I'm off to the pub for a quick half."

Kate was startled. Where on earth was Robert? He'd been gone for ages. He was bringing Alison back and here was Seb preparing to bolt again.

"I don't suppose you'd come with me. You seem to have been temporarily abandoned."

"Of course I haven't. I'm expecting Robert any moment."

With relief, she heard the crunch of wheels on gravel. "Oh, here he is now."

Nervously she realised that if Robert came upstairs and found her with Sebastian half naked he might not be too pleased. He might also misjudge the situation. With a muttered excuse she pushed back the chair and hurried from the room. It was time for Sebastian to face up to Alison and Kate found herself hoping that for once he might meet his match.

Seven

Ten minutes later the four of them were together in the sitting room. Faced with the likelihood that Sebastian would slip away, Alison had insisted that she was well enough to talk. Alison had asked Robert and Kate to be there. Kate had agreed, hiding her dismay, and now sat apprehensively on the sofa beside Robert.

Sebastian spoke up first. "Right, let's all agree that I'm a total bastard and that—"

Robert said, "Watch your language! And yes, you are. It's unanimous."

Alison said, "But it wasn't all his fault. I should have stopped it before it went too far. I'm the married one."

"We're not actually here to fix blame," Robert said. "We're here to decide what's to be done. You're having Seb's child and as the father he has a right to—"

Seb said, "I'll waive my rights, if that's any help."

Three heads turned towards him with identical expressions.

He held up his hands. "Sorry. Forget it."

210

Kate turned to Alison. "Does Bernard know all the facts?"

"Yes. He knows about the child and who the father is."

Robert sighed. "And how did he react?"

"He was ... he was disgusted."

It silenced them all. Robert recovered first.

"We're talking about my grandchild," he said. "Or rather I should say our grandchild." He reached out and gave Kate's hand a squeeze.

Alison looked at Sebastian. "If Seb and I decide to marry ..."

"We won't," said Sebastian, "it would be a terrible mistake and we all know it. Even you, Allie."

"Why would it?" She was struggling to remain in control. Kate gave her a reassuring smile.

Sebastian shrugged. "Because it was an affair not a lifelong passion. You know it meant nothing, Allie. We enjoyed it while—"

"I didn't know that, Seb. You said you loved me. That you always had. You said you'd always known I'd married the wrong brother. I believed you."

Robert said, "Rule one, Alison. Never believe a man who is trying to get you into bed!"

Kate groaned inwardly.

Alison ignored the remark. "So you're

going to let me down, Seb? Is that what you're saying? You don't want your child?"

There was another silence. Seb looked cornered, his expression resentful, and Kate found herself hoping he was suffering some guilt.

At last he said, "Frankly, no. Not very nice of me but I'm not the fatherly type."

Kate took one look at Robert's face and closed her eyes.

"I never thought I'd hear any son of mine—"

Kate intervened. "Alison, how would you feel about staying married to Bernard *if* he was willing to bring up Sebastian's child?"

"I don't think he would be – and I don't think I'd want that."

Sebastian said, "You could have the child adopted."

"No she can't," Robert said, "I'm not having my grandchild farmed out to complete strangers. Vi would turn in her grave."

"I don't think Alison would want to part with her child." Kate took hold of Alison's hand. "She's always longed for a family."

"I couldn't part with it." Alison gave Sebastian a poisonous look.

"Then Seb will have to maintain it. He'll have to get a job and make regular payments. We'd have to go through the courts." He rubbed his eyes tiredly. "We have to try and look ahead. If Alison decides to bring the child up on her own, she will need plenty of support from us."

Kate had a sudden thought. "We should really have included Alison's parents in this discussion." She looked at Alison. "They do know, I take it."

She nodded. "I told them this afternoon. It ... it didn't go well. I spoke to my mother and she kept crying and she said she'd tell my father and ring me back and then ..."

Her voice faltered and Kate crossed her fingers.

"My father rang and he was – he said terrible things about me – that I'd shamed the family and that I wasn't their daughter any more and I couldn't ... that I'd made my bed and I was no longer welcome there."

Kate and Robert exchanged glances. So *that* had been the final straw. That was when Alison decided to end her life. Kate swallowed hard then put an arm round Alison's trembling shoulders. Sebastian was staring fixedly at the floor and Robert was heading for the drinks cabinet. He poured himself a large whisky.

"Anything to drink? Kate? Anyone?"

Kate shook her head and Alison did the same. Seb said, "I'll have a whisky," but Robert ignored him. He took a few mouthfuls and sat down again.

Alison looked at Sebastian. "I wish I'd never set eyes on you, Seb. You said you

213

knew what you were doing when we were ..." She blushed. "You said nothing would go wrong." Her voice hardened. "You're such a liar!"

"And you're Miss Innocent, are you?" he snapped.

Robert glared at them. "Stop that! It gets us exactly nowhere. Alison, you've had your say and now you'd better go and lie down. The doctor should be here within the hour." He turned to Seb. "You just get out of my sight before I say something I'll regret."

Kate watched as Seb left the room, his head held high, his expression defiant. Alison stood up and Kate rose with her. "I'll see you into bed," she said.

But suddenly there were raised voices in the passage outside and Caroline burst into the room.

"So what's this then?" she demanded. "A family conference behind my back. My opinion's not needed but Lady Kate must be included! Well, thank you Father for that vote of confidence! Now I know where *I* stand in this family. I count for absolutely nothing!"

Kate stammered, "You weren't here, Caro, and we had to—"

"Don't you Caro me!" Her voice was shrill with anger.

Robert said, "Jesus Christ, here we go again!"

She rounded on her father. "Don't think I don't know what's happening around here because I do. And so does Seb. I know what you said to her!" She shot a venomous glance at Kate. " 'From now on it's just you and me, Kate!' "

Kate froze. So Seb *had* overheard them and the chickens were coming home to roost.

Robert protested. "But it wasn't like that. Seb only heard part of it. It wasn't that we don't want you and Seb here, Caro—"

Caroline's eyes blazed. "You liar! You want Kate and Highstead all to yourselves – and when you die you'll leave everything to her. And that's what she's waiting for." She turned to face Kate. "Oh, don't bother to deny it. We guessed days ago!"

Kate said hotly, "But it's not true. Not a word of it."

"I'm not listening to you!" Caroline snapped. "I'm talking to my father and I'll thank you to stay out of it. You're not part of this family yet and I hope you never will be. We were fine until you came along."

Robert shouted, "That's *enough*, damn you!" He grabbed her by the arm. "You'll apologise to Kate *now*!"

"I *won't*!" She snatched her arm away.

Kate said, "It doesn't matter, Robert. Truly it doesn't."

Caroline glared at her. " 'It doesn't matter, Robert!'" She mocked Kate's voice. "How too, too understanding! How too, too generous. Sweet little Kate understands nasty old Caro! Well you can go to hell for all I care. You can—"

Alison protested. "Honestly Caro, Kate only wants to help. She and your father—"

"Who asked you, Alison? You're partly to blame for all this. Carrying on with Seb like a dirty little tramp!"

Robert seized her and shook her violently. "You'll apologise for that crude remark, Caro, and you'll apologise to Kate. No daughter of mine—"

"Oh, shut up, damn you – and let go. You're hurting me."

Kate put a hand on Robert's arm. "Robert, I don't want to hear her apology."

"Good," cried Caroline, "because you're not going to." With a final effort she jerked herself from her father's grasp and ran back towards the kitchen where she slammed the door with great force. They heard something break.

Alison fell back into the armchair and began to sob anew. Robert closed his eyes and sucked air into his lungs while Kate tried not to join Alison in the relief of tears.

There was a ring at the front door.

Robert said, "Oh God! That'll be the doctor."

Kate rallied. "You take Alison upstairs while I let him in."

As she walked to the front door she wondered how things could possibly get worse. It seemed unlikely, but it seemed equally impossible that they could get better.

Twenty minutes later, in the hay loft above the stable, Caroline glanced up as footsteps approached her hiding place.

"Caro?"

It was Sebastian.

"I'm up here."

He climbed the ladder and sat beside her on the hay. For a few minutes they stared at each other wordlessly then he said, "Cheer up." He tried to see her expression but she covered her face with her hands.

"Worse troubles at sea!" he said.

"Oh God, Seb!" She drew a long shaky breath and uncovered her face. "I'm going to kill that woman! She's going out of our lives forever! Once and for all."

"Bit extreme, isn't it? Murder's a criminal offence, in case you didn't know."

"Of course it's extreme. Killing people *is* extreme. But I mean it, Seb. She's turning our own father against us and I'm not standing by while she does it."

"Ask her to leave then. Shame her into going. That's not a criminal offence."

"I tell you I don't care, Seb." Her voice had risen to an undignified squeak and she swallowed hard. "I just don't know how to do it."

She watched him closely as he put his head on one side and pretended to consider. He wasn't taking her seriously but she was past caring.

Seb said, "Let's see now ... you could stab her. Shoot her. Or maybe poison her? That's it! You could grind something up and add it to her tea ... or what about an ambush?"

She had known he would make light of it. "Trust you to be silly. You'd like to see the back of her, but you're not prepared to do anything. You said you were going to seduce her but you haven't."

"For heaven's sake, Caro! I may be a fast worker but not that fast. I have to be careful or she'll suspect. I've already put the idea into her head."

She eyed him with suspicion. "You're getting rather keen on her. Admit it."

"She's a nice-looking woman. I won't deny that. If I met her at a party, as a stranger, I'd spin her a line. Any man would."

Caroline was aware of a deep sense of betrayal. She wanted him to hate Kate the way she did. Instead, knowing him, he was probably falling in love with her. So would that help or hinder? She said slowly, "If Kate

218

fell in love with you, Father would send her away."

Seb gave a short laugh. "He'd kick me out too!"

"That might be the best thing that ever happened to you."

"Meow!" He grinned. "Just the teeniest bit jealous, are we?"

She was suddenly fearful that he *would* fall for Kate Harper. "I hate her. She's a thief. She's stolen my life, my father, my future ..."

"Oh come off it!" He gave her a brotherly pat on the knee. "You're exaggerating and you know it. All Kate's really done is fall in love with Father. That's hardly a crime. Don't do her in, Caro. They'd find out. Ways and means. This is nineteen thirty-four. They have up-to-date methods of detection. It's not just a magnifying glass and a spark of inspiration these days." He shook his head. "Sorry, Caro, but it won't work. I can see it all. You'll be 'hanged by the neck until you be dead' and I'll be languishing in a prison cell as an accomplice. I want to be an artist, not a felon."

She gave him a withering look. "Why don't you just push off and leave me in peace."

She hoped he'd insist on staying but he jumped to his feet. "I won't be in for supper, Caro. I can't face Father and Alison's staying the night. I think I should make myself scarce."

"Where will you be?"

"Book into a pub or something. Don't worry. I may be a rotten apple but I do have a few friends." He wanted her to argue about that but she wouldn't do so. His shining image had been tarnished in her eyes and she felt cheated. "I can always bed down somewhere."

She shrugged. Go, she thought irritably. If you're out of favour you have only yourself to blame. She watched his retreat down the ladder in an aggrieved silence and listened as his footsteps receded. Loneliness swamped her and she shivered. Then, with an effort, she put him out of her mind. Forget Seb, she told herself. The real enemy is Kate Harper.

For Kate, Monday morning came as a welcome relief. She filled Muriel in on the events of the weekend after first swearing her to secrecy.

"My God, Kate!" Muriel had listened throughout with rapt attention. "I must say married life promises to be less than boring with Robert!"

Kate rolled her eyes. "At least he saved Alison. That would have been a terrible tragedy. If he had been ten minutes later ..." She shook her head. "The doctor thinks the baby will probably be all right."

"Only probably?"

"They won't know until it's born. Thank goodness the poor little thing is oblivious to all the dramas going on around it. If I were Alison's child I wouldn't fancy the outside world! As for Sebastian ... words fail me."

"I can see where Robert Dengaul gets inspiration," Muriel laughed, "he just studies his immediate family!"

Kate laughed with her. "He assures me they aren't always so troublesome but I have my doubts. I was so pleased when Sebastian took himself off. That only leaves the two girls for Robert to cope with."

"And will he cope, d'you think? We don't want our favourite author cracking up – especially before Wednesday."

"Wednesday?" Kate looked at her in alarm.

"The literary luncheon in Hastings. I hope he hasn't forgotten."

Kate groaned. "He hasn't mentioned it and *I'd* forgotten. I'll remind him when I ring him."

"Which reminds me, Gordon asked if you would go with Robert because Sarah's got a meeting with Hank Smillie, our new American author."

Kate nodded. At least in Hastings she and Robert could spend some time together away from his family. It would be good for both of them. Her glance fell on a brown-paper package strategically placed on her desk blotter. "I hope that's not what I think it is!"

Seeing her glance Muriel rolled her eyes. "I'm afraid so! Another of Gordon's friends. He wants you to read it yesterday!"

Kate tutted. "I've got a backlog already."

"Haven't we all!" Muriel stood up.

"I suppose he'll want a very diplomatic report if it's no good. Do I return the manuscript to Gordon himself?"

"No. He wants you to return it direct to the author."

Kate groaned. "We know what that means, don't we!"

"That he's already read it," said Muriel, halfway out of the door, "and it's no good!" She closed the door quietly behind her.

Kate made a few phone calls and then settled down to read the manuscript, making notes as she went along. It was nearly four hundred pages and long before she had finished she knew it would never be publishable. A pity. Discovering a new writing talent was every editor's dream.

"Oh dear!" she muttered.

Being diplomatic was going to be difficult. A letter turning it down, no matter how sensitively written, would be a bitter blow.

She glanced at the accompanying letter,

saw a telephone number and on impulse picked it up.

"Medvale 330."

"Is that Mark Seager?"

"Yes?"

"I'm Kate Harper, an editor with Gordon Brett. I've just read your manuscript. I'm afraid we can't make an offer for it, but I would like to help you if I can." She rushed on, allowing him time to recover from the disappointment. "I wondered if you would consider talking to a retired colleague of mine. Her name is Lottie Morgan. If you are committed to a career as an author, Lottie could advise you. She's very experienced."

"How much would it cost?"

"I expect it's negotiable. I'll give you her number anyway, and let her know she might hear from you. My letter will—"

"Has Gordon Brett read it?"

"Yes, he has. He didn't feel it was ready for publication in its present form and he passed it on to me for a second opinion." She tried to sound brisk without being unsympathetic. There was no way a rejection could be made bearable.

There was another silence. Then he said, "Fine, then. I'll wait for your letter. Do you think I have any chance – if I work with this colleague, I mean?"

"There is certainly hope, Mr Seager. You have persevered and produced a finished novel, so you have commitment and you will have learned a great deal by writing this first book. All that is in your favour, you see." She thought suddenly of her own abandoned novel. "If it makes you feel any better I wrote a novel myself some years ago but it was rejected. But I'm not giving up." She frowned. What *was* she talking about? "I'm going to make time to try again. If you're a writer you just keep going until you get it right."

She waited but he didn't reply. She could imagine him on the other end of the line, dejected and undecided. "I'll ring Lottie Morgan, just in case. And I'll keep my fingers crossed for you. Goodbye, Mr Seager."

His "Goodbye" sounded a little brighter. She hoped that a personal call from an editor would give him something positive to tell his friends.

As she rolled a sheet of the firm's notepaper into the typewriter she was surprised to realise that she really was going to start writing again. She smiled broadly.

"News to me!" she said, aware of her growing excitement. She would take her own advice, re-read the novel. If she liked it she would make a fresh start. The idea pleased her tremendously.

While Kate worked on, Bernard, John and

Jasper left the road and set off across a large sloping field. The July sun cast dark shadows beneath the trees as they made their way beside the hawthorn hedge towards the woods. There were rabbit holes along the edge of the field and Jasper snuffled eagerly at each one, his stubby tail wagging with wild enthusiasm. Bernard, tramping along in wellington boots and old clothes, breathed in the tranquillity and felt the tightness in his shoulders lessen. He knew that without John he would be in far more distress emotionally. His friend had asked very few questions and had given little by way of advice. He had simply opened his home, providing shelter and comfort when it was most needed.

But now Bernard was ready to talk about it. He was simply waiting for the right moment – a time when he could talk without breaking down and making a fool of himself.

Cows at the far end of the field suddenly took an interest in the trespassers and ambled clumsily towards them. Bernard eyed them nervously.

Seeing this, John smiled. "They're attracted by Jasper but they don't intend any harm. They're curious animals. We brighten their day, that's all."

"If you say so." Bernard slackened his pace as five cows surrounded them.

Jasper barked and they backed away, tossing their heads and rolling expressive brown eyes. John picked up a stick and hurled it, shouting, "Fetch boy!"

The dog bounded away and the cows immediately lost interest.

Bernard said, "We were chased by a bullock once. I've never forgotten how frightened I was. I'd read about legs turning to jelly but mine really did! I was terrified." He shook his head. "It was Seb's fault. He wasn't a very nice child. No brotherly love between us, I can tell you! Caro was wearing a bright-red dress and he dared her to dance in front of the bullock. Of course she did. When it ran towards her she ran back to us and we were all targets."

"It sounds as though your brother's always been a bit of a troublemaker."

"Always. They're as bad as each other." He shook his head. "Caro was very wild and totally fearless. Of course, Mother used to hold me up as the perfect example. Seb must have hated it. 'Why can't you be sensible like Bernard?' she used to say. Once Seb said 'Like Bernard? Ugh!' and she slapped his legs. They got even with me, though. They locked me in a cupboard for what seemed like hours."

John said, "God! Makes me glad I was an only child."

Bernard hesitated. This might be the

moment for confidences. If it was, the chance was suddenly lost when Jasper began to dig furiously at a large hole.

John whistled to him. "Come here! Leave it, Jasper! Leave it!" He looked at Bernard. "A badgers' sett, but don't tell anyone. They're shy creatures and easily disturbed."

"Have you ever seen one?" Bernard asked.

"Only once. I spent several hours late one night watching from over there." He pointed. "There was a bright moon that night and I saw a mother with three young ones. Fascinating creatures. You feel very privileged just to catch a glimpse of them."

Bernard was still seeking a way to confide in John when they reached the wood and came to a halt. John ducked under a length of barbed wire and held it up so that Bernard could follow. Jasper slid under the wire with ease his tongue lolling happily. John said, "Silly old dog! He loves his walks."

Bernard swallowed hard. "John, I need to talk. Could you bear it?"

"Of course."

They crunched across last year's dead leaves, shaded now by large oaks. There was a faint smell of dry rotten wood and a hint of woodsmoke from an invisible fire. Bernard could see no recognisable path but John seemed to know exactly where he was going while the dog ran around in circles, trying to look purposeful.

"Alison's expecting his baby," Bernard said.

John shook his head. "Why are women so gullible?"

Bernard shrugged. "I think I could have forgiven her the – the rest of it but a baby ... What am I supposed to do? Bring up Seb's –" his bitterness surfaced – "bring up my brother's child? I have to leave her, but I don't know where to go or what to do. Seb has got me tied in knots as always." He bent down, picked up a stick and threw it for the dog. Jasper brought it back and Bernard patted his head absentmindedly. "Damn Sebastian! I'd like to throttle the little sod and that's the truth!"

John glanced at him. "Look, I don't want to interfere in any way, Bernard, but I will just say this. There's always room for you at my place. That spare bedroom is yours for as long as you want." He paused. "For ever, if need be."

Bernard stopped in his tracks, staring. "John!" He was astonished at the man's generosity.

"Purely altruistic, I have to admit. I rattle around there with just the dog. It gets lonely and I've enjoyed your company. We get along OK, don't we?"

"Yes but ..." Words failed him.

"I'm just making the offer, Bernard, so you know what your options are with your wife. I won't be upset if you don't take me up on it, so you just please yourself."

Bernard drew a deep breath. "Well, I don't know what to say ... how to thank you ..."

"Then don't. Finish telling me about the problem."

They walked on.

After a few moments Bernard said, "It wouldn't be fair, would it, to lie to the child for years and then suddenly announce that I'm not the father. And suppose it's a boy and looks just like Seb. I might hate the poor child and – and all the time I'm going to wonder if Alison's secretly pleased that it's his and not mine. And Seb will be his uncle. Good old Uncle Seb. I just can't see how any of this is bearable or how Alison thinks I can do it. I'll be good old dutiful Bernard if I stay with her and a rotter if I don't – Christ Almighty, I can't win, John, and I don't – I can't—" He stopped, suddenly choked. Tears threatened but as his eyes blurred with tears he felt the sudden weight of John's arm across his shoulders.

"Come on, old lad!" John said gently. "You can get through this. Just hang on."

At that moment a large black Labrador came rushing through the undergrowth in pursuit of an invisible quarry, and two elderly ladies appeared round a bend in the path. Bernard blinked back the tears and produced a lopsided smile.

John lifted his cap. "Mrs Brake. Miss Simpson. Lovely weather."

Jasper appeared and ran up to them to be patted.

"How old is Jasper?" one of them asked.

"Getting on for twelve."

"Oh, a good age for a spaniel."

"Indeed – and your Lab?"

"Oh, Blackie's only a baby. Two years old next March."

The niceties exchanged they all moved on and Jasper disappeared again.

John grinned. "Blackie! Now that's original!"

Bernard managed a smile. He had seized the chance to gain control of himself and felt able to continue. He went on. "The house belongs to Alison's parents. Well, actually it was a wedding present, but the mortgage is theirs. So she'll always have a roof over her head. Sebastian will have to pay something towards the baby's keep."

"Has he got any money?"

"Not at the moment."

"Will her parents help?"

"I don't know. They're very strict churchgoers. I imagine it will crucify them."

"The Sebs of this world! They don't know what havoc they wreak."

"But they *do* know!" Bernard said vehemently. "They know and they don't give a damn!"

A frenzied barking broke out somewhere nearby and John said, "Oh no!" and whistled for his dog. "Jasper hates black dogs," he explained. "Don't ask me why. I bet he's gone after Blackie."

As though to confirm this guess, the spaniel came hurrying back, the fur on the back of his neck still bristling. John bent to pat him. "Picked a fight, did you? Silly animal!" He threw a stick which Jasper ignored.

For a long time they walked in silence. Then John said, "It might work itself out somehow."

"It won't. I've gone over and over the possibilities and nothing works. I think she wants Seb. I'd always be second best." He sighed.

John said, "Look, I was unfaithful to my wife once. It lasted about six weeks and then she found out. She was terribly cut up about it and I was sick with regret. The other woman meant nothing to me. It was an adventure, nothing more nor less. My wife took me back."

Bernard glanced at him hopefully. "And it was OK?"

"Not really. I wish I could say it was. She forgave, but she couldn't forget and there was always the hidden resentment on her part. I never felt she trusted me and I resented that. We spent another sixteen years together, but in the end we simply tolerated each other. Looking back she should have thrown me out. With hindsight it would have been best for both of us."

They stopped to watch a grey squirrel on a nearby branch.

John shook his head. "Interlopers!" he muttered. "Pretty creatures but they're going to drive out the reds. You see if they don't."

John gave him a crooked grin. "Down with all interlopers! My sympathies are with the reds!"

Kate sat on the floor with her novel spread out in front of her. She was reading a chapter at a time with frequent groans. It was worse than she remembered but the editorial knowledge she had gained in the intervening years convinced her that it did show promise. She was halfway through it when the phone rang.

"Kate!"

She smiled at the sound of his voice. "Robert. How are you surviving? You looked so tired on Sunday. I hated leaving you." Almost true, she reflected. She had been sorry to abandon him to his problems but deep down she had been grateful for the excuse to extricate herself. "I wish I had been more help but I seemed to be making things worse just by being there."

"Nonsense, Kate. You were a tower of strength. You know, of course, that Seb has pushed off. Packed a few things and departed. Can't pretend I'm sorry. I also had a letter this morning from Alison's father, telling me what he thinks of my sons. Not very pleasant reading and slightly hypocritical I thought. Nothing about his daughter who co-operated with Seb. Very arrogant tone. He says that if Bernard won't take Alison back he's no longer on the executive board. In other words he's fired."

"Sounds like blackmail."

"It's exactly that. I'm so weary, Kate! I wish you were here. No I don't. I wish I were there."

Kate waited. He needed to unburden himself, she thought.

"I'm keeping Alison here for a few days because I'm afraid to let her out of my sight. I wondered if I should tell her parents about the suicide bid. They're entitled to know. D'you think they'd be moved to come and take her back with them if I did?"

"I don't know if they'd go that far but perhaps they should be told. If she tries it again and succeeds it might look as though we were negligent in *not* telling them."

After a long silence he asked, "So what are you up to?"

She explained about the early novel and her decision to try again and he was very encouraging. Then she said, "Don't forget Wednesday is your literary do in Hastings. Yours truly will be accompanying you. I think they rather fancy the impact we will make together now that the news is out. The press will want to see the two of us."

He laughed. "Still we'll get a few hours together! Wonderful. Gives me an excuse to walk away from Highstead without feeling guilty and Caro can keep an eye on Alison. Can't disappoint my public, can I?"

"Certainly not."

Buoyed up by the news of their imminent meeting, Robert listened cheerfully as she explained the travel arrangements and for a while his family problems were firmly relegated to second place.

"So I'll see you under the clock," Kate said. "Sounds rather naughty, doesn't it!"

"I thought Brighton was the place for naughty weekends."

"So it is," she laughed, "but Hastings is better than nothing."

"I suppose you wouldn't like to spend the night with me. Travel back on the milk train?"

She hid her surprise. "I'd like to, Robert, but I won't!"

"I'm losing my touch."

"Never!"

In a different tone, he asked, "Will it ever come right for us, do you think?"

"Darling, of *course* it will!"

"We'll be together, married? We'll be happy?"

"Of course we will. What's got into you?"

"Nothing. Forgive me. I'm not feeling so confident at the moment. You said once that we could have a Register Office wedding."

"And you said we couldn't." She was beginning to feel distinctly uneasy. "Is there something wrong, Robert? You would tell me, wouldn't you?"

"No! There's nothing wrong!"

"There's no need to shout, darling. If there is something you're not telling me—"

"I've got to go. Caro's just come in with a face like thunder. See you Wednesday."

Kate stared at the receiver in disbelief. He had hung up on her.

Eight

The following afternoon, Kate's office phone rang.

"Kate Harper."

"Oh, Mrs Harper! Robert Dengaul's just arrived!"

It was the new receptionist. Still easily impressed, thought Kate with a smile.

"Robert Dengaul, your fiancé. He's on his way up now."

"Thanks, Daphne."

Her immediate pleasure was somewhat dulled by the memory of their last telephone conversation and its abrupt conclusion. She had made up her mind that she would not refer to it unless Robert mentioned it first. He was under considerable pressure and, in his shoes, her own patience would be wearing a little thin. She pushed aside the manuscript she was working on and rose to greet him.

The door opened and a large bunch of red roses was thrust round the door.

"A peace offering!" he cried. He came into the room, tossing them carelessly on top of the nearest filing cabinet.

"Robert!" Kate threw her arms round him. "What a lovely surprise. And the roses – they're beautiful!"

His arms tightened round her, preventing further talk. "I had to come. I'm sorry about yesterday. It was a bad moment." He released her and settled himself in a chair.

Making himself at home as usual, Kate thought with a smile. In a way Gordon Brett's was a second home to him. He had certainly known the place for far longer than she had.

"I can offer you a cup of tea?"

He grimaced. "No whisky stashed away anywhere?"

"Afraid not. Is it that bad?"

He shrugged. "Not really. Alison's mother turned up unannounced on the doorstep this morning. Vi described her once as 'a woman in full sail'! You'll meet her one day. She had come to take her daughter home – not to her own home but to Alison and Bernard's place."

"Ah!" Kate raised her eyebrows.

"Exactly! Father disowns daughter. Mother issues ultimatum. If Alison can't come home then she, Mother, will go to Alison. Big row. Father won't budge." He whistled, shaking his head. "I had the whole sordid story, blow by blow. Plus tears, hysterics, the lot! I gave her a double brandy in the end. That brought the colour to her cheeks!"

"Poor woman!"

Robert bristled. "Poor woman, my eye! It's about time someone else felt the brunt of it. Alison's their daughter after all. If they brought her up to commit adultery—"

"Robert! You don't mean that, I hope."

"You know what I mean." He had the grace to look slightly discomfited. "It was time somebody else had to deal with the dramas. God knows, I've done my share. She told me what a rat Seb is to take advantage of her innocent daughter and what a rat Bernard is not to have seen what was going on and what a rat her husband is not to be full of Christian forgiveness! She stopped short, just, of calling me a rat!"

"I'm sorry to laugh, darling, but you—"

He grinned. "Laugh if you must but it *wasn't* funny. She couldn't make up her mind whether or not to be pleased there's a grandchild on the way but I expect she'll come round to the idea. Probably started knitting already." He threw up his hands with a despairing gesture. "Anyway, they've gone and the house is strangely quiet. No Sebastian, God knows where he's gone." He grinned again. "I bet this interruption is just what you need when you're in the middle of a manuscript."

"I'm sorry I wasn't there to help you."

"No you're not! You're glad to be out of it." His look was quizzical.

"Very glad! Robert, you said yesterday that Caro had a face like thunder. What was that about?"

"Oh God, yes! Someone's stolen some tack from the stable. The horse blanket was missing and so was the second saddle. It's not the value of the items so much as the thought of an intruder – or intruders – sniffing round the place. We've never had anything like that and we've lived there for donkey's years."

"What did the police think?"

"They weren't very interested. Local plod. What do they care if the rich get robbed?" He sighed. "Look, I know you're busy. If I could have the key to your flat I'll see Gordon and then make myself scarce."

Kate reached for her handbag, rummaged within it and, beaming, held out a key. "Yours," she told him. "I had it cut yesterday. Treat the flat as your own home." She could see that he was touched by the gesture. "Help yourself to whatever you want and I'll be home around six."

"I'm taking you to the Ritz. I've booked a table."

"Maybe I'll make that five forty-five!"

He was on the point of leaving when Muriel arrived. "I heard you were here," she told him. "Daphne couldn't wait to tell me.

Incidentally she'd like an autograph but is too shy to ask for it."

Robert smiled. "I'll see her as I leave. We're dining at the Ritz tonight at eight. Would you and Eddie like to join us?"

"Would we?" Muriel rolled her eyes. "I don't need to ask Eddie. We'll be there – best bib and tucker! And thank you, I was having a rotten day but it's suddenly looking brighter!"

"What's the problem?" Kate asked.

"It's the new Derek Carr press release. He doesn't like it apparently. According to him, we're giving away too much of the plot and not saying enough about him."

"Sounds par for the course!" said Robert. "You never get mine right either!"

He departed hastily as the two women rounded on him in mock anger. When he'd gone Muriel looked at Kate with concern.

"He doesn't look at all well," she said. "Is he losing weight?"

Kate sighed. "I wouldn't be surprised. All this squabbling can't be good for his nerves. Never mind. He can eat his fill tonight at the Ritz. A mix of good food and good company. Robert thrives on it. I'm so glad you and Eddie will be there. It will stop us from talking about his family. The latest is they've been burgled!"

"Oh no! Poor things. Have they lost much?"

"Horsey stuff," she said. "Reins and bridles and things. I forget. Poor Robert. It makes you wonder where it will all end."

That evening, after a cheerful meal with Muriel and Eddie, Robert and Kate arrived back at the flat and let themselves in. Kate felt tired but happy. She had enjoyed the company and Robert had been the perfect host. No one had mentioned Highstead or the problems there and for that Kate was grateful. She had looked carefully at Robert and thought perhaps he had lost a little weight, and had made a mental note to fatten him up once they were married. As soon as they switched on the light, Robert said, "I hope you don't mind, Kate, but I read some of your novel. It's good, you know. Why didn't you tell me you wanted to write?"

For a moment she was disconcerted. "Why? Because I didn't know myself." She crossed to the sofa, kicked off her shoes and sank down into the cushions. Robert sat beside her. She went on, "I once wanted to write, but it was years ago and now I have a career in publishing and—"

"But you have talent, Kate. I'm not pretending that that particular novel would have found a publisher, but there's enough there to tell me – Oh, Kate! I could have helped you!"

"Could have? You still can, can't you?"

"Of course I can," he said hurriedly. "What I mean is you've wasted so much time. I'm not being biased, Kate. That novel was almost there! Your dialogue's believable, the time gaps are handled well, you have obviously done your research."

"Stop!" She smiled. "You've convinced me. I am going to have another try but right now I'm dog-tired and—" She stopped, surprised by the intensity of his expression.

He said abruptly, "I want you, Kate. I want you tonight. I can't wait for a piece of paper that says I'm allowed to sleep with the woman I love."

Kate faced him, her heart suddenly thudding.

He went on. "You've been married. You understand, Kate. Don't you want me?"

"Yes, but ... I always thought – that is, I always imagined that we should start married life with a clean slate. It's only a few more weeks."

He put an arm round her shoulders. "I can't wait, Kate. There's so little time left for us."

Her eyes widened. "So little time? What's that supposed to mean?"

"That – that I'm so much older. I want us to have a child, Kate, as soon as possible."

She was confused, she longed to say "yes", but wasn't sex before marriage the classic mistake? She and Will had waited. Most decent people did. Presumably Robert and Violet had waited also.

Robert stood up and crossed to the cabinet and poured two brandies.

She protested, "I drank too much at dinner, Robert. I've got to go to work tomorrow. It's fine for you but—"

"No it *isn't*!" he cried. He thrust the glass into her unwilling hand. "Don't you see? Nothing is fine for me. I'm old. I'm running out of steam. Can't you see?"

A great coldness seized her. What on earth was he saying? That he was too old to father a child? But that was nonsense.

"You're *not* too old," she said. "Lots of men of your age have children." She took hold of his free hand. "Robert, you are becoming paranoid about this. Believe me, you *are*."

He pulled his hand from hers and swallowed his brandy. "Drink up!"

After a moment's hesitation Kate followed his example and in silence he refilled the glasses.

She said, "It's Caro, isn't it? She's said something to you about us."

"No, no!" He shook his head.

"Seb then. They don't want us to have a child. That's it, isn't it?"

"No, Kate."

"Then why the hurry? I don't understand,

Robert. We were fine. We had our plans. Now, since I came to Highstead, everything's different." She looked at him with a deep feeling of foreboding. "It's about your inheritance, isn't it? Your children are afraid that—"

"It's not them, it's me. I'm ..." He drained his glass. "Drink up."

"I don't want—"

"Drink up, damn you, Kate!"

Her apprehensions were crystallising into fear. Pointedly she put the glass down without taking her eyes from Robert's face. Already her head was beginning to spin. She closed her eyes. When she re-opened them he was staring at her with desperation.

She said, "Darling! Tell me!"

He stared at the floor. "I'm ill, Kate. I'm dying. I may have a couple of years. I may not."

The room seemed to whirl around her as the words echoed in her brain. *"I'm dying ... dying ..."*

She let out a cry of anguish. "Oh Robert! Oh my God!" She couldn't breathe and clutched her chest where her heart pounded painfully. "I don't believe ... Oh my poor darling!"

For a long time they clung together wordlessly while she sobbed and Robert did his best to comfort her. Then it was time to talk.

"I suspected something was wrong," he told her, "but the tests showed that it was worse than I expected. Nephritis. Ghastly word." He looked at her with wild eyes. "How did it happen? Where did it come from? Oh God, Kate! It's knocked me over."

He stumbled on through the doctor's diagnosis while she held him in her arms, kissing his hair, making soothing noises while all the time she tried to quell the terrible trembling inside her. His obvious terror undermined her attempts to be strong and for a while she dared not speak in case he saw how frightened she was. Robert was going to need all the help she could give him. If she could be positive she might be able to give Robert courage and Kate felt intuitively that that might alleviate his symptoms.

Gathering all her resources she said, "Darling, we can fight this together. You're not alone with it. You've got me and I'm a fighter!" Somehow she forced a smile. "I'll talk to your doctor. Find out exactly what we can do to slow it down."

He drew a long breath. "You think it might ... we could ...?"

"I don't think, I *know*. You and me, Robert. We'll be invincible."

She was rewarded by the ghost of a smile. "You're bloody wonderful, do you know that?" he whispered.

"I've always known it!"

They laughed shakily and Kate realised that the worst was probably over for both of them. Robert had finally unburdened himself and now Kate understood the strain he had been under for the past few weeks.

"Well, in view of the latest evidence, Robert Dengaul, perhaps you do have a case. I don't think we should waste tonight. Do you?"

He shook his head. "Should I do something gallant? Carry you over the threshold perhaps?"

She considered, her head on one side. "I vote we skip the preliminaries and go to bed."

On Wednesday they reached Hastings just after eleven thirty and made their way to the Castle Hotel where the lunch was being held. Inside the foyer there was a large display board with a photograph of Robert taken at least ten years earlier.

"Very suave!" said Kate.

They would talk again about Robert's illness but for today they had agreed to try and forget the problem. Kate was putting on a brave face but she had been sleepless for most of the night and her head ached. Her eyes were red rimmed but she had applied a little more powder than usual to her blotched cheeks. A dab of lipstick had also helped bring a little colour to her pale face.

Robert studied the photograph. "The poor devils are in for a nasty shock."

A middle-aged man came forward to greet them, introducing himself as the organiser, Steven Hardy. He looked suitably impressed as he shook hands with Robert and delighted when he realised Kate's identity.

They were led into a large function room where half a dozen waiters were busying themselves with the tables – adding napkins, polishing the glassware, checking the ashtrays and bringing in small vases of flowers.

There was a bar at the far end and their host found them a small table and brought them drinks and a dish of peanuts. He left them alone for a moment then reappeared with a younger man who sported an immaculate blue blazer. Kate forced another smile as he greeted her.

"Adrian Betterson is the man who suggested your visit," Mr Hardy told them and there were more handshakes while Mr Betterson collected a drink and joined Kate and Robert at the table.

He was thin with a freckled face and smooth sandy-coloured hair.

"I can't tell you what a thrill it is to have you here," he said to Robert. "Because it is such a special occasion we shall be quite a large crowd. They'll start to arrive at any

247

moment and we'll start the meal promptly at twelve thirty. We usually allow an hour and then the speaker takes over at one thirty."

Robert nodded. "That's fine. How long do you want me to speak for? I usually reckon forty minutes with another fifteen for questions. After a big meal with wine, people's concentration begins to wane."

As they discussed the details people drifted into the room in twos and threes. At ten to twelve Kate excused herself and made her way to the ladies room to freshen up. At twelve thirty precisely a gong sounded and everyone took their seats. As usual Kate found herself next to Robert on the "high table" with various members of the committee.

She was astonished that he appeared so normal but reminded herself that he had had several weeks in which to recover from the doctor's prognosis. In her heart she was still unable to accept the gloomy verdict and intended to ask for a second opinion. There was no way she could lose Robert so soon. Sitting with him beside her it seemed impossible that he could die, but she knew it happened. Will had died. Somehow she forced down the salmon, asparagus and summer pudding but she tasted nothing.

Just before Robert was due to speak he whispered to her, "Take notes! This'll be you one of these days!"

He gave her a large wink and she smiled back but, without warning, tears threatened and she bent her head as she blinked them back. Outwardly calm, she was still in a state of shock and grief, still finding unexpected tears in her eyes.

Steven Hardy rose to his feet and the hum of voices was gradually hushed.

"Ladies and gentlemen, it is my pleasure today to introduce our guest speaker whose name is known to millions of readers worldwide. His novels have kept those same millions glancing over nervous shoulders –" There was a ripple of laughter. "– or listening for noises that go bump in the night. Who doesn't enjoy a good crime novel? And who does it better than our honoured guest who only last year was awarded the Centurian Prize for Literature? Ladies and gentlemen, a rousing welcome please for Robert Dengaul!"

The applause was generous as Robert rose to his feet, a glass of red wine in his hand. "My thanks to you all for inviting me to talk to you."

Kate looked round the hall. All faces were turned towards Robert, and she felt tremendously proud to be sitting alongside him. As he began to speak she realised just how clever he was with words, how totally in control. Nobody fidgeted as he began to outline a normal day in his life. He spoke effortlessly without any notes, making them laugh, making them pause for thought, making them love him. What had he said? "Take notes, Kate." Oh no, she thought, she would never be able to hold a hall full of people in the palm of her hand the way Robert did.

On her right Steven Hardy leaned towards her, his face aglow, and whispered, "He's absolutely brilliant!"

She nodded. Robert was telling a joke and the audience erupted with delighted laughter. Kate was aware of a tightening in her throat. How could he put on such a show when he knew his days were numbered? Of course he had done it many times before but now it was different, surely. He had told her he didn't want anyone else to know about his illness. Certainly not the family. Nearer the time, he had begged, when it was impossible to hide his frailty, they could be told. Until then it was going to be a secret between them and life would be what he called, "business as usual".

"Don't think that an author has it all his own way," he was saying. "We labour over the book and lavish our attention on it so that we can eventually hand it over to the publishers who will have their evil way with the precious manuscript." He glanced down at Kate with a smile. "I have to step carefully here since my fiancée, Kate, is an editor with Gordon Brett!"

Finding all eyes upon her, Kate said, "My lips are sealed!" and the audience laughed.

Robert went on. "The publishers decide the quality of the paper, the size and shape of the print on the page, the print run, the budget for publicity. They decide whether an author is worth an author tour. They can also decide to change the title. 'Not marketable, Mr Dengaul' and change the length – 'Too short, Mr Dengaul' or 'Too long!' The whole process is rather like giving birth and then handing your baby over for adoption ..."

Giving birth. The words jolted Kate. Suppose she were pregnant. It was what Robert wanted but it would mean big changes in her life. She would have to give up her job, but then she would do that anyway. She would insist on a Register Office wedding and she would move to Highstead to care for Robert and to spend as much time as possible with him. A year was such a short time. Please God, she prayed silently, could you stretch it to two? I will do anything if you will allow us two years together. I want him to see his child. I want photographs of us as a family to remember him by.

She pulled a handkerchief from her purse and dabbed her eyes where more tears waited to spill over. Steven Hardy whispered, "Are you all right, Mrs Harper?"

"Something in my right eye," she muttered and forced herself to look up at Robert once more. The realisation came to her abruptly that when Robert died she would spend the rest of her life alone. No other man would take his place. Will had satisfied her youthful yearnings but Robert satisfied her soul in a way that no other man could hope to do. We will spend every possible moment together, she vowed. Certainly every night. A faint smile touched her lips as she recalled the previous night's intimacies. Robert had been a surprisingly gentle lover with a sure but delicate touch. He was confident without being arrogant, eager without being selfish. It was unfair to Will to compare them. Robert was a mature man, Will had been as inexperienced as she had.

Somehow, too, Robert had managed to drive away the anguish which had earlier filled her mind. For the duration of their love making she had been able to forget. Another burst of laughter brought her sharply back to the present. A lady near the front was laughing so much that tears rolled down her face. Kate looked round at the sea of faces and saw rapt attention. They were devouring every word, she thought. In more ways than one, Robert Dengaul would be an impossible act to follow.

Caroline was unsaddling Nutmeg when Alison came into the yard looking pale and unhappy. She's not the only one, thought Caroline. She said, "If you want Father he's not here, he and Lady Kate are in Hastings for a luncheon."

"I just wanted a break from my mother," Alison admitted. "Did you have a good ride?"

"It's a bit hot to be togged up." This was the ideal time to plant the seed in Alison's mind. But don't rush it, she told herself. Wait for the right moment. It has to sound perfectly natural. "Sorry about the other day. What I said."

"Forget it. We're all on edge at the moment."

"Actually I'd rather ride in the evening but Nutmeg gets lonely. I wanted to buy a young donkey or a goat to keep her company but Father's not keen on the idea. The only thing he is keen on at the moment is Kate Harper. I bet they sleep together when he stays in town – not that I care tuppence."

Alison said, "Mother's driving me mad." She leaned against the wall, obviously wretched and, in spite of herself, Caroline felt sorry for her. Her sister-in-law had brought disaster crashing down on her own head but she was paying a high price for her mistakes.

"Honestly Caro, I don't know what's going to happen – I mean, my father might relent and then we'll go home."

"Leaving Bernard, are you?"

"I can't leave him. He's already left me." She hugged herself as though she were feeling the cold. "Mother keeps crying. I never thought having a baby could be so miserable."

Caroline carried the saddle into the tack room and came out with the curry comb and brush. "I never thought you'd be having Seb's baby but you are."

"You'll be the baby's aunt."

"Am I supposed to jump for joy?" She turned her back and began to groom the horse. Curious about the mysteries of pregnancy she asked, "So are you being sick every morning?"

"Yes. It's not much fun." Her voice shook.

"So do you have to go to a clinic or some-thing? Or have visits from the district nurse?" She had heard vague whispers of "internal examinations", whatever they amounted to. It sounded rather embarras-sing so she decided not to ask.

Alison shrugged. "I suppose so. Mother's coming with me to the doctor tomorrow. She keeps on about twins. They run in the family apparently."

"But you're not a twin."

"I was. The other one died at birth. A little

boy. Mother's only just told me. I should have had a brother."

"Count yourself lucky you didn't! They're nothing but trouble."

Nutmeg tossed her head and skittered on the cobbles. Caroline said, "Stand still, girl!"

She concentrated on the horse's flank, her movements smooth and firm. Alison stroked the horse's muzzle, watching her unhappily.

Caroline took a deep breath. "Did you hear we'd been burgled? We lost some tack. Good thing we're insured."

"Not very nice though. Strangers creeping round. Doesn't it make you nervous?"

"These things happen. I'm just pleased no one was hurt. If I'd disturbed him ..."

Alison nodded. "I didn't think to bring Nutmeg a carrot. I just had to get away so I made a dash for my bike when my mother wasn't looking." She patted the mare's neck.

Caroline softened towards her. Anyone who was kind to Nutmeg couldn't be entirely bad. But she couldn't afford to spoil the opportunity. She said again, "If I'd surprised him he might have gone for me."

"It might have been more than one. Did the police say there'd been any similar robberies in the area?"

Caroline shook her head. "D'you want to stay for lunch? Seb's vanished so it's just us."

Ten minutes later they were sitting on the

terrace in the shade with a plate of ham sandwiches and a jug of lemonade on the table between them.

For a while they munched steadily, staring moodily across the grass.

Caroline broke the silence. "It's fine for Father to keep staying with Kate but with Seb gone that leaves me here alone. It's a big place. If they come back they might get into the house. I could be attacked." She glanced at Alison. By her expression, she was miles away, wrapped up in her own problems, no doubt. Caroline said carefully, "What I'm saying is that if he comes back one day and finds me stretched out cold with my head bashed in ..."

Alison said, "If it's a boy I'm going to call him Donald after my uncle. If it's a girl I thought about Althea. Thea for short."

Caroline wanted to shake her. Instead she said, "After an old aunt?"

"No. After my best friend at boarding school." She lowered her voice. "Have you seen anything of Bernard?"

Caroline pulled a face at the sharpness of the lemonade. "No, but I know he's staying with John Somers."

"Does that seem a little odd to you?"

"No. What's odd about it? Somers seems a decent sort, from what you hear."

Alison let the subject drop. She said, "If you don't like Kate, why don't you move out? Find a job in a stables or something. Take Nutmeg with you."

Caroline let it pass. It wouldn't be an issue but she could hardly say so.

Alison brushed crumbs from her skirt. "Are you going to the wedding?"

"I don't want to but I can't hurt Father. Will you go?"

"I expect so – if I'm invited. I quite like Kate."

Caroline let the remark pass. She was seriously considering Alison's suggestion about the job. It would be fun to have her own money and to earn it working with horses. She wondered if she knew anyone who was looking for staff.

Alison said, "You could work in a racing stables. Then you'd be able to take the horses to race meetings and walk them round the ring. Bernard took me to a meeting once. I lost three shillings and he won half a crown! But it was such fun. All those gorgeous horses and the jockeys in the colourful silks. Bernard said that when we're rich he's going to buy a racehorse." Her shoulders slumped. "But now that will never happen. Poor Bernard."

"You ought to try and get him back."

"He wouldn't come back – and I don't want him to." She gave Caroline a challenging look. "If you must know, I'd rather have Seb."

On Thursday afternoon Robert returned alone to Highstead, determined to talk to Bernard. He found Caroline in the kitchen and saw with surprise that she was mixing a fruit cake.

"That looks interesting," he remarked.

He was even more surprised when she smiled at him. "I thought we'd need something nice for tea over the weekend. I expect Kate's coming down." She added another handful of sultanas and stirred again.

Robert looked at her suspiciously. "You don't like Kate," he reminded her. "You were damned rude to her last time she was here."

"I know. I was very upset at the time. Stupidly jealous. I really am sorry."

"You'd better tell her that."

"I will. And she'll forgive me because she's that sort of person."

He stared at her, eyes narrowed. This wasn't a Caroline he recognised. She had always been quick to insult and slow to apologise – if she ever did apologise. He wondered if it was that time of the month. Vi had always made allowances for that. Poor Caro. She was probably missing her mother more than the boys did. Womanly bond and all that. Perhaps he had been too hard on her.

She said, "I found the last of the pheasants in the ice house. I'll do a casserole for Sunday with apple and herbs."

"Sounds ideal."

"And we could invite Alison and her mother. Cheer them up a bit."

Now he was really worried. "You called Alison a tramp, remember?"

"We've patched things up."

"Good ..." He said suddenly, "I still miss your mother. I'm sure you do. D'you think she's ever around us in spirit?"

She gave him a quick glance. "That doesn't sound like you but yes, I think she may be. She used to believe in that sort of thing and –" she swallowed – "a week or so before she died she talked to me. She said she'd be near us."

She was looking at him for confirmation but he had already regretted the question, which he fancied smacked of a betrayal of Kate. "I think she and Kate ..."

"Would have been friends? Yes, I think so."

She was giving all the right answers, he thought with surprise. It made a welcome change. Perhaps she really had had a change of heart. "We'll get through this, Caro, won't we?"

"Oh yes." Her smile was serene. "We'll get through this."

Half an hour later the sound of a mower

stopped abruptly and Robert, waiting on the doorstep, practised his greeting. John Somers opened the front door. He wore shabby shorts and a pair of ancient sandals and his face gleamed with sweat.

Smiling, he said, "Your son's at work, Mr Dengaul, but I'm sure you knew that."

Robert put a hand to his head. "Oh Lord! I should have known that, but to tell you the truth the days are beginning to blur. I can't concentrate on my writing and I hardly know which day it is." He felt a wave of self-pity as he said this and hoped it didn't sound as trite to John Somers as it did to him.

"Come on in if you've time, and I'll brew up some tea. I daren't drink anything stronger or I'll never finish mowing the grass. I thought a big lawn would be easier than lots of flower beds but I was wrong. Mind you, the mower's on its last knockings."

He led the way into the large kitchen where an elderly spaniel slept in a basket near the Aga. Curiously, Robert followed him and sat in the chair indicated.

While Somers fussed with the tea making, Robert tried to size him up. The friendship between his son and this man had begun to worry him.

As though reading his mind Somers said, "In case you're wondering, I have no designs on your son's body, Mr Dengaul. I'm just a lonely widower who's enjoying his company. I don't know what he's going to do about his wife, but I do know he may divorce her. If he does he will probably lose his job and his home. I've told him he can stay here if he wishes. We seem to get along. Obviously if it became a permanent arrangement – a sort of lodger – he would chip in with the rent and stuff like that ... not that I'm hard up. I was in business for myself and retired early. I can't see myself remarrying. I'm getting set in my ways and I don't think any woman would want to take me on." He gave a short laugh then waved the teapot. "How d'you like it – strong or weak? It's a blend I get in London. Rather scented but not to everyone's taste."

Robert said, "As it comes. I'm not fussy." He glanced round the kitchen. "You've made it very cosy."

"Lemon?"

"Lemon? Bit Russian, isn't it?"

"On my maternal grandmother's side."

"Milk, please."

Somers smiled as he picked up the two mugs. "Let's sit in the garden, shall we?" He whistled and the dog looked up. "Come on Jasper."

Seeing a visitor, the dog ambled over and Robert bent to stroke him.

They settled themselves under an old

apple tree and Robert clutched his mug with both hands. "I want to help Bernard but I don't know how," he said without preamble. "He's always been such a decent lad. No trouble. Worked hard at school. Good at games. I'll be honest, Mr Somers, I don't know what to do. Has he talked to you?"

Somers nodded as the dog settled at his feet. "He doesn't know either. It's knocked him for six."

Robert relaxed a little. It was a relief to talk to someone who had no axe to grind. Somers was in effect an onlooker and as such probably saw most of the game. He said, "I rather fancy having a grandchild – boy or girl." He almost said "before it's too late", but he stopped himself in time. The time factor was between himself, Kate and the doctor. "Seb should take responsibility, but he's a feckless blighter although I say it myself. Says it would end in disaster and with that attitude it probably would."

Somers shrugged. "On the other hand, sometimes it takes responsibility to settle a man."

"God only knows! I certainly don't."

A white dove landed in the middle of the lawn and Jasper leaped to his feet with surprising agility and chased after it, barking furiously. He trotted back with a jaunty wag of his tail and Somers made a great fuss of him.

"What a brave boy you are! Chased off that nasty big bird." He smiled at Robert. "I envy you the child. An investment in the future."

Robert snorted. "We thought that about our own children but look where we are now!"

Somers sipped his tea. "How's Alison dealing with it? I saw them together once before I knew Bernard. She seems a nice little woman."

"She's nice enough ... or maybe nice is the wrong word."

"Easily led?"

"That's for sure!" Robert looked at him thoughtfully. "I suppose I daren't suggest you and Bernard come to Sunday lunch. We've invited Alison and her awful mother. Get them all together and try to be civilised."

"Very daring of you." He considered the idea. "I take it Seb won't be there."

"No."

Somers looked doubtful. "I'll put it to Bernard but I very much doubt it. If we're coming I'll get him to ring you this evening but don't get your hopes up. Will Kate be there?"

"Oh, yes." Robert grinned self-consciously. "I already feel lost without her."

Meanwhile, in London, Kate had returned

from work. She kicked off her shoes and investigated the larder. She had decided to cook a meal for Robert when he arrived back from Highstead. No doubt his nerves would be frazzled and his spirits low. She would cook something comforting, she decided. What her mother had called "nursery food". But what exactly? She found a couple of bananas. Banana custard. The perfect pudding. Then she found bacon and some tomatoes and a lump of cheese. Maybe a savoury flan.

When the doorbell rang her first thought was that Robert was earlier than she expected and she hurried to open the door. Her landlady peered shortsightedly over spectacles which to Kate's knowledge had never been cleaned.

"There was a young chap called," she informed Kate without preamble, "said he was a friend of the family."

"Young?" So it wasn't Robert.

She nodded. "Very nice-looking. Bit gingery, his hair, and lovely blue eyes. Said he was a close friend but I said you was out because you'd be at work and he said, Oh how silly of him of course you would but you wouldn't mind him waiting inside but I said that wasn't allowed because I didn't know him from Adam. I hope I did right." She paused for breath. "I mean he could've been anybody."

A horrible suspicion was forming in Kate's mind. "Did he give his name?"

"Not that I recall. It wasn't your fiancé, though. Not Mr Robert Dengaul. I'd have recognised him straight off." She smiled at the mention of his name. Kate knew how thrilled she was to have a famous author visiting.

Her tone was mildly accusing, Kate thought. She said, "Well, thank you for telling me."

"He had a bunch of flowers. Pink carnations. I said they're lovely and he said it was your birthday but I said I thought that was in March because I remembered—"

"Yes, it is in March." It had to be Sebastian, she thought.

"So, Mrs Harper, should I let him come up if he comes again? I mean, should I—"

She was interrupted by a shout from below.

"Kate! It's me, Seb."

Kate forced a smile. "I do know him," she told the landlady. "He's my fiancé's son."

The woman's eyes widened in delight. "Mr Dengaul's *son*? Oh, how exciting!" She hurried back down the stairs.

Cursing to herself, Kate took the opportunity to whisk round the flat, which she had left in a hurry that morning. Alarm bells were ringing. Whatever the excuse for his visit, she must get rid of him as quickly as possible. Probably come to borrow some money, she thought uneasily. What should she do if he did ask? What would Robert want her to do – and should she tell Robert? If she did it would sound like criticism of his son and if she didn't it would be deceit.

Seb knocked and came straight in. She looked at him in surprise – no lazy, confident grin. For a moment they regarded each other warily. Neither spoke.

Kate attempted to lighten the tension. "So what happened to the carnations?"

He didn't answer and looked uncharacteristically nervous.

"The pink carnations for my birthday!"

"I had to say something."

Kate could see why Sebastian had impressed the landlady. He looked very attractive in pale slacks with a blue open-necked shirt. A linen jacket was slung casually over one shoulder and his hair was slightly dishevelled.

"I gave them to a woman at a bus stop. She went pink with surprise."

Kate could imagine it. "So ... to what do I owe this visit? I have to tell you I'm rather busy."

After a long pause he said, "Can't you guess?"

"I hate guessing games."

He glanced around. "Aren't you going to ask me to sit down?"

She waved an impatient hand but he remained standing.

"Kate, I want to tell you something without you getting angry or upset."

"I can't promise that, can I?" She felt a frisson of alarm.

"I have to tell you ..." He tossed the jacket on to a chair. "I just wanted to see you again."

"To talk about what exactly?"

"Just to *see* you."

Her mind raced. What was he up to? "Is this how you softened up Alison?"

"I suppose I deserve that." A silence lengthened between them until he threw up his hands in mock surrender. "So I must be all bad. Is that it? I've let Alison down so that means I can't be sincere."

"It means I suspect your motives, Seb. I don't want to be unkind but 'just wanting to see me' is hardly reasonable."

His expression changed. If this is all an act he's very good at it, she thought. She didn't want to make an enemy of him but she couldn't be seduced by his apparent desperation. "Look, Seb," she said firmly. "I've no time to listen to any nonsense from you. I'm expecting Robert shortly and I have a meal to cook."

"This won't take long. If you'll just spare me five minutes."

Exasperated, she retreated into the kitchen

but he followed her. She turned to face him. "Don't try it on, Seb. Your charm won't work with me. I can see how your mind works. You want to come between us and—"

"No I don't."

"There will never be anyone else in my life except your father, Seb, and when he dies I will live alone."

He seemed to be considering this information. Kate reached for a bowl and took three eggs from the larder. Go away, Seb, she begged him silently.

At last he said, "I could have any woman, married or single. Why should I choose you?"

She took a mixing bowl from the dresser. Damn and blast him. She thought she had dealt with this stupidity but she had underestimated his powers of perseverance.

"You'd better go," she said. "I don't want you here if you are going to talk like this. I'm sorry about that because you're Robert's son and I wanted us to be friends."

"You said we *were* friends."

He actually looked upset.

He moved between her and the table, blocking her way. If she stepped within range she was afraid he might try to kiss her again. She faced him as calmly as she could. "We can be friends, Seb, but nothing more. Unless you persist in this kind of talk every time we find ourselves alone. What do I have to say to convince you?"

He ran fingers through his hair, never taking his eyes from her face. She was shaken to see what looked like real anguish in his eyes.

"Kate, you'll be alone soon."

She pounced on the word. "Soon? What does that mean?"

"Father is dying. I know you know. I've just come from Harley Street. I managed to convince the lovely Nurse Brown that I needed to know the truth."

Kate sat down abruptly, shaken. "You shouldn't have done that, Seb. You had no right. He didn't want any of you to know." She was desperate not to cry because Robert was due and he would see her reddened eyes. She took out a handkerchief and pressed it to her eyes, willing back the tears.

Sebastian said, "A bit of a blow for you both. I'm so sorry."

She could only nod.

"When did you find out?" he asked.

"A few days ago. He told me himself."

"I guessed some time ago that something was wrong." He sat down on the opposite side of the table, his expression bleak. "That fall on the stairs. He didn't trip although he tried to pretend he did. You see, it wasn't the first time. I was there one evening a couple of weeks ago when he was in the garden and I was standing by the window. I saw him stagger and recover himself. He put a hand to his head – and then he keeled over. By the time I reached him he was on his feet again, denying that anything was wrong. And he's looked so pale for months now. I asked him if he should get a check up but he snapped my head off. Caro asked him and got the same response. It was fairly obvious he was worried but he's so stubborn."

Kate put a hand to her head. "So do they all know how bad it is? Bernard and Caroline?"

"No. Just me."

"So little time!" she whispered.

He swallowed. "And we're all making his life hell! That's what you're thinking, isn't it? Well, it's true, but none of it was planned. Families are all the same. They bicker among themselves. They disappoint each other. Make mistakes."

"*Are* all families like this?" she asked with genuine dismay.

He gave a short laugh. "Some are better but some are worse. When we were children Mum used to be at her wits' end and Dad used to rant and rave. He was always threatening to sell us to the first bidder. I was the biggest thorn in his flesh. Then when I was eleven I went to boarding school. I was a little horror and after about eighteen months they asked Dad to take me away. He talked them round – the Dengaul charm again! – and they gave me a second chance."

Kate, trying to imagine the young Sebastian, said nothing.

"Bernard, naturally, had been a prefect and then head boy." He sighed heavily.

In spite of herself, Kate was fascinated by these revelations. "And Caroline?"

"She was seven when she caught pneumonia and she spent several months in a convalescent home in Bognor. When she came back she kept calling Mother 'Nurse'. They started to spoil her, of course, and she became devoted to Father. Obsessively so." He paused. "Why am I telling you all this?"

"You were telling me about families." Kate, watching him as he talked, became convinced that for the first time she was seeing the real Sebastian.

He shrugged. "I was always a problem and now I've excelled myself! I'd do anything to turn back the clock and walk away from Alison. The trouble was the old rivalry was still there. I saw her first, you see." He gave her a wry glance. "But she didn't take me seriously. Thought I was too young and rather wild. So she threw in her lot with big brother Bernard."

"And you saw a chance to even the score?"

"Something like that. But the timing is

terrible and it's hurting Father when he really can't deal with it. I won't tell the others what I know. I'm only telling you because I want you to know how I feel about you." He smiled faintly. "The fact that he's fallen in love with you doesn't rule out the fact that somebody else might do the same. No!" He held up a hand. "Let me finish, Kate. I want you to know that you can call on me in an emergency. If Father is taken ill suddenly, you can rely on me for help. Anything I can do for the two of you I will."

"That's very sweet of you, Seb, but—"

His expression changed. "It's not 'sweet' of me at all. I want to be there for you both."

"Thank you, Seb." She found herself staring at him. Sebastian wasn't the sort of man she could ever trust, but there was so much of Robert in him. The same eyes, the same voice, even. And he was undeniably attractive. Briefly, guiltily, she allowed her imagination to run, imagining herself in bed with him, waking in the morning to find him beside her. With a start she realised how easy it would be to fall in love with him and she knew how impossible it had been for Alison to resist him. With an effort she forced the romantic images from her mind and stood up.

He said, "I'll do anything to make you happy." He watched her closely.

Kate felt her face burn. Had he read her

mind? Distractedly she began to assemble the ingredients for the flan. "Don't talk to me like this, Seb," she begged. "I have to get on." She tied an apron round her waist then faced him squarely. "You couldn't make me happy, Seb, because I've watched you break Alison's heart, because you're too good-looking for your own good and, unlike Robert, you have no real respect for women."

He said, "People change, Kate. How do you know what Dad was like when he was younger? Very much like me, actually, according to Mother. She always said we were two apples from the same tree."

Kate stared at him. She had to admit there was a certain logic to it. She had always suspected that the youthful Robert Dengaul had been a bit of a hell-raiser.

Before she could speak again Sebastian reached across the table and took hold of her hands. "If you must know, I planned to seduce you. I thought it would be fun. Something to crow about – to prove I could do it."

"Seb!" Kate pulled her hands away, shocked. She was angry, too. How dare he keep her off balance this way.

He watched her closely. "Isn't that awful? Well, it's true. You think I'm making it all up? Sorry to disappoint you. Call it a confession. Now you know the worst, you

273

can forgive me and we'll start afresh."

Kate couldn't answer. In a strange way she felt as though she were rejecting a young Robert. Confused, she began to measure flour into the bowl.

Afraid that he would sense her confusion, she said, "You'd better go. Your father will be here soon. I won't say you were here."

"Or that I know about his illness."

She nodded. If only she could rely on Sebastian but she dare not. This might be one big bluff and she couldn't afford to make a mistake.

Sebastian picked up his jacket. "Maybe you're my punishment for what I've done to Alison," he said quietly.

Kate concentrated on the pastry, avoiding his eyes, then raised floury hands as though in self-defence. "Please ... just go," she said.

Nine

Sunday morning at Highstead was a dismal affair in spite of all Robert's efforts to the contrary. Kate had known from the beginning that inviting Alison and her mother had been a mistake but she clung to the hope, quickly dispelled, that with enough goodwill it could at least be bearable. Alison was tongue-tied, her mother tearful. John and Bernard had declined the invitation.

While Robert strolled in the garden with their guests, Caroline masterminded the casserole and Kate prepared the vegetables. Caroline confided that she was missing Sebastian, was worried about Bernard and was furious with Alison. She referred to Alison's mother as a "stupid woman" and grumbled about Robert. Kate bore it all as well as she could, determined to remain as cheerful as possible for Robert's sake but at last Caroline went too far. She dropped a broad hint that she knew Kate and her father were sleeping together and made her disapproval clear.

Kate, peeling potatoes, rounded on her. "I hardly think that's any of your business."

Caroline tossed her head. "In view of what's happened to Alison I should think he'd set a better example, that's all. He's nagged us all these years about behaving decently and—"

Kate said coldly, "Be careful, Caroline. You might say something you'll regret."

Caroline glared at her, then picked up the casserole, thrust it into the oven and slammed the door. She turned back to face Kate, her face flushed, her eyes glittering. "I mean, you don't want to find yourself in Alison's predicament – or perhaps you do!" She twisted the oven cloth fiercely.

"What I want, and what your father wants, is our business. Robert and I are free as birds. We are to marry in a couple of weeks. You may not approve, but I advise you not to meddle in our affairs."

"That sounds like a threat!"

"Take it how you damned well like!"

Immediately regretting her show of temper, Kate drew in a long breath. Don't be drawn, she urged herself, Caroline is as dangerous as her brother. "Your father is in no mood to listen to—"

Caroline threw down the cloth. "Don't you dare try to tell me about my own father! I've known him all my life and I understand him better than you! If you must know I wish he'd never met you. We all do. We were—"

"Don't give me that nonsense about how happy you all were!" Once again Kate felt her control slipping but she was losing patience. "All I ever wanted was to make your father happy. I wanted us all to be friends, but it's becoming impossible. I can't win, can I? I'd say the cards are stacked against me, Caroline, but there is no way you are going to get rid of me."

"Don't be too sure!" Caroline's eyes glittered with malice.

"There's nothing you can do to turn us against each other."

"And you'll turn Father against us!"

"You're being paranoid. I'm simply saying that I shan't allow you to spoil what Robert and I feel for each other." She was breathless with anger; at Caroline, for her behaviour and at herself for losing control.

Caroline raised her voice, "D'you think I don't know—"

Robert, appearing in the doorway, looked from one to the other. "Know what? What's happening?" he asked.

Caroline said, "Nothing." She turned away and began banging saucepans around on the stove top.

He looked enquiringly at Kate.

Refusing to lie, Kate swallowed and drew breath. "A difference of opinion."

He threw up his hands in a gesture of despair. "Well, Alison's mother is in tears again." He crossed the room to put his arm lightly over Kate's shoulder. "Are you all right?" he asked softly.

Kate nodded, struggling to regain her composure.

He said, "Something smells good."

"It's Caroline's casserole."

He gave Kate a quick smile. "Fancy a walk?" he asked. "If Caro can spare you."

"I can!" said Caroline, a trifle too readily. "I've been cooking Sunday lunch ever since Mother died. I don't need anybody's help."

Kate and Robert made their escape. They walked in silence for a while then he said, "Trouble with my darling daughter?"

She smiled. "Nothing I can't handle." She took his hand in hers and they wandered towards the stables.

"Kate, I'm worried," he told her. "Alison's mother wants the child adopted. Says she can't bear the scandal. She's suggesting Alison should go to Austria where they have a family friend who will look after her until after the child is born."

"And you don't want that to happen."

"Of course I don't. The child is a Dengaul."

"Can't Alison be persuaded to keep the child? We could help her financially, couldn't we?"

278

"I've suggested that. It wasn't well received."

"And Alison?"

"She's chaff in the wind. Doesn't know what to do for the best. She wants Seb but he's never going to agree."

No, he's not, thought Kate guiltily.

At the stables they made a fuss of Nutmeg and Kate mentioned Caroline's desire for a companion for the mare. "A goat would be enough," she suggested.

He looked at her, his head on one side and she laughed.

"Yes, Robert, Caro *has* mentioned it once or twice. She obviously hopes I have influence."

He said, "Oh, tell her she can have her blasted goat." He stopped to hold her close. "I know how difficult she can be."

Kate recognised his reference to the trouble earlier. "She's had her say, Robert, and I've had mine. As far as I'm concerned, that's the end of it. Why should they love me? I'm a threat."

"Because *I* love you and you're not a threat. You're the dearest person in the world and I'm a lucky so-and-so."

They walked back ten minutes later in time for Kate to help with the last-minute chores and to help Caroline carry in the tureens.

The food was delicious but sadly no one

was in a mood to appreciate it. Alison was subdued, Caroline icily polite.

When they were clearing away the dishes Kate caught Caroline in the kitchen.

"Shall we try and forget that little argument?" she suggested. "I think we both said more than we intended."

To her surprise, Caroline's expression darkened ominously. "You might have done," she snapped, "I meant every word."

Later that night, when Kate opened her eyes, the room was very dark and it took her a few seconds to realise she was at High-stead in Robert's bed. Someone was shaking her arm and she peered into the darkness.

"It's me, Caro. Wake up."

Kate sat up, her mind clearing instantly. She glanced down at Robert who still slept beside her, snoring softly.

"What is it?" she asked.

"There's someone in the grounds again. Heading for the stables. I'm going down there."

"We must wake Robert!"

"*No*! He looked very tired. All we have to do is scare them off."

Her outline was becoming clearer as Kate's eyes adjusted to the dark. She saw that Caroline was fully dressed and carried a torch.

Kate said, "Hang on!" She fumbled for her

shoes, put them on, then threw on her dressing gown. "Maybe we *should* wake Robert," she whispered but Caroline shook her head.

Caroline said, "He sleeps so heavily with those sleeping pills." She was hurrying along the passage and Kate followed.

"Sleeping pills?"

"He doesn't think I know, but I've seen them. You know what he's like. He hates to show any sign of weakness."

"Shouldn't we call the police?"

"I already have but they're so slow. We can't wait. I'm so afraid they'll take Nutmeg." As they let themselves out of the back door she stopped. "I think all we need to do is make a bit of noise. You go past the vegetable garden and I'll go round by the roses. Crash about a lot and call out the men's names. We don't want them to know we're just two women."

Kate hesitated, shivering slightly in the cool night air. It sounded reasonable but she was not sure it was the best idea. If the burglars were frightened off tonight they'd come back again. "Don't you want the police to catch them? If we scare them away—"

"Oh for heaven's sake, Kate! If you don't want to help go back to bed!"

She disappeared into the darkness and Kate could hear her stamping along. After a moment Caroline called out, "Sebastian! Quick! I think they're heading for the stables!"

Tightening the cord of her dressing gown, Kate set off towards the vegetable garden as instructed, moving as noisily as possible, shaking overhead branches and scuffling her feet on the gravelled paths. Her shoes were untied but she didn't want to stop to tie the laces.

She shouted, "Robert! Where are you? Can you see them?"

There was a gruff "Not yet" from somewhere to her left. It sounded exactly like a woman pretending to be a man.

Kate stumbled on, convinced that this plan of Caroline's was a mistake. The police were the professionals and they should have waited for them. Not that she didn't understand Caroline's dilemma. The police would be of no use if the thieves had already taken the horse. She pressed on but now she could no longer hear Caroline. Hopefully she wasn't going to do anything stupid like tackle the men herself. Kate stopped and listened. No sound. She was very near to the stable but there was no sign that Nutmeg was alarmed. Surely they hadn't worked that fast, she thought anxiously. If they found the stable empty Caroline would be beside herself. She stepped a little closer and at that moment the moon shone through a gap in the clouds. To her relief the stableyard appeared to be deserted. The stable door was closed and she could hear faint sounds from within. Perhaps they had scared the intruders off.

"Robert! I'm at the stables!" she shouted, ready to move at the first sign of trouble. She stared into the surrounding darkness. Where on earth was Caroline? And more to the point, where were the police?

"Caro?"

Still no answer. Her uneasiness grew. Had Caroline run into the intruders and been silenced? There had been no call for help and Kate had heard nothing to suggest a struggle. If Caroline had been caught then she, Kate, would probably be the next victim.

"Caro! Where *are* you?"

It occurred to her suddenly that maybe Caroline had been attacked inside the stable. She turned to unlatch the upper half of the door when a slight sound made her pause. She spun round. "Is that you?"

Another silence. Thoroughly alarmed, she swung open the top of the door but suddenly sensed someone behind her. Reacting rapidly she bent double and swung round. As she did so something heavy slammed against her neck and shoulder causing her to gasp with pain. The man swung the weapon again and this time it landed across her back.

Through the fear and pain, Kate's temper flared. As she struggled to retain her balance she caught sight of a wellington boot. Foremost in her mind was the realisation that this wretch meant to kill her. Her mind raced. What had she and Will been taught? Never turn your back on your assailant. She butted the man in the stomach. It was not as hard as she would have liked but as he gasped for breath she felt a rush of adrenalin followed by deep satisfaction. She must get him off balance. But he had other ideas. He straightened up and raised his arms. Before he could strike her again she lunged forward with as much speed as she could muster and drove the rigid fingers of her right hand hard into his thigh. Before he could recover, she stabbed at his eyes and scratched his face.

At the same moment she heard a male voice call, "Police! Anyone around?"

Aware that help had arrived she opened her mouth to shout and her attention wavered for a few seconds. It was long enough. Her assailant's weapon caught her a glancing blow on the side of the head and she slipped at once into unconsciousness.

When she came to, someone was leaning over her, shining a light in her face.

"You're going to be fine, Miss Dengaul. I'm Sergeant Crewe. Can you sit up if I help you?"

Kate stared up at him dully. It was a moment before she remembered what had happened. At least she was still alive, she thought gratefully. Her head ached, her back and neck were painfully stiff but she struggled carefully into a sitting position with the sergeant's help.

She said, "I'm Kate Harper. Where's Caro? Is she all right?"

He crouched beside her. "Now you take your time. Come round slowly. Then tell me what you can."

Kate raised a hand to her head and a groan escaped her. "He tried to kill me!" she said. The realisation terrified her.

"Well, he failed, miss. You may be a bit knocked about but you're still in one piece."

Kate breathed slowly in and out, trying to calm her fear. He had meant to kill her. She was sure of it.

He said, "The message was a bit garbled. Poor Alice – that's my wife – sent me off to Ben Gore's place. Had me knocking on the door of Barley Cottage. Frightened the life out of them, this time of night. When I got back to Alice I thought if it wasn't 'Ben Gore' it might have been 'Dengaul'. Came here on the off chance."

At that moment they heard footsteps and Caroline limped into view from inside the stable. "Oh Lord!" She rushed forward. "The wretch knocked me in the holly bush.

I might have lost an eye! He got you too, did he? Or were there two of them?"

The sergeant stood up and began to repeat the muddle over the telephone call but Caro, crouched beside Kate, wasn't listening. "What happened, Kate? How many men were there? I only saw one but—"

The sergeant interrupted them. "We'd better get you two ladies back to the house and send for the doctor. While we wait for him you can give me some details."

With Caroline and the policeman's help Kate made her way slowly back to the house and into the kitchen. Caroline looked in better shape with nothing more than a few scratches on her face, and she quickly rallied. While Kate gave her version of what had happened, Sergeant Crewe took notes. Caroline put the kettle on and then hurried upstairs.

"So you didn't get a good look at this chap, Mrs Harper?"

"No. He was wearing a mask."

"Tall? Short? Any idea?"

Kate tried to recall her impressions. "Not tall ... slightly built but strong. I think he had a club of some kind."

Caroline returned, shaking her head. "No chance of waking my father. He's dead to the world."

Kate said, "You said something about pills."

286

Caroline fussed with the teapot. "He sometimes doubles the dose."

She poured tea as she gave the sergeant her own version of events. "I lost track of Kate and then I tripped over something and went sprawling on to the path. I moved nearer to the stables and then got that creepy feeling that someone was near me and froze. Then I heard a scuffle – it must have been Kate and her attacker – and the next thing I knew someone ran straight into me and I went down again – straight into the holly bushes!"

The sergeant was writing furiously. "And was this the same assailant or another man? Did you get a glimpse of him?"

Caroline sat down at the table and sipped her tea. "Not really, but I'd say he was tall and burly. He breathed heavily as though he'd been running, or maybe he has asthma or something like that."

"So there must have been two men." He added to his notes then stopped to blow on his tea. "Got a spot more milk, have you?"

"Help yourself." Caroline pushed the jug towards him. "Oh yes! He was wearing leather gloves. I smelled them as he tried to cover my mouth – to stop me from screaming. And I smelled brilliantine from his hair."

The sergeant looked up. "So after you fell

into the bushes he grabbed you? He didn't just run off."

"Well, yes. I suppose he did. Grab me, I mean. Yes, he did. He began to drag me along. I remember wriggling free. I was frantic with worry."

Kate was surprised. Had Caroline really been concerned for her or was this for the sergeant's benefit?

Caroline went on. "If they'd laid a finger on Nutmeg ..." She shook her head.

Kate said, "Excuse me," and made her way out of the kitchen. Somehow she dragged herself up the stairs and along the landing to the bedroom. Once there she sat down gingerly on the edge of the bed.

"Robert?" She leaned over and shook him gently. "Wake up, darling." To her surprise there was no response. She tried again but he lay with his face half in the pillow, breathing noisily.

"Robert?" She was aware of great longing for the reassurance which only he could give her. The shock was settling in and she felt desperately weary. She could feel herself trembling and tears were near. But she mustn't break down. Caro had also been attacked and she was behaving with great courage.

"Wake up!" Now her attempts to rouse him were hardly gentle but he remained asleep. She sat up, making an effort to concentrate. Why had he had taken so many pills – and when had he taken them? She had no recollection of it. Did he suffer from insomnia? If so, he had never mentioned it. With an effort, she walked into the adjacent bathroom and looked in the cabinet but saw nothing she recognised as sleeping pills.

She stood for a while by the bed, looking down at the man she loved. She felt curiously betrayed by his inability to help her.

"Why, Robert?" she whispered. They had made love. Afterwards she had heard him slip into a relaxed sleep. Nothing made any sense – unless he had woken later and taken them. Still deeply puzzled, she longed to slide under the bedclothes with him but the sergeant would be expecting her back. She went carefully back down the stairs, clinging to the banisters, aware of the various pains developing in her body. As soon as she entered the kitchen the sergeant turned to her.

"I know you must need your rest but if I could summarise these details it would be a help."

Kate said, "Could we leave the doctor's visit until the morning? Neither of us is bleeding or seriously hurt. I mean, nothing that might threaten our lives. I just want to go back to bed."

To her surprise Caroline agreed. They

listened to the sergeant's summing up and both agreed it was accurate. Two men had apparently attempted to steal the horse but had been scared off. They had attacked the two women separately.

Sergeant Crewe closed his notebook. "And you will call in the doctor first thing in the morning just to be on the safe side. We shall send two of our men to search the area for clues. Might strike lucky."

Caroline showed him out. Kate waited in the kitchen.

"He says we'll have to sign the statements tomorrow. He'll be back about nine. He says we mustn't walk around too much or we'll wipe out the footprints but I shall go down to feed Nutmeg."

Kate said, "You really are remarkably cool considering everything that's happened. I'm shaking inside." She finished her tea, conscious of Caroline's eyes upon her.

"If you'd grown up with brothers you'd have learned not to show your feelings."

"I suppose so."

"Are you going to be all right? I mean, do you need anything – witch hazel for your bruises, maybe. Arnica?"

Kate forced a smile. "If you have a gallon or so of the stuff! If not I'll wait for the doctor, but thanks anyway." She stood up carefully. "See you in the morning."

Back in bed Kate made one more

unsuccessful attempt to wake Robert then lay wide awake replaying the events of the past hour. The attack and the foiled theft she could understand. What worried her was Robert's dependence on the pills. As sleep finally claimed her, one question nagged at her mind. What else was Robert keeping from her?

Next morning, just after eleven, Kate was getting ready to rush for the train. Robert finally surfaced and she smiled as he sat up with a grunt of discomfort.

"You've finally woken up," she said.

"God, my head!" He stared at her. "What have you done to your face?"

Kate started to tell him what he had missed the night before, making light of her injuries. Halfway through her account he said, "What d'you mean you couldn't wake me?"

She stopped brushing her hair. "The sleeping pills. Caro said you must have taken a double—"

"Sleeping pills? I never take sleeping pills."

They stared at each other, perplexed.

Kate thought quickly. She was determined to go up to London and mustn't miss the train. "It's not important, Robert. We'll talk—"

"Not important? Of course it's important. I've never—"

Pulling on her hat, she fought down impatience. "Darling, Caro found some in your bathroom cabinet once. She didn't like to—"

"There are *no* sleeping pills in my cabinet." His tone was aggressive. "What's she talking about?" He fastened the top button of his pyjama jacket, frowning with the effort of concentration. "They must have been Vi's. She was always a poor sleeper."

Kate shrugged then regretted it. "I was only quoting your daughter, Robert. I have to catch that train."

"Do you *have* to go in? Can't you pretend to be ill? Dammit Kate, you *are* ill!"

"I want to go in, Robert, so please don't argue. I need to talk to Gordon Brett about giving up my job." She watched for his reaction and saw him brighten.

"You're giving up? Oh darling Kate, that's wonderful!"

"They might need time to find a replacement so it may not—"

"You can start writing again, Kate. I'll help you if you'll let me."

The idea of Robert looking over her shoulder all the time was totally unacceptable but this was not the time to say so. Wincing a little she reached for her clutch bag and tucked it under her arm.

Robert said, "You should rest, Kate,

especially with that bandaged shoulder. Do please stay here."

She looked him squarely in the eye. "The doctor's already been and he says there's nothing that won't mend given a little time. I want to give in my notice personally, Robert. I want to do it today – before I change my mind." She smiled at his expression. "I'll tell them about last night and I'll stay home tomorrow."

He was shaking his head. "When I think you might have been killed. Or Caro! You're sure she's OK?"

"She's fine. Just a bit of a limp. She got off fairly lightly, thank goodness."

He pushed back the covers and stood up. "There's no end to it, it seems. Someone up there –" he rolled his eyes upwards – "has it in for us!"

She leaned towards him to kiss him goodbye but he gave her his usual fierce hug. She gave a little scream and pulled free.

"*Sorry*, darling!"

She smiled reassuringly through the wave of pain. "I'm off."

"Are the police coming back? They have to look for clues, don't they – footprints and the like?"

"They're out there already."

He rolled his eyes. "Much good may it do! They'll drink gallons of tea, trample the flower beds and discover precisely nothing!"

She uttered a small prayer that Robert would be helpful and not censorious and said, "Sergeant Crewe was very efficient and quite charming."

"A charming policeman? Oh God! My head! Have we got any aspirins?"

"I don't know, Robert. It's your house." She glanced at the alarm clock but at that moment a car pulled up in the driveway below and someone sounded the horn.

"My taxi!" Kate said and made a hasty exit.

When Kate entered her office she was surprised to find Muriel already ensconced, reading a newspaper. She looked up and was immediately concerned. "Your arm! Or is it your shoulder? Oh poor Kate. It must have been awful."

Kate blinked. "You *know*?"

Muriel grinned. "Didn't *you* know? You made the headlines at last! The early editions." She turned the newspaper so that Kate could read the front page.

AUTHOR'S FIANCÉE ATTACKED!

"Oh no!"

Muriel surrendered the newspaper and Kate sat down behind her desk to read the article.

"...Late last night Mrs Kate Harper was savagely attacked at her fiancé's home in Kent ..." It then gave a reasonably accurate account of the abortive theft and ended: "Author Robert Dengaul apparently slept throughout the incident ..."

Kate laughed. "Poor Robert. He's going to hate that!"

Muriel regarded her solicitously. "Seriously, Kate, how are you? – apart from looking like death with one half of your face swollen. Should you have come in today? Surely the doctor should have—"

"I had to, Mu. I can't explain now but I will later."

"Was it the way they said?"

"The report? Pretty accurate. There seemed to be two men involved."

"Trying to steal the horse."

"Presumably. It seems rather odd, though, because inside the house there are items worth more than the horse. Some beautiful paintings, not to mention the silver." She smiled. "What Robert calls his 'nouveau riche' collection! He's surrounded by landed gentry and he says he had to retaliate. Poor Robert!"

"Poor? Hardly, Kate. Wealth and fame and you! What more could he ask."

Try as she would, Kate could not think of a flippant reply, instead she said, "Nutmeg is a nice horse – four legs, a head and tail – but nothing special. It's not as though she's a valuable racehorse."

"But stealing the silver would have meant

breaking into the house. This way they might have led the horse away and Bob's your uncle."

"Imagine I'm shrugging, will you! I have to remember what agony it is to make sudden movements!"

"I'm so dreadfully sorry, Kate. We might have been reading your obituary!"

"When your number's up! That's what they say, isn't it?"

"Only if they're very unoriginal!" Mu answered with mock severity. "I'll make you a cup of tea."

Kate set the paper aside. "What really worries me is Robert. He really did sleep through it all. We both tried to rouse him but he was out for the count." She sighed. "Caro insisted that he often takes sleeping pills. Robert flatly denied it." She picked up a memo.

"Not very manly, I suppose, sleeping pills."

"Maybe ..." She straightened carefully, biting her lip as she did so. "So the eleven o'clock meeting was cancelled."

"Yes. Marie Jayne's agent is tied up in Scotland with her lawyer over that stupid plagiarism claim. Gordon decided to call it off."

Kate frowned. "I keep wondering whether coma could be a symptom of—" She stopped abruptly but Muriel turned sharply towards her.

"A symptom of what, Kate?" she asked quietly.

"Nothing."

"Kate?"

"Nephritis. An old aunt of mine." She cursed inwardly, furious with herself for the slip. Muriel had known her too long to be deceived by such a feeble lie. She wondered frantically if there was some way to retrieve the situation but her friend was regarding her with such concern that she couldn't bring herself to follow one lie with another. She was also aware of a desperate longing to share the terrible news with a loving friend. She stammered, "Oh God, Mu!"

"Tell me, Kate." The words were an invitation rather than a command.

Kate drew a long breath. "It's not an aunt. It's Robert – but you mustn't tell a soul." She looked at Muriel, her eyes full of pleading. "Please promise me you won't tell anyone."

Muriel put down the teapot and stared at her. "Robert has *nephritis*?"

Kate nodded.

Her friend sat down with her and took hold of her hands. "I promise I will never repeat that, Kate, but you must promise me something in return."

"Of course. Anything."

"You must promise to come to me for help when you need it."

297

In the garden at Highstead, Detective Sergeant Lane was shaking his head and Caroline was looking agitated. Robert, watching them both, was feeling distinctly uneasy. His head still ached from his heavy sleep and he was mortified that when Kate had needed him most he had been of no help.

Caroline said, "It was here. I'm pretty sure – but it was dark."

They were standing by the edge of the lawn where the rhododendrons encroached on the grass. Overhead, the trees cast a welcome shade from the midday sun.

The detective examined the ground. "Then where are the tracks made by your heels? There are no signs at all that someone has been dragged against their will."

Robert looked at his daughter. "You must be mistaken."

"Perhaps I am," she agreed with an abrupt about turn. "Yes, it must have been somewhere else."

DS Lane tried to hide his impatience. "Let's go back to the beginning again."

He set off across the grass and they trailed after him, Caroline looking thoroughly bad-tempered and harassed.

"You're not helping very much," Robert told her in a low voice. "You're coming across as confused. It's not like you at all."

"It was *dark*. I'm doing my best."

"Are you?" He looked at her suspiciously. "I'm not so sure. And why did you lie about the sleeping pills? I told him I never take them. You insisted that I do. How d'you expect the wretched man to solve anything?"

"I don't. He's as dim as they come!" she answered. "It's all a waste of time anyway. They'll never catch him."

"Him? I thought it was 'them'. You've told the police there were two of them."

"I meant 'them'. Don't keep trying to trip me up. They're bad enough."

They caught up with the detective at the edge of the terrace. He was talking to his detective constable who looked at Robert and Caroline with triumph.

DS Lane said, "They've found footprints. Wellington boots – which ties in with what Mrs Harper told us. But there only appears to be one set. In other words, there was only one assailant."

They all looked at Caroline.

She said, "Well, you're wrong. The hefty one was going for me and the slightly built one was hitting Kate with a – with whatever it was. There were two men."

DS Lane consulted his notes. "And you're sure you didn't hear either of them speak. They were totally silent the entire time. Not very likely, is it?"

She hesitated. "How would I know? I think I'd have remembered voices."

"It's surprising what people forget – especially the victims. It's as though the mind blocks things out."

Robert was watching her closely. For some reason she was being deliberately unhelpful. He said, "Take your time, Caro. Think carefully." He found himself wishing Kate was present. She would certainly have proved a more reliable witness and Caroline might have followed her example.

She gave the policeman a withering glance but frowned dutifully. At last she said, "I think one of them shouted something. It could have been a name."

"Which one shouted?"

"The other one. Not the one who collided with me."

The policeman waited, pencil poised. "Then yours must have answered."

"He didn't. At least he – I think he muttered something. To himself."

Robert said, "So you must have heard what the other one shouted."

The detective sergeant said, "If you don't mind, sir. I'll ask the questions."

"Sorry."

They both looked at Caroline.

She said, "It was a name."

"Which was?"

"I'm not sure."

"Then how do you know it was a name?"

Her mouth tightened. "What else could it have been?"

"A command. A question. An oath, even."

"For heaven's *sake*!" she snapped. "It was a name. Albert. It was Albert. Satisfied?"

The two men exchanged glances. Robert began to speak then bit his lip and remained silent. Was his daughter deliberately trying to confuse them? She certainly appeared to be concealing information. If he could see it, the police would have registered the fact. What the hell was she up to?

As though reading his mind, the policeman gave Caroline a look that spoke volumes.

"Miss Dengaul, you and Mrs Harper were both assaulted last night. One or both of you might have been killed. Perhaps I should remind you that withholding information from the police is an offence. I don't think you're being as helpful as you might be in the circumstances."

Robert looked at his daughter. She was flushed but her expression was stubborn.

"I don't care what you think!" she snapped.

He stiffened. "That attitude will not help you, Miss Dengaul. I might consider it an obstruction and would then need to take you into the station for further questions."

Robert realised with horror that it was a direct threat.

"For God's sake, Caro! This is so unlike you. The man's only doing his job. We all want the blighters found."

She didn't answer and the silence lengthened uncomfortably. Caroline fidgeted, her expression sullen.

DS Lane said, "Mrs Harper's attacker was wearing a mask of some kind. Possibly they both were. I'm wondering why. Did they expect to be recognised? I had assumed originally that they expected to creep in, take the horse and go, without meeting anybody. The stable is a longish way from the house. So why should one of them come armed with a weapon? Nothing seems to add up." He looked at Robert.

He said, "You're right. It is odd."

Caroline shrugged. "I don't see anything odd. Obviously we surprised them and their plan didn't work out."

The detective scratched his head. "What about his hands. Were they rough? Workingman's hands?"

"Yes. Rough. And he smelled sweaty – or his clothes did."

Robert turned away, smothering a groan. The policeman had laid a trap for her and she had fallen straight into it.

The detective went on, "This voice calling 'Albert'. Did it sound like a young man or an old one?"

"No, not particularly old. Not hoarse

or raspy or wheezy."

"Now let me see ..." he consulted his notes again, "yesterday you said that Albert was wearing gloves but—"

"Who's Albert?"

"The man who attacked you. You said the other man called him Albert."

"Oh, yes. That's right."

"You said he was wearing leather gloves so you couldn't have known that his hands were rough."

Robert said quickly, "I think she's had enough. You're confusing her."

The detective gave him a cold look. "I have a job to do, sir, with respect." He turned to Caroline. "What made him release you?"

"I don't know."

"Yesterday you said there was a whistle – that you thought was a signal of some kind."

"Did I? Then there *was* a whistle."

Robert looked at her with displeasure. In her slacks and blouse she looked very young – like the difficult daughter she had once been. Her attitude of non-co-operation was horribly familiar to him. It had driven both him and Vi to distraction over a long period. Now, for the first time in years, Robert longed to slap her. Kate had narrowly escaped serious injury, Caroline herself had been attacked and her precious mare might have been stolen. So why was his daughter proving such a very unreliable witness? Already suspicious, his mind raced unhappily. Was she shielding someone, he wondered. If so, who was it?

Frustrated and angry and with a throbbing head, he decided he had had enough. Leaving them to it, he made his way back into the kitchen then went slowly up the stairs to his study, trying to decide whether or not to call the doctor. His unnaturally deep sleep worried him. Was it a symptom of his disease that the doctor had omitted to mention or had he been wrongly diagnosed? He sat down at his desk and stared blankly at the first few pages of his novel. A year or two. That was all he could expect.

"Oh God!" He had never been a religious man although his parents had sent him to Sunday school and they had all attended church on Sunday morning. Until he reached the age of fourteen and had faced the hurdle of confirmation. He had rebelled against the idea of communion, suggesting to the head master that everyone sipping wine from the same chalice was unhealthy. The vicar, informed of this heresy, had been secretly delighted when the arrogant young pipsqueak had refused to attend further classes.

Now Robert put his elbows on the desk, closed his eyes and tried to redress the balance.

"Please forgive me. I will lead a blameless life henceforth if you will only help us all to some kind of happiness."

Even to his own ears it lacked the ring of truth and he straightened up, aware that God was probably unimpressed.

The shrill of the telephone startled him.

"Kate! I've missed you!"

"It's not Kate."

"Sebastian." He tried not to sound too disappointed.

"I've just seen today's paper. How is she?"

"She wasn't hurt but she's being difficult as usual. Hopeless witness."

"I meant Kate. It says she received injuries."

"Her shoulder, back and neck are badly bruised, also her face."

"Jesus Christ!"

"One blow caught her across the side of the head. She looks as though she's gone three rounds with a heavyweight!"

"Thank God it's no worse! Is she there? Can I talk to her?"

"No. She insisted on going in to work." He sighed heavily. "I suspect she was glad to get away from us."

There was a pause. "Would you mind if I gave her a ring? I mean, I'd like to say how sorry I am and all that."

"By all means, Seb!" Robert's spirits lifted a little. His son was concerned for Kate!

305

Had God actually been listening? He smiled. "Where are you, Seb? I mean, you needn't tell me if you—"

"I'm at Reggie's place in Tunis Road. Remember Reggie? Carrotty hair and rabbit teeth? Useless at sports but always top of the class. He's something in the city now, married to this gorgeous blonde. They're expecting their first baby."

Robert said, "So are you, remember?" and after a moment the line went dead.

Ten

Nurse Brown picked up the receiver and smiled at the invisible caller.

"Doctor Harris's office How can I help you?"

"It's Mrs Harper, Mr Dengaul's fiancée. I need to see the doctor. Is he in yet?"

Nurse Brown's smile faded. Of course! The poor woman had been attacked in her garden and half murdered "Oh dear," she said. "I'm so sorry. I don't think he's taking any new patients at the—"

"No, no! It's not me. I'm fine."

"But the paper said you could have been killed! A frenzied attack, they said."

There was a pause. "It was rather frantic, I suppose. I try not to think about it. I'm in London at the moment and I want to talk to Doctor Harris about my fiancé's condition. If he's there, nurse, I'll have a word now. If not I'll make an appointment."

It would be rather nice to meet Mrs Harper. She said, "The doctor's due in but he's late – I expect he missed his train. I'll see if I can fit you in."

307

Nurse Brown reached for the appointments book and ran a slim finger down the page. "I do have a slot at ..." She waited. "Mrs Harper? Are you still there?" There was no answer. "Are you all right?" Perhaps she had fainted! Pressing her ear closer to the receiver, she waited. She heard a voice say "Sebastian? Oh no!" That would be Mr Dengaul's handsome son. Her smile faded. She had been indiscreet and Doctor Harris had been annoyed with her. Smothering feelings of guilt, she listened again. She heard Mrs Harper say, "On his way up? Oh, damn!" Whatever was happening? she wondered. She said again, "Mrs Harper?"

"I'm here. I'm so sorry. I have an unexpected visitor." She was speaking hurriedly. "I'll ring back later. Ten minutes should be enough. Thank you."

Nurse Brown replaced the receiver carefully. So Sebastian Dengaul had gone to see his father's fiancée. Maybe *he* had told her about the nephritis. What an interesting family. She carefully pencilled in Mrs Harper's name.

Back at Highstead, Caroline sat alone in the kitchen staring at a packet of Bath Oliver biscuits. Her mouth was dry and her pulse was racing. Her head ached but her mind was clear as a bell. The police suspected her. They had persisted in their stupid questions

– the same ones over and over again. Now they were on to a new tack. Had their been any animosity between her and Kate? Why had she given the police such a garbled message? Ben Gore sounded remarkably like Dengaul, did it not? Yes, it damned well did and she had meant it that way but she had never expected them to figure it out. She had never intended that Kate should be alive to tell her side of the story – an account which provided inconsistencies when compared with Caroline's own version. More than anything she regretted the fact that she hadn't hit Kate hard enough. All three blows had failed to reach the target squarely but had glanced off. Somehow Kate had avoided the damage the cricket bat should have inflicted. Kate had also driven her fingers into Caroline's thigh with horrific force. The bruise was enormous and her whole leg ached abominably. Damn and blast her to hell! She had no right to be causing Caroline all this anguish.

Outside in the garden three policemen toiled, searching for incriminating evidence while Caroline sat in the kitchen, pretending to have her lunch, pretending to be calm and reasonable and unafraid. She had deliberately not offered them any lunch although her father would have done so. He'd gone to see Kate, however. As always, it was Kate he was concerned about. Never mind that his own flesh and blood was dangerously near to hysteria, clinging to sanity like a drowning man to a rope.

And where was Sebastian when she needed him? she thought with growing bitterness. All these years she had been there for him, but he was leaving her to her fate. She poured herself another measure of brandy, which she swallowed with a grimace. She hated the stuff but it was supposed to be medicinal. Good in emergencies. Well, she had an emergency now. She was all alone with the police barking at her heels.

Suddenly she stood up on shaky legs and snatched up the bottle. She would go where the police would never find her and she would stay there until her father or Bernard or Sebastian turned up to support her. Slowly she made her unsteady way to the top of the house and stepped out on to the roof. She closed the door behind her and stumbled towards the chimney stack. There, she sank down gratefully and took another mouthful of brandy straight from the bottle. The July sun was very hot and the leads reflected the glare. Around her the air shimmered, softening the view across the surrounding land and distant rooftops.

"Bloody Kate!" she muttered thickly.

After a few moments she crawled to the edge of the roof and stared down. She could see policemen moving carefully across the garden, probing the undergrowth with sticks. Looking for the weapon, she thought. Well, they wouldn't find it. She finished the brandy with three large mouthfuls, the last of which made her choke and she withdrew hastily to lean against the stack once more. Her leg ached beneath the slacks which she wore to hide the bruise and her stomach rumbled uneasily. She should have eaten some lunch but her appetite had deserted her. Self-pity overwhelmed her. Today should have been a time for celebrating. She should have been ringing Seb to share the good news instead of cowering on the leads alone with the stench of failure in her nostrils. Sighing, she was aware of a deep longing for her mother. For the mother with whom she had clashed so often as a girl; the mother of whom she had been unbearably jealous. Unbidden, an image arose in her mind of her mother passing her father's chair and smoothing his hair. He had reached up, caught her hand and kissed it. It was the only tenderness between them she remembered and even now it provoked a wave of irrational envy.

"You shouldn't have died," she told her absent mother. "You shouldn't have left Father on his own."

By dying, her mother had abandoned Robert to his fate. A fate in the shape of

Kate Harper who had swooped down from a great height.

"Damn, *damn* Kate Harper!"

From below she heard a shout but felt too tired to make any further effort. They may have found something, she reflected, but it would mean nothing. They knew she had done it but they had no evidence and they never would. She had got away with it. Smiling, Caroline closed her eyes and drifted into an uneasy sleep.

A voice said, "So you did it, Caro!" and she recognised her brother's voice. She nodded without turning her head. He materialised before her, his outline blurred by a combination of brandy and sunlight.

She squinted up at him. "But she didn't die. I'll have to try again."

He took the bottle from her hand. "Drinking at your age, Caro! Tut tut!" and leaned across and kissed her.

She said, "Oh Seb!" His kindness unnerved her and suddenly her lips trembled.

"So what did you use?" he asked.

"Your cricket bat."

He sat beside her. "I spoke to the detective. He said they had a strong lead. That means they have a suspect."

Caroline wasn't listening. "She kept moving, Seb. I couldn't get a good swing at her. Then she jabbed me in the leg. Spiteful cow! I've got an enormous bruise."

He was giving her a strange look. "There was no need. I told you I was going to fix everything. That I was going to seduce her."

"But you didn't ... Don't look at me like that, Seb. I hate that look."

"Father will be furious when he knows. He'll never forgive you."

"How will he know?"

"I might tell him. You're such a little fool, Caro."

She swayed. "You told Mother when I broke that jug. I know you did."

"For heaven's sake! That was years ago."

"You must have told her or else how did she know? You told her. I could see it in your eyes." She yawned. "But you won't tell Father I tried to kill Kate because he won't believe you and you can't prove it."

For what seemed an eternity, neither of them spoke. Caroline was falling asleep, her head on her brother's shoulder. It was a long time since she had felt this close to him and it reminded her of their childhood alliance.

"But I've seen your hiding place," he said. "The mask and the bat; hidden in the hayloft. All I have to do is show the police and you'll be arrested. They'll find you guilty of attempted murder – quite definitely premeditated – and you'll go to prison for a long time." He began to play with her hair. "You'll hate that, Caro. You'll be locked up and you'll never see Nutmeg again."

She opened her eyes, alerted by his tone. "It was *your* bat, Seb." She gave him a crooked smile. "They'll think it was you."

"No they won't. I have an alibi. I was at Reggie's."

"They might not believe you."

To her surprise he put an arm round her shoulders and it felt wonderfully reassuring. It felt the way it had done all those years ago when she curled up on her mother's lap. Tears filled her eyes but she brushed them away.

"You wouldn't tell them, would you?" He had been such a dear little boy. So trusting, so full of love.

"Of course not. I was only teasing. You know I wouldn't let them lock you up." Soothed, she relaxed against him, then sat up. "That milk jug. Seb, you *did* tell her, didn't you, that I broke it?"

"Yes. I'm sorry."

"You told a lie, Seb, but ... but I forgive you." Her words were slurred but nothing mattered. It was just the two of them together on the roof and everything was going to be all right. The sun was scorching her face, her legs were hot and she was beginning to perspire. She felt delightfully dizzy and wondered why she had never tried brandy before.

He said, "Do you remember how we used to walk along the edge? I don't think you could do it now."

"I could," she whispered with a faint smile, "of course I could."

"I dare you then. Go on. Walk along the edge."

She opened her eyes and his face was very close to hers.

He kissed her again. "Prove that you love me, Caro."

"Why should I?"

"Because you tried to kill Kate." He lowered his voice. "It was a wicked, *wicked* thing to do but I'll forgive you if you do as I say."

Caroline sighed. "I don't feel like it, Seb. I just want to sleep."

She lolled happily against him, her eyelids drooping, her thoughts spinning off into oblivion. But someone was shaking her and she was forced to open her eyes. She tried to say "Stop that" but no words came to her trembling lips.

"Get up, Caro."

With Seb's help she rose unsteadily to her feet and stumbled towards the end of the roof. With his hand on her arm she stepped over the rail to the narrow ledge.

He said, "I'll hold you, Caro. Take it steady. You can do it. I know you can."

Caroline smiled shakily at his hazy image.

"Of course I can do it. You don't need to hold me."

She took a step and then another. It was ridiculously easy. From below she heard a shout which distracted her attention and for a moment she wobbled but Seb's hand was steadying her. She said, "I can do it, Seb!" and he took his hand away.

Now several people were shouting somewhere in the distance. It sounded like "Get back!" but she ignored the voices because she *knew* she could do it. She was halfway along and she smiled with a deep satisfaction. From behind her she heard the sound of footsteps coming up the stairs and a man's voice shouting, "Grab her, for God's sake man!"

At that moment a white bird swooped close into her line of vision and instinctively she tried to step back. She screamed and felt Seb catch hold of her sleeve. He tugged her backwards but she lost her footing and she felt herself tilt to the left. In a split second she was unbearably sober, staring down at the drop fifty feet below.

"Seb!" she screamed.

In desperation, she reached out and her frantic hands fastened on his arm. With horror she realised that he was trying to detach her fingers, trying to free himself.

"Seb! Don't!"

He was going to let her fall!

316

Hurriedly she tightened her grip as her weight threatened to carry her over the edge. Then he, too, lost his balance and lurched towards her. She screamed his name for a third time and it hung in the air. The sight of his horrified face was the last thing she saw as they plunged together on to the terrace forty feet below.

When Kate returned to the office after her appointment with Doctor Harris, she found Muriel waiting for her.

"The police rang for you," she told Kate. "They asked you to ring back urgently – and Robert arrived but you'd already gone out. We offered him a snack lunch – but he said he'd be back some time this afternoon."

"The police? Maybe they've caught someone. I'll ring them now."

"Let me know if it's anything I can help you with. I'll be in my den."

Detective Sergeant Lane sounded hesitant and Kate felt a frisson of fear as she waited.

"I was hoping that Mr Dengaul might be with you. We need to contact him rather urgently. There's been an accident."

Kate closed her eyes. She had an immediate picture of Caroline falling from her horse. "Is it Caroline? Is she badly hurt?"

"I'm sorry, Mrs Harper, but I really need to speak first with Mr Dengaul. It's rather serious news, I'm afraid."

She thought, Oh God! Hasn't he got enough to contend with? "And you can't tell me?"

"I shouldn't. Our policy is to inform the next of kin."

Kate felt as though a lump of ice had formed inside her. *Next of kin*? That could only mean one thing. She said, "He's due back here later this afternoon. Shall I— Oh, wait a moment. This might be him now." The footsteps came to a halt outside her door. It opened and Robert put his head round it.

"Darling Kate! You're ..." He registered her expression and came in, closing the door behind him. "What it it? What's happened?"

She said, "The police are on the line. Detective Sergeant—"

He had snatched the phone from her hand.

"Have you caught them?"

Kate watched helplessly as his expression gradually changed. He groped for the desk and sat down on the edge. His eyes stared unseeingly and he could only nod his head. At last he said, "Caro! *Caro!*" then clapped a trembling hand to his mouth. He turned his head and stared beseechingly at Kate as though somehow she could change things.

"What's happened?" she whispered.

He put a hand over the receiver. "It's Caro. She's been killed."

318

Kate stared at him speechlessly. She heard Robert say, "The *roof*? What in God's name was she ...?" Puzzled, Kate waited. Suddenly Robert uttered a cry of pain and slammed the phone down. Tears burst from his eyes and he sank down on to the nearest chair.

Kate rushed to him. "Darling, tell me? Talk to me!"

It seemed he could only sob, dry anguished sobs from somewhere deep within him. Kate hugged him close but there were tears in her own eyes. Caroline was dead. Robert, who had lost his wife so recently, had now lost his only daughter. But what had he said about the roof? She waited until his distress was lessening and then said, "Can you tell me about it, Robert?"

He nodded. He took a handkerchief from his pocket, wiped his eyes and blew his nose. "Caro and Seb fell from the leads – the edge of the roof. They think Caro was drunk. I can't believe that, but there was—"

"You said Caro and Seb? Are they both ..." She couldn't bring herself to utter the dread word.

"As good as. It seems he was trying to save her and they both fell. The police watched it happen, but couldn't get there in time to do anything. Seb's in hospital with various injuries. His legs and his back ... broken –"

he shuddered – "but he landed on top of Caro. He may not survive – they don't hold out much hope – but if he does he'll be crippled for life. Stuck in a wheelchair. Seb – in a *wheelchair*! Oh God, Kate! It's impossible to even think about it."

"I'll fetch you a brandy, Robert. Mu keeps some for clients."

She rushed along the corridor, burst in and dived for the cupboard, promising to explain later. Minutes later she was back in her own office and Robert was holding the brandy in shaking hands.

"Drink some," Kate told him, "before you spill it."

She was overwhelmed by the disaster and completely at a loss to know how to help. Was there anything to be said or done after such a tragedy? If she said, "At least Seb's alive" it would smack of disloyalty to Caroline. While Kate searched her mind for something positive to say, Robert struggled to retain control of his emotions.

He said dully, "They're treating it as an accident. That's what he said. Treating it as an accident." He turned his face up to hers. "What's that supposed to mean? That it might have been deliberate? That it was a suicide pact? Or that Seb tried to *push* her off? That's too bloody ridiculous! Of *course* it was an accident!"

Kate wanted to cry. Perversely tears

wouldn't come but in their absence her eyes ached with grief. She looked at Robert despairingly because from now on nothing could be the same for him and she was powerless to help him. Nothing she did or said would bring Caroline back and no words could undo the damage to Sebastian. Robert's spirit was mortally wounded and all she could ever do as his wife was to save him from the worst of his depression. The future stretched ahead bleakly and Kate sighed. The man she loved had so little time in which to recover from his loss, however long he had left would be shadowed by the double tragedy.

She decided that the only possible course was action. Anything to keep the dreadful thoughts at bay.

"We should get down to the hospital," she said, "and sit with Seb. He must be in a terrible state, actually *being* there at the time his sister died. And no doubt the police will want to see us. I'll call a taxi. There's no way we can hang about on station platforms."

Robert nodded, seemingly only half aware of what was happening. Shock, thought Kate. She kissed the top of his head and said, "Robert, I'm in this with you, remember. You don't have to suffer it alone. You must talk to me. You must let me help you."

He nodded again without speaking and she reached for the telephone.

The next day, in his hospital bed, Sebastian murmured his sister's name over and over. He opened his eyes but she wasn't there. He was in a small room, a private room presumably. It paid sometimes to have a wealthy father. There was another bed but it was empty. Slowly he moved his head and felt no pain. He had never been in hospital before. Beside him was a tall contraption with a fine tube reaching into his arm. Blood, probably, so he must be bleeding from somewhere. He seemed to be floating on air – a rather nice feeling. Closing his eyes, he relived the moment when they had fallen. He had *wanted* her to fall. He had allowed it to happen. But had he *pushed* her or had he merely witheld help when she needed it? He saw again her face as she toppled backward – the open mouth, the wide terrified eyes. She knew in that instant that she was going to die. He was glad that he had no recollection of her lying on the terrace, broken and bleeding. Yet *he* was alive. Battered and bruised but alive. It felt like a miracle. And he felt no pain, that astonished him – but then in all probability the doctor had given him morphine.

For a few moments he drifted again then his mind cleared. He wondered if his father had been told yet. If so he would come to the hospital to see him.

He said aloud, "Caro, I'm sorry!" but in his heart he knew that he had done the best he could for her. He had removed her from the clutches of the police. Caro had tried to kill Kate and the police knew it. Eventually they would have arrested her. Caroline could never have survived a lengthy prison sentence and his father would have broken under the strain. Death was the kindest way out for Caro but he hadn't expected to be involved.

A nurse appeared at the doorway and, seeing that he was awake, hurried towards him. She wore a grey dress with a white bib apron and a white headdress. Sebastian wondered what it was about a uniform that was so attractive on a woman.

"Mr Dengaul! How wonderful to see you awake. We weren't sure whether or not you would regain consciousness."

"Am I going to live then?" His voice sounded very distant.

"Of course you are!"

"I feel very strange. I can't feel my body at all."

"That's the morphine." She smiled. "You've got a visitor. Mrs Dengaul is here to see you."

That must be Alison.

"She's been waiting for hours."

"What time is it?"

"Just before six."

He tried to sit up but she laid a hand on his arm. "You have to remain flat. How you survived is a miracle. Doctor Summers couldn't believe it. A trick of fate, Mr Dengaul – or else you've led a blameless life!"

When Alison came into the room, Sebastian felt very calm. Watching her cross the room towards him he felt an unexpected wave of happiness. Dearest Alison. They had been so good together. Shame it had all gone wrong, but that was life for you. He remembered her little sideways glances and the way she laughed at his jokes – always afraid she wouldn't understand them. He gave her a broad smile as she sat down beside him, her hair as immaculate as ever, her knees tidily together, hands clutching a small purse. So *neat*, Alison. Like a small bird. It was one of the things that had intrigued him. He had wanted to ruffle her feathers from the moment he first set eyes on her.

The sister said, "Only ten minutes or the doctor will be after me!"

"I should think he already is!" Seb replied.

She said tartly, "All the men say that!" but he was rewarded with a faint blush as she withdrew from the room.

"Trust you!" said Alison. "You'll be cracking jokes at your own— Oh, sorry! How stupid." She looked mortified.

324

"Don't apologise. It's such a relief not to be dead that nothing seems to matter. I thought I was a goner when we fell." He watched her, waiting for any response – a flicker of the eyes or a tell-tale twitch of the mouth.

She said, "Caro's dead, Seb. She didn't suffer at all. How you survived is – well, it's incredible." She took a quick breath and looked at him steadily. "I think, Seb, that you were saved for a purpose. I've only got a few minutes so I'll say what I have to say and leave you to think about it, and don't think anyone has put me up to this because they haven't. Even Mother doesn't know what I'm going to say."

He smiled lazily at her. She was so pretty when she was excited, with the colour mounting in her cheeks. Her silk dress was buttercup yellow and it suited her.

She said, "You love me, Sebastian, and I love you. We're having a baby and I want you to be with me while he or she is growing up. I know there can't be any ... there won't be any brothers or sisters but it's not important. I'm an only child and it has its compensations."

She paused, expecting some reaction, but he could only smile and nod. She was such a dear.

Alison went on, "As soon as I heard what had happened I did some hard thinking.

325

Your father won't live forever and I can't see Kate dedicating her life to looking after you. Why should she? With poor Caro gone there'll be no one else. I'll never let them put you in a home, Seb, so you're going to need me." She was leaning towards him and he could see the curve of her breasts against the yellow silk. "I went round to see Bernard and he's going to allow me to divorce him on grounds of desertion, so there'll be nothing nasty to upset the parents. It's very decent of him in the circumstances." She frowned. "Are you listening to me, Seb?"

Poor Allie. She took life so seriously. He said, "Of course I'm listening! Don't I always?" He smiled. "I could do with a cigarette. You couldn't get me—"

"No. Just go on listening." She fiddled with her hair, a sign that she was nervous. "As soon as I'm free we'll get married, Seb. Mother will make no end of a fuss but I'll deal with her. She'll come round to the idea. Father never will but ... but I don't give a fig. I don't care if I never set eyes on him again. If he never sees his grandchild that will be his loss."

She looked so earnest. Sebastian laughed and the sound echoed in his head. He was laughing. He was happy. He wasn't dead.

She put a hand on his and squeezed it. "And don't say that you can't marry anyone because ... because of what's happened to you. I love you and I want to look after you. It doesn't matter to me, Seb. I mean that, hand on my heart! My uncle ended up in a wheelchair but he still managed to enjoy life. It's not the end of the world, Seb, and you're still the man I want." She swallowed. "That's about it really. You think about it and I'll come and see you again." She looked suddenly as though she might cry.

Sebastian smiled. "You're so sweet, Allie. D'you know that?"

The sister came back into the room. Before Alison left she bent down and kissed him, not on his lips but on top of his head.

When she had gone Sebastian shook his head. "What was all that about?" he asked.

The sister shrugged. She adjusted the drip feed and said, "Now you must rest. No more visitors for at least an hour but I couldn't turn your wife away. Are you quite comfortable?"

"She's not my wife," he said.

"Well, future wife." She picked up his wrist and timed his pulse.

"How can I call you? I might need help to reach the lavatory."

She avoided his eyes. "All that's been seen to. All you have to do is rest."

"Really?" He closed his eyes and breathed gently. Future wife? He shook his head. It was all a bit confusing, but he was alive. He felt so cherished.

He said, "My sister's been killed. Isn't that dreadful?"

"Terrible!"

At that moment there was a knock on the door. Sebastian turned his head carefully and saw a policeman framed in the doorway.

"I've already told you. Not today!" the sister told him sharply.

"I was told he was conscious."

"He *is* conscious, that is true, but that is not the same as being rational. Mr Dengaul has been through a terrible ordeal and is lucky to be alive. He is badly shocked and—"

"We are investigating an attempted murder and it's my job—"

"It's my job to care for the patient, Constable."

"Detective Constable."

"For the last time, you cannot interview the patient today. Mr Dengaul is in a critical condition and is under heavy medication. He'll answer your questions as soon as we consider he's well enough."

Sebastian smiled as the policeman withdrew. So he was in a critical condition. Odd, really, because it always sounded so dire yet he felt wonderfully happy and relaxed.

The sister fussed with the sheet and patted his arm.

A critical condition? He smiled happily and closed his eyes.

In the small interview room, Kate and Robert rose when Detective Sergeant Lane entered. He waved a hand and they all sat. Kate's heart ached for the man beside her, knowing how much this was hurting him.

Robert said brusquely, "Just get on with it, please. You don't have to pull any punches."

The policeman nodded. "Then I'll tell you straight, sir. We were on the point of charging your daughter with the attempt on Mrs Harper's life."

There was a silence. Kate had had her suspicions: her attacker had been very slight and Caroline's story so hopelessly unconvincing. She had also learned from Robert's doctor that coma was not a symptom of his disease but that a large amount of sleeping pills could have accounted for Robert's inability to waken. Caroline had slipped them into his cocoa, she was sure of it. Kate would never have expressed her doubts, but had Robert worked it out for himself? Now she waited, expecting Robert to show surprise and anger but instead he put a hand over his eyes and uttered a soft groan.

The detective continued, "My men have discovered a pair of boots that fitted the footprint we had taken from the scene of the attack. Your daughter could have worn them to add to the confusion."

"That's preposterous!" Robert glared at him but to Kate's ears his rejection sounded what it was – a token denial. She understood what this dreadful knowledge was doing to him. His own daughter had tried to kill the woman he loved. She longed to help him but could think of nothing to say or do. The facts were damning.

"I'm sorry, Mr Dengaul. This can't be pleasant for you but you must hear me out. Later, about fifteen minutes after the fatal fall, we turned up further proof, hidden under hay in the loft above the stable. A cricket bat and the mask Mrs Harper described. Hardly likely that outsiders would decide to hide incriminating evidence in such a place. I appreciate how you feel, Mr Dengaul, but there really is no doubt in our minds."

"Oh God! My own daughter!" He groped blindly for Kate's hand and she held his in hers. "Kate! She wouldn't, would she?"

Kate could only shake her head. Proof that Caroline had hated her enough to want her dead was difficult for her to accept. She watched the detective brace himself for further revelations and prayed that these crushing blows would not precipitate the final stages of Robert's illness. She had told Gordon Brett that she must have time off and he had offered indefinite leave of absence. Now she knew that she could never go back. She would devote the next few years to Robert. With an effort she forced her attention back to the policeman.

"Mr Dengaul, I have to tell you that we also believe that your daughter's fall was not an accident; that your son was probably involved. From where my men were—"

Kate interrupted him. "You couldn't be sure. You couldn't have seen *exactly* what was happening."

Robert said, "It's all right, Kate. I can deal with it."

But you *can't*, she thought despairingly. His face was ashen, his eyes dark with horror and the hand she held was trembling.

The detective shrugged. "It looked as though he pushed her or—"

Kate said, "He was trying to catch hold of her – to save her."

He ignored the interruption. "Or else she jumped."

"No! She would never ..." Robert faltered.

Kate could almost read his mind. He was seeing quite clearly that if Caroline *had* wielded that murderous cricket bat she might well decide to take her own life when threatened with discovery and retribution.

"When your son is well enough to be questioned, he might throw some light on the problem."

Robert rallied. "He will never fully recover."

"I understand he could make a – a partial recovery."

Robert shook his head, unable to answer. Kate could imagine his mind, filled with unimaginable horrors. The blackest day of his life and one from which he would never fully recover.

The detective looked at Kate. His expression was apologetic but she recognised the gleam in his eyes. To him it was simply a fascinating case which they had solved. It might never come to court but they had triumphed. She could understand that. With one part of her mind she could also admire his professionalism.

Supressing her sympathies, however, she said, "It could look very different, though. I think Caroline did it while she was under some kind of emotional pressure – jealousy or fear – and then she regretted it and ... and was glad I survived." She glanced at Robert whose chin had sunk to his chest. Kate ploughed on. "She drank to dull the remorse and in an unstable state of mind decided to walk along the ledge. When she wavered her brother tried to save her."

She glanced at Robert.

Picking up his cue, he said, "Why not? You can't prove otherwise. There's certainly no reason for Sebastian to kill his sister. They were very close."

The detective said, "But that might also be

why he pushed her – to save her from the consequences of her own actions."

Kate said, "Sebastian will tell you he fell while trying to save her. You'll never get a conviction." She hoped she sounded more confident than she felt.

"We'll see." He stood up.

Robert remained seated, staring into space until Kate took his arm. "Darling, we can go." She half pulled him to his feet.

When they stepped out once more into the street, Kate's own despair was growing. Robert looked dazed and weak and she held his arm tightly. They stood together, isolated by grief, while the July sun shone and the rest of the world was bright.

The seventeenth of July arrived. A week had passed. Half the year gone, thought Bernard. He stopped pushing the mower and wiped a handkerchief over his face. Without the mower, the sounds of the countryside reasserted themselves. A dog barked, children chattered on their way home from school and overhead a lark sang.

John called, "Tea's up!"

Bernard grinned. "Tea's up" meant a pot of tea, scones and jam and a slice of the cake made by the local bakery. He had put on weight since leaving Alison and he blamed it on John's love of all things sweet.

In his pocket was a letter from his father-in-law who, threatened with his wife's permanent defection, had now decided to reinstate Bernard in his good books. He had written to say that his place on the board was safe and that he hoped to open a new shop in East Grinstead. Was Bernard interested in managing it? Bernard was and he had broken the news to John over breakfast.

Now he joined his friend at the rickety table and wiped his face again.

John said, "We need a new mower. That one's on its last legs."

Bernard poured the tea. "I went over to Highstead. Thank God for Kate, that's all I can say. She's a tower of strength and Father's in such a state. He relies on her for everything at the moment."

"He's been through a great deal, poor chap."

Bernard nodded. "The police have released Caroline's body and Kate's arranged the funeral for this Friday. Could you bear to come?"

"If you want me there."

"Of course I do. Hard to believe what's happened to this family in the past few weeks." He shook his head and bit into a scone.

"Life goes like that. You drift along for years in a comfortable rut and then suddenly it's all upside down. I remember one year – I was about twenty. My father died, my mother's mind collapsed under the strain and she was taken into a nursing home and I failed my exams. It felt as though the sky had fallen in!"

"Now it's fallen on me!"

"You'll get over it. I'm pleased about the job offer though. Bit of a change of heart, isn't it?"

"Yes, it's a great relief but I don't know whether to take it or not."

"Because of me?"

"Yes."

"That's not a problem, Bernie. We can move to East Grinstead. I quite fancy a change."

Bernard stared at him. "You'd come with me?"

"Why not? I can be happy anywhere except in a town. I only came here to please my wife. There are other churches and other choirs. Pastures new. I'm game."

A smile spread over Bernard's face. "That's tremendous!" he exclaimed. "That's really made my day! I'll take you up on that. The new shop's a challenge and it would probably mean more money in the long run." He was positively beaming. "I can't believe it, you know. A few weeks back I was in deep despair and now everything's working out for me. Alison wants a divorce and that's agreed. I get a new start some-where else."

"Someone up there loves you!" John told him.

Bernard sighed. "I'll feel like a rat, though, leaving a sinking ship. Seb in a wheelchair for the rest of his life, Caroline dead and Father so ill."

"Not your doing though, Bernie. Don't start blaming yourself for any of it. Alison's got the child she always wanted – or she will have in a few months. Seb's got Alison, whether he likes it or not!" He laughed. "Your father's got Kate. You're stuck with me." He raised his tea cup. "Here's to East Grinstead!"

Bernard raised his cup also. "I'll drink to that!"

Two days later Kate walked along the hospital corridor, trying to prepare herself for the coming ordeal. The consultant was going to break the bad news to Sebastian and had requested that a member of his family should be present. Robert had been the most natural choice but Kate had offered to take his place.

The nursing sister, large and reassuring, greeted her at the door. "Oh, there you are, Mrs Harper. Mr Carpenter, the consultant, will be along shortly."

She led the way into the room where Sebastian was still the only occupant. He was lying flat on his back, trying to read a novel, but he put it aside when he saw Kate.

She smiled as cheerfully as she could. "Seb! You're looking so much better!"

The sister moved a chair so that Kate could sit beside him. She was not looking forward to the consultant's revelation because Sebastian was going to be devastated. Since his accident he had refused to believe the extent of the injury to his spine. He knew his legs had been damaged and was trying desperately to reconcile himself to the possibility of artificial legs. That in itself had required great courage and a huge leap of faith. As far as Kate knew, the thought of being permanently immobilised had never entered his head.

Now Sebastian winked at the sister. "It's all this loving care! Sister's an angel."

The nurse glanced at Kate. "This young man is quite a handful! He has all the young nurses in a flutter!"

As Kate sat down, a small bespectacled man entered the room, a clipboard in his hand, a harassed expression on his round face.

Kate rose to her feet, but he said, "Don't get up. You must be Mrs Harper."

Sebastian said, "Soon to be the second Mrs Robert Dengaul!"

Kate didn't meet his gaze.

Mr Carpenter consulted his notes,

frowning slightly as he riffled through the pages. The sister brought up a second chair and withdrew as soon as the consultant had sat down.

"Mr Dengaul," he began without preamble, "the news is not at all good but considering you should by rights be dead by now, I think you'll appreciate that it's as good as can be expected. In the circumstances."

Kate saw a small muscle flicker in Sebastian's jaw and knew he was not as calm as he pretended.

The doctor continued. "The best news is that we have decided against amputation of either leg." He waited. When there was no response he said, "We can put them back together again after a fashion."

Sebastian said, "Well, that's reassuring."

He turned to Kate.

"That's wonderful news!" She smiled at Sebastian. "I was praying for that, you know. Losing a limb must be very demoralising. I didn't want that for you."

The doctor said, "I have to admit it was touch and go – they really are very badly broken but in the circumstances it didn't seem too important if—" He stopped abruptly.

Sebastian said, "In the circumstances? Which circumstances? Have I missed something?"

Kate reached out and put a hand over his.

The doctor said, "Mr Dengaul, what I mean is that since you won't be able to walk on them, it won't matter quite so much if—"

"Whoa! What was that?" Sebastian's face had lost its colour. "I won't *walk* on them? What the hell does that mean?"

Kate said, "Seb, it won't be—"

Ignoring her, he stared at the doctor. "I won't walk again? Is that what you meant?" Panic-stricken he glanced to Kate for reassurance.

"Seb, I'm sorry."

Mr Carpenter said, "Mr Dengaul, I'm afraid I *did* mean that. It's difficult to bear, I know, but even if we could restore your legs, your spine won't co-operate. Your back is irreparably damaged. It's a mercy you can use your arms but—".

Seb cried, "Kate! Tell me it isn't true!"

Kate steeled herself. All the bad news had to be offered today. There was no way she could soften the blow. "Seb, the doctor's right, I'm afraid. There's nothing they can do for your spine. You fell from a great height and—"

He had one hand on his heart and when he spoke his voice was faint and breathless. "I won't walk again? Not *ever?* No! I *can* do it, Kate! I can do anything. Exercises. I'll have treatments. Operations." He looked at the consultant who shook his head. "Jesus Christ! You can't tell me that I'll *never* walk again. You can't *know* that!" He turned abruptly back to Kate. "What's the point of keeping my legs if I can't walk? Oh God! This can't be happening!"

Kate willed herself not to cry. "Seb, you'll be *whole*. That matters, doesn't it? And you'll have all the help we can give you."

"I don't want your bloody help! I want to *walk*!"

The doctor pursed his lips, his eyes on his notes.

He's dealt with this situation before, Kate thought, envying him his control.

"It's a terrible shock, Mr Dengaul," Dr Carpenter said, "but in time you'll learn how to cope. Believe me, you'll be grateful you are still alive."

"But a cripple!"

"A cripple? That is largely in the mind, Mr Dengaul. I suspect you are a fighter and will make more of your opportunities than many of our patients. You have many advantages – not least a supportive family."

"What's left of it!"

His tone was full of bitterness and Kate longed for words that would help him through the next terrible hours. All she could think of were trite phrases of condolence which he would reject. She wondered what Robert would have said in

340

the circumstances. Nothing diplomatic, she reflected wryly. Tact wasn't his strong point.

Seb's face was changing as fear gave way to an unreasoning anger. Colour flared in his cheeks and his eyes glittered. "You send us home with patronising words to a future that's ..." He groaned. "Never walk? I can't spend my life in a wheelchair!" His voice cracked.

The doctor rose to his feet and looked at Sebastian with compassion. "All we can ever do is pick up the pieces, Mr Dengaul. We do our best with broken bodies but we can't perform miracles."

"Well, your best isn't good enough!" Seb shouted. "Damn you all to hell!"

Kate said gently, "Seb, please stop this! The doctor is quite right. The hospital staff are doing all they can. They've saved your legs so you're still in one piece. You're still alive. You have to thank God for that."

"I'll call by in a day or two. I'm sorry, Mr Dengaul, that the news wasn't better." He smiled at Kate and walked to the door. Then he turned back, directing his words to Sebastian. "Last night we amputated the leg of an eighty-year-old man who has no one in the world to care for him. His home is a room above a shop – reached by a steep flight of stairs. He has no money for a private nurse."

He closed the door quietly behind him

and Sebastian stared after him.

"Pompous prig!" he muttered.

"I wouldn't like his job," Kate remarked. "Pretty thankless sometimes."

"Save your sympathy, Kate. I'm sure he gets well paid for it."

There was a long silence. A quick glance at Sebastian showed her that he was breathing fast. His fingers clutched the bedclothes and his eyes were unnaturally bright. "If you're waiting for my tears," he said, "forget it!"

She ignored the words. Clasping her fingers she rested her chin on her hands.

"It looks as though you and Father are stuck with me after all."

Kate gave him a steady look. Nothing she could say would undo the damage to his body but she dare not let him slide into self-pity. He was going to need all the Dengaul spirit to survive the coming months. The kindest thing she could do for him was to paint an accurate picture of the future.

"Seb, I think you should marry Alison. She still loves you and she wants to care for you."

Astonished, he cried, "You're throwing me out of Highstead?"

"Of course not, but you have to see that Robert has very little time left. I want the two of us to be together. We're entitled to that. Please go to Alison, Seb. She loves you and she's expecting your child."

"She's not expecting a cripple to care for as well!"

With her heart full of pity, Kate took both his hands in hers. "She's not just *prepared* to spend her life with you, Seb, she *wants* to. So why not give it a chance?"

"Because I love you."

"I love you, Seb, but not in that way." She had to convince him that his best hope for the future was with Alison and the child. But how? "I'll never love you that way. Nothing's perfect. It never is."

"We could have been happy together."

"We can still be very good friends, Seb."

"And you'll be my stepmother!" He rolled his eyes with a pathetic attempt at humour

Kate took heart. "You're not the only one with problems, Seb. I'm going to lose Robert – the person who is dearer to me than anyone else in the world. He's going to die." Her voice shook but she pressed on. "You're not going to walk. Caroline is dead and your father will never stop grieving for her. He's already blaming himself, wondering where he went wrong. It's *life*, Seb. It's the way things are. We all have to ride out the storms."

He drew in a long breath. "You're saying that I'm a selfish bastard!"

"Seb!" The word hung in the air between them.

"I'm sorry ... Mother said once that

343

Father was just like me – self-centred and arrogant."

"I wouldn't have loved him, then."

"Mother did."

"She must have seen the potential." She tried to see the young Robert in this difficult son of his and sure enough he was there. So there was hope for Seb. "Look Seb, you need time to think, but I believe you can survive this and make a new life for yourself. I have to do the same. I hope your father will give me a child to love. I'd settle for that."

His expression changed. "I'll marry you and bring up his child."

She smiled. "Dearest Seb, you have your own child to bring up. You had a loving father. Your child deserves the same. Just imagine, we'll be going through the trials of parenthood together."

For a while he said nothing while his fingers plucked nervously at the blanket. "Not much of a catch now, am I?"

"Alison adores you."

He sighed deeply, then leaned forward and kissed her hands. "I suppose I'll have to settle for friendship – if that's all that's on offer."

"It is, Seb."

"I'm sorry – about Father."

She nodded. She got up to go but he kept hold of her hand.

"Kate, I want you to know that I didn't push Caro."

"That's a relief. May I tell Robert?"

"Yes ... but ..." he swallowed hard, "I have to tell you something, Kate."

Alarmed by his tone she said, "I don't think I want to hear it."

He said slowly, "I didn't push her but I meant to let her fall."

Kate froze. Her instinct was to snatch her hands away from his but somehow she resisted it. "You meant to ...? I don't believe it!"

"I wanted her to die ... because of what she had done to you."

She stared at him, shocked and sick at heart.

"Because she tried to kill you and she meant to try again. I wanted to punish her ... and to stop her. And I couldn't let her go to prison. Up there on the leads, I saw the perfect way out!"

Horrified, Kate tried to imagine what this would do to Robert. She said, "You must never tell another soul, Seb, and certainly not Robert." She saw his mouth open and hurried to forestall an argument. "Telling him just to ease your conscience isn't fair, Seb. I think we must spare him this."

He hesitated. "I want his forgiveness."

"But suppose he can't give it? You will have deepened his grief to no purpose."

His face contorted suddenly with the burden of guilt. "I let my own sister die when I could have saved her. I *am* a murderer in a way."

"No, Seb! There's a difference. I don't think it's a crime to *allow* someone to have an accident. I admit we're drawing a fine line but—" She faltered to a stop, unsure of her argument.

His face crumpled. Kate tried to speak but there was nothing to be said. Gently she squeezed his hands as pity engulfed her. His guilt must be overwhelming and would haunt him forever.

"Do you forgive me, Kate?"

"It's between you and God. But for what it's worth, I forgive you." Unable to control her own grief, she feared she would break down. "I have to go," she whispered. "I'll come in again tomorrow."

Bending forward, she took his face in her hands, turned it gently towards her, and kissed his cheek. She was trembling as she closed the door. Behind her she heard his first sobs.

"Oh Alison!" she murmured. "I do hope he's worth it!"

Eleven

Robert and Bernard were seated in the front row. Alison and Kate sat behind them in the second row. Robert, bowed down with misery, had not demurred and Kate was content to be with Alison whose mother had gone home for a few days. Sebastian was still in the hospital. Behind them the pews were filling up with acquaintances and friends and more than a few curious or sympathetic villagers. At the rear of the church Kate had seen Detective Sergeant Lane. He was seated in a discreet position behind a column and was scrutinising the faces of each mourner. What was he expecting to see? Kate wondered wearily. With the main suspect dead and an official verdict of accidental death, there were no other suspects to be discovered. Only Seb might be of interest: although he could not prove his innocence with regard to Caroline's death, the police could not prove his guilt.

Ahead of her Kate looked beyond Robert to the mahogany coffin – the best money could buy – with its highly polished surface, elegant inlaid design and shining brass handles. Not that much of it was visible – it was half hidden by Robert's enormous wreath of white lilies. Kate was so thankful for the flowers. Occasionally she had attended a funeral where there were 'no flowers by request' and mournful affairs she had found them.

The choir was in place and she saw John Somers for only the third time. She was pleased that Bernard had found an ally, and understood the attraction. Somers' face was good-natured and, according to Robert, he was a man at peace with himself. Bernard would find that a great comfort, she told herself.

Alison whispered, "I wish Seb could have been here."

Kate nodded although she was far from convinced that a meeting between the two brothers would have been wise. Alison was clinging to the thought that Seb would accept his fate and marry her as soon as it was possible. She was keen for him to move in with her immediately he left the hospital and was arranging for the small dining room to be converted to a downstairs bedroom for him. Being pregnant affected women in different ways and Alison was blooming. There was a bright colour in her face and her skin was clear. The morning sickness had lasted only a few weeks and now she was full of energy and plans for the future. Kate didn't envy her but she was full of admiration.

The vicar took his place and turned to face them and a hush descended on the congregation as he announced the first hymn.

Everyone rose and Kate saw Somers throw a quick glance in Bernard's direction. As they began to sing her thoughts reverted to her own situation. Her body was beginning to interest her more than usual – showing what Kate suspected were tell-tale signs. She had missed a period and her breasts felt unnaturally sensitive. She had decided to wait another week or two before going to the doctor for confirmation. She and Robert had brought forward the date of their wedding and had obtained a special licence. They would be married secretly in London in two days' time with Muriel and Eddie as witnesses. Kate wanted to be a married woman before she saw the doctor so that no awkward information could leak out to the ever-hungry journalists. There had been enough revelations already over the past ten days and Robert was cracking under the strain.

As they sang, Kate watched him with growing concern. His shoulders were bowed, his head bent. Bernard leaned forward and whispered something to him.

Kate had insisted that as soon they were married they would spend a few days in her flat. They would walk in the park and she would invite Mu and Eddie to supper. Anything to remind Robert of the simple pleasures of everyday life. She would ask his advice about her novel to distract him from the recent nightmare.

There was a clatter as Robert dropped his hymnal. As Bernard stooped to retrieve it, Robert turned to her. Kate saw the tears running down his face and threw her arms around him.

And at that moment her confidence plummeted. All she wanted was to make this dear man happy but all the fates were conspiring against her.

On a cold day in February Kate walked slowly along the churchyard path. Seven months had passed since they buried Caroline and some of the worst memories were fading. A chill wind blew erratically, swirling the dead leaves around Kate's legs and carrying the smell of distant wood-smoke to her nostrils. Her feet crunched across the gravelled path and she raised a gloved hand to a woman who was walking in the opposite direction with a small bunch of early daffodils.

"From your garden, Mrs Beddowes?" Kate asked with a smile.

"Yes. He was a great bulb man, my father. Daffodils and tulips everywhere! I used to tell him it was like living in blooming Holland!" She laughed then studied Kate. "Mrs Dengaul, isn't it?"

"Yes." Kate was becoming used to being recognised. Despite the quiet ceremony at a London register office, their marriage had made the front pages.

"Baby all right?"

Kate smiled. "Kicking a lot!"

"Oh they do! Most likely a boy."

"The midwife seems to think so."

"No problems, then?"

"A bit of backache today but I've been lucky so far."

She gave Kate a sympathetic smile. "Best thing that could happen after – well, you know."

"Yes. We're thrilled."

"Your husband well?"

Kate hesitated. "As well as can be expected. Caroline's death was a great blow."

As she walked on she hugged her coat closely round her thickening body and thought about the child which would be born in a month's time. They were counting the days. It was the brightest star on their horizon; the promise of joy that was helping Robert to rise above his agonised depression.

He still made a weekly pilgrimage with flowers to his daughter's grave and Kate understood that the weekly ritual was a part of his atonement for what he saw as his failure. He believed he hadn't loved Caroline enough, hadn't given her enough, hadn't valued her enough. He blamed himself because he hadn't recognised the signs of recurring paranoia.

Another feature in his recovery was the novel which Kate was reworking under his expert guidance. Not that she was allowing him to write a single word, much to his disappointment, but she valued his opinion and was willing to rewrite wherever he could show her a better way. She wrote throughout each morning and then offered it to him for comments after lunch. In fact, she would have preferred to stumble through it alone, making her own mistakes and hopefully learning from them but she knew that it was important to him to be of use. His own novel would never be finished and finally Gordon Brett had acknowledged it too. It took all Robert's energies to get through each day and survive the often sleepless nights. His own particular demons were with him at all times although Kate fancied she saw a reduction in the number of his deepest moods and congratulated herself that tender loving care was beginning to heal the emotional wounds.

She found him beside Caroline's grave, his head bent, his hands thrust into the pocket of his greatcoat. Moving to stand close to him, Kate slipped an arm through his.

"Caro loved you, Robert," she said softly. "Don't you think she would have forgiven you by now – if there ever was anything to forgive?"

"Maybe." He didn't move.

"I think she'd want you to forgive yourself."

He turned at last and kissed her.

She said, "My back aches. I feel a hundred years old!"

"You still look good to me."

"Thank you, Robert."

They walked back towards the gate hand in hand. Robert's face had lost its haunted look and he had put on a little weight.

"I popped in to take Alison the matinee coat and bootees," Kate said. "The baby was gurgling away as usual. A happy little soul, bless her!"

"The famous matinee coat!" he teased. "How long has it taken you? A year?"

She laughed. "Don't mock, Robert. You know I can't knit for toffee! It took two months actually but only because I had to undo some of it. Luckily it still fits her. And Alison showed me the christening gown – the one *she* wore as a baby. It's beautiful. White silk trimmed with Honiton lace."

"And Seb?" He sighed.

Kate knew how much it cost him to ask the question. The sight of his son in his wheelchair was almost more than he could bear.

"He was quite cheerful today. He's been sketching the baby and he's good, Robert. Really. Do you think we might pay for someone to give him art lessons."

"A private tutor, you mean?"

"Yes. A year's tuition could be his birthday present so he needn't feel he was accepting charity."

"That never troubled him in the past!"

Kate took heart at the flash of irritation. Two months ago she would have been lucky to receive any answer at all. This sounded more like the old irascible Robert. Ignoring the jibe she went on. "Alison showed me a sketch he'd done of her in pastels. A portrait. He's very good at catching a likeness. You'd be impressed, darling. I said I'd sit for him one day next week. There might even be a market for portraits. A way for him to earn some money. A chance to contribute."

Kate was, as ever, trying to bring father and son together. Robert had found it impossible to face his son in the months following Caroline's death but Kate had continued to visit Sebastian. Alison had brought the baby to Highstead on several occasions and Kate had vowed never to give up on a reconciliation.

They crossed the street and climbed into the motor. As the car rolled smoothly through the streets she said, "Alison's coping very well. She's better since her mother went home. She can make her own decisions."

Robert said abruptly, "I had a letter from Bernard this morning."

"I thought I recognised his handwriting."

"He's got that shop up and running, but then I knew he would. He's got a flair for business, that boy. I always knew he'd do well. When Bernard sets his mind on something ..." After a moment he said, "He's not much good with women though."

She smiled. "I'm very impressed with Bernard. He's no longer bitter and he's behaved like a gentleman throughout. He even sent a card when the baby was born. He has the makings of a very good uncle." She took a deep breath. "Alison has invited Bernard and John to Althea's christening. I'm looking forward to seeing them both again."

She dared not glance at her husband's face but saw his hands tighten on the steering wheel.

He said, "Is that wise? People are bound to talk."

"Let them. I'm perfectly satisfied in my own mind that they are simply friends. Two women can live together, why not two men? The main thing is that Bernard's happy."

"Easy for you, Kate. He's not your son."

"He's my stepson and I'm very fond of him." She decided to press home her advantage. "Alison's father won't be there. Sad, don't you think? I've always believed that families should stick together."

"You're an optimist, Kate. I'm a realist."

They stopped at the crossroads and a middle-aged man tugged at his wife's sleeve and pointed to Robert with excitement. Seeing him, Robert raised a hand in greeting and smiled.

Kate looked at him. "I shall never get used to that," she told him. "Being recognised by strangers."

"You will when you're famous!"

He turned and grinned and immediately Kate felt better. Her days were spent in trying to make her husband happy and for so long a smile had been a rarity.

"I don't expect to be famous but I do hope to see my book in print. Just to see it on the shelves of a bookshop. I don't need literary lunches and launch parties."

Robert swung the car off the road and into the drive. "They'll creep up on you," he told her. "You'll enjoy it. Your novel is going to make waves, you know. It might happen earlier than you think."

"Then you'll be around to hold my hand!"

"Will I?" His tone was wistful.

"You'd better be, Robert. Promise me!" Something else for him to look forward to, she thought; something to live for. The doctor had said that willpower had a part to play and a month earlier he had declared that the rate of Robert's illness had slowed. Kate counted every day as a bonus.

Robert raised his right hand. "I promise. God's honour!" Another smile.

Kate breathed a sigh of relief. She looked up at Highstead with an affection she had never expected to feel. It felt like home – another surprise. In spite of the tragedy she had shared here with the family, the house was part of Robert. His success and his self-esteem were lodged within these four walls. She had been so naive to imagine that he would ever leave it.

He walked round in front of the car to open her door and still her heart ached at the sight of him. Neither illness nor sorrow had changed the wonderful eyes or the strong mouth. *Oh, Robert!* She was going to lose him. She had forced herself to accept that but she dare not think about it. Daily she thanked God that she was carrying his child.

As she climbed from the car she gasped with sudden pain.

"It's nothing," she said uncertainly. "At least ... I don't know." It was a sharp pain unlike any she had ever had before.

She waited while he closed the car door and then leaned towards him as he slid an arm around her waist.

"Kate? You look bemused."

"Did any of your children ever come early?"

"The boys did. Why?"

"How early, Robert?"

"About three weeks, I think. It was a—" He stopped abruptly and stared at her excitedly. "Kate! You're not thinking ..."

She caught her breath as another identical pain hit her. "I don't know, Robert but I think your fourth child has decided to arrive." She felt shocked and unprepared. "Can you help me to the house. I think I need to sit down."

Inside, Kate quickly decided that sitting down was of no help. Neither was lying down. As the pains developed a distinctive pattern she was forced to the conclusion that they *were* contractions. Another Dengaul baby was eager to face the world. She listened while Robert telephoned the midwife. Fortunately the room upstairs was ready – she had made preparations in plenty of time. She watched her husband's face light up as he spoke into the telephone and closed her eyes against another pain. Uttering a silent prayer of thanks, Kate knew the best was yet to come.